MURDER BY CHAMPAGNE

AN INVESTIGATION BY
COMMISSAIRE

DENISE CARON
and the
POLICE JUDICIAIRE DE REIMS

KEITH SPICER

MURDER BY CHAMPAGNE

An Investigation by Commissaire Denise Caron
and the Police Judiciaire de Reims

**This book is entirely fictional. It bears no relation whatever to
any person living or dead.**

EAN-13: 978-1481985611

ISBN-10: 1481985612

Publisher: Éditions Censier
51 rue Censier
75005 Paris
Printed by CreateSpace
Author contact:
E-mail: kspicer22@gmail.com

OTHER BOOKS BY THE AUTHOR

For Dag, Vivi and Nick...

Champagne, if you are seeking the truth, is better than a lie detector. It encourages a man to be expansive, even reckless, while lie detectors are only a challenge to tell lies successfully.

-- Graham Greene

CONTENTS

CHAPTER ONE
Shock and Awe

A soft late-summer morning light crept over the stone streets and façades of ancient Reims, a short train ride east of Paris. Once the second largest city in the Roman Empire and later coronation seat of twenty-nine kings, it was now the capital of France's Champagne region. Its signature product evoked love, elegance and celebration.
But not today.

Hubert Repentigny teetered at the top of the long steep stairway. His ancient chalk champagne caves lay twenty-eight meters below. As he looked down, the steps began to blur. The round brick walls revolved in a slow, solemn dance around him. Dizzy, then losing his footing, he toppled backward down the dark tunnel. Rolling sideways, his head crashed against each stone step. There were over a hundred of them, every second one lit by a soft yellow-orange lamp. On the shadowy, slow-motion careen downward, he silently screamed, expecting each step to smash him into oblivion.

Helplessly he rolled, the half-lit steps fading into leisurely revolving champagne bottles. They turned unaided, executing the traditional champagne-maturing quarter-turn in sync with the crashing of his head on each stair. Rolling steps and churning bottles meshed in his brain, casting him suddenly into a huge white room with a high ceiling. Hidden lights dazzled him. Was this, he thought, the end of his terrifying slide to nothingness? His rib-cage collapsed, piercing his organs. His brain ached as if stabbed by an ice-pick. Dying would be deliverance.

Half-conscious, he fought to understand. He willed his eyes to open. A grey-and-white cloud floated over the eerily turning bottles.

Gradually, the images focused into something rectangular: the foot of a hospital-bed. Shadowy figures were watching him. Squinting, he guessed he was not dead. Rolling down the stairs must have been a delirium. A trauma-induced nightmare.

Worried voices whispered: "What happened? They found him behind a bottle-rack, deep in the caves? Who would do this? Will he live? For how long? How is his family? Will he ever work again?"

Thoughts flickered and faded. Slowly he grasped that something or somebody had gravely hurt his head. That someone had tried to murder him.

Throbbing surged at the back of Repentigny's head, piercing and pitiless. He groaned. He struggled to assess his pain. But it blinded him to any image of his fate or future. Soon he sank back into a soft welcoming place. A place without name or contour.

Hôtel de Police, Reims... 8:43 a.m.

The call flashed from the caves to the 24-hour, 10-screen police call center. The duty officer, *l'officier de quart*, sent a patrol-car to the Repentigny caves to check that the call reported a real crime, not a prank. Within 22 minutes, the patrol confirmed a major crime with Repentigny as victim. The victim being still-but-barely alive, *le quart* sent a SAMU medical-emergency ambulance to meet police investigators at the crime-scene.

Office of Commissaire Denise Caron, Hôtel de Police, Reims... 9:05 a.m.

Commissaire de Police Denise Caron reacted quickly to the confirmation this melancholy morning of October 1 -- feast-day of Saint Remi, the town's legendary fifth-century bishop. Caron was Reims's chief murder investigator. She instantly understood that this could prove the most complex, spectacular case of her career. Somebody had tried to murder the most powerful and controversial baron of champagne-land – who was a top regional politician as well. And fingers pointed in all directions at plausible suspects.

Commissaire Denise Caron was a 32-year-old rising star of the Reims regional Police Judiciaire (a branch of the Direction Centrale de la Police Judiciaire (DCPJ). She held the key position of Chief of Operational Divisions – overseeing all investigations. Her gray-brushcut, seen-it-all regional director Georges Baraquant was her fan and protector. Today, he was away on an end-of-term Interpol seminar in Lyon. His number two, ebullient assistant director Philippe Duroselle, kept a close (and appreciative) eye on Caron.

Like Baraquant, Duroselle allowed Caron a loose rein on the minute-by-minute operations of her thirty investigators. Every day, usually in early evening, she held a brisk, all-hands debriefing session, using a big white-board in the upstairs meeting-room.

Caron's job was demanding, unpredictable, multi-faceted and often dangerous. But she felt fully up to it (except on the very rare day when her fleeting imposter complex clicked in).

She was also proud of being a cop's daughter. Twelve years before, her dad, police captain Gilles Caron, had taken a bullet in his spine during a robbery. Now he followed his daughter from a wheelchair as a fingerprint expert in the downstairs lab. Denise's father gave her "street-cred," as well as unusual respect from most colleagues.

Being brilliant, cultured and head-turningly pretty, Caron was used to flak from the old boys.

Several times a day, she walked the wide halls of the cavernous Hôtel de Police in tailored slacks and elegant white shirt and sweater. With her slim, well-molded figure and flaming-red hair in no-nonsense page-boy cut, she overheard their sniping: "She's a knockout, but she's far too green to handle this job," grumbled one of them. Another muttered that "broads belong in police PR or work with kids. Maybe parking fines." Another handed her a two-edged defense: "But at least she studied in Reims, and must have tossed back a few bubbles."

Most cops did their job loyally under her direction. But a handful didn't go out of their way to make Caron look smart and in control. A few colleagues used the put-down that French males love to play with in the name of gallantry. "You're *so* beautiful," the odd officer would leer, to take the focus off her competence. "You must have a *very* interesting private life." Knowing the species, Caron either ignored the remark, rolled her eyes, or froze the offender with a Vladmir Putin KGB stare.

The case at hand stopped such trivia. Its extraordinary complexity would demand consummate investigative and diplomatic skills. The victim's enemies were legion: business, politics, personal -- each category rich in variety. Much of the antagonism was mere jealousy. As a *notable* – a well-known local personality – Repentigny would draw in senior players of the judicial and political establishment.

Office of Regional Police Assistant Director, 9:09 a.m.

Alerted from the start, Duroselle and Caron needed routine legal cover: an official order to proceed from the *Procureur de la République* Alexandre Simon. To gain time, they hastily pulled together a team of seven of Caron's thirty investigators to work with her in the caves. French police culture favors collective efforts. Caron stood out as a star, but she always acted with and within a group.

Of course, the mid-sized Reims police operation knew mankind's inevitable rivalries and personality conflicts. But it worked smoothly and informally, with high morale.

Caron's Repentigny team included most of her specialists: *police technique et scientifique*, the chiefs of judicial identity, of the criminal division (including anti-gang and anti-drug police), of background files, as well as two *enquêteurs* or investigators. Each team member, including Caron, threw on a sleeveless black bullet-proof *gilet* with handy pockets and handcuffs. On its back: the huge white words *POLICE Judiciaire*. The team raced to the Repentigny caves in a small convoy.

The state prosecutor, by French law guarantor of the legality of all major police actions, immediately grasped the crime's import. Repentigny being a famous – for some, infamous – man, the prosecutor quickly authorized Caron's plan to investigate at the crime scene. He jumped in his car to go there himself.

Caron dashed to the site with her team, as well as with Duroselle, her supervisor. She immediately ordered the entire Repentigny property cordoned off, above and below ground. With her photographers and technicians working closely with her down below, she took charge of the immediate crime scene around the blood-spattered bottle-rack.

"Guard this whole scene," she ordered, "including the caves for 100 meters in each direction. Don't disturb a single grain of dust before the *police technique et scientifique* finish their work."

The only outside people allowed below were the three SAMU-sent staff: a doctor, a paramedic-anesthesist, and a driver-stretcher-bearer. All three wore temporary hygienic boots. Only this "SAMU/SMUR" team – guided by scientific police to avoid crime-scene pollution – could advance cautiously to examine the body and inject a cocktail of painkiller and anti-inflammatory drugs.

This first aid completed, along with photos of body position and state, Caron let the ambulance team remove the victim to the waiting ambulance upstairs.

She turned to Sébastien Painteaux, the blond, 51-year-old *chef de cave* who had made the police call. He looked frightened and distraught. After sounding the alarm, he had waited for the police to arrive.

"Tell me, *monsieur*, when and how you found him."

"It was at about 8:40 a.m. this morning. I discovered him on my early walk from our blending area down to the underground storage area," said Painteaux. "I passed through the large, well-lit room over there where Madame Repentigny has displayed her impressive art collection. Monsieur was lying crumpled and unconscious behind this rack of champagne bottles. His feet were sticking out from behind the bottle-rack."

"Monsieur Painteaux, I will have many more questions to ask you in formal interview at my office. Meanwhile, perhaps I will see you at the hospital."

"Of course, Commissaire."

Now she and her team could refocus on the crime scene. At this stage, her key players were the *Police technique et scientifique.* Their leader, a sturdy, serious 35-year-old *Normande* with hair in bun, designer glasses and thick-soled shoes, was *Commandant de police* Dominique Flochard. She ruled her domain of ghastly crime photos, micro-scopes and finger-print screens with a proud se-renity. "You get used to the horror," she would say amiably, "and learn to sleep with it."

Flochard and her staff wore regulation hood-ed white body-suits, light-blue gloves and large moon-walk boots. To the unwarned, they looked exactly like NASA astronauts. They photographed everything in sight, took blood and DNA samples, dusted for chemicals, and – her passion -- lifted fin-gerprints from plausible and implausible places.

Among their notable take-aways: the bottle-weapon with bloodied bottom and a black head-scarf.

Treading cautiously, Caron memorized the scene, studying the body's chalk outline on the cement floor and the ugly splash of blood on the wall. As if to mock the police, the assailant had drawn a rough "R" for Repentigny in the blood. And he had crossed it out top-to-bottom with a large angry line – apparently to make the vengeful proclamation: "I have killed Repentigny!"

After her people had worked for two hours, Caron let them continue alone. The prosecutor, seeing the police were following proper procedures, had already left. So had Duroselle: he had urgent reports to write for higher-ups.

Caron raced with two colleagues in her Peugeot 308 SW to the Centre Hospitalier Universitaire (CHU) de Reims, the city's huge conglomerate of eleven hospitals. In the emergency trauma department, she spotted Madame Repentigny.

France 3 – Regional TV news, Champagne-Ardenne, 10:53 a.m.

"Flash: Reims police confirm that the victim of an assault in the Repentigny caves is Monsieur Hubert Repentigny himself. The victim is in grave condition at the CHU de Reims. For the time being, police have no leads, but are looking at all hypotheses."

L'Union daily newspaper, Reims, 10:55 am....

The news hit the region's daily newspaper editors at 5 rue de Talleyrand from their "cop-shop" junior reporter at the Hôtel de la Police. Anne Rondache immediately got through to the editor-in-chief, Jean-Philippe Couvreur.

"They found Repentigny about two hours ago," she told her boss breathlessly. I tried to get the Commissaire divisionnaire, but he's away on a seminar. But I hear the officer assigned to this is Commissaire Denise Caron – their top murder investigator. She has already checked out the caves, and is at the hospital."

"This is sensational news, and for now you should stay at the Hôtel full-time to try to get HQ information – official statements, and especially any unofficial stuff you can dig out of individual officers. We'll put a team of four or five on this. But once Caron gets back, you can glue yourself to her."

"Will do."

"Having a top female cop leading this will make a fantastic story – and don't be shy about fleshing her out with some personal color. Don't embroider; focus on the facts. But remember that personalities sell stories. A young red-haired heroine would almost justify those expensive Goss presses we bought."

"I hope you're not thinking of running a color bikini shot."

"Well, not right away."

"Disgusting. You guys still amaze me."

"Now you go and amaze us old guys with brilliant coverage."

"That's my plan."

"Bye now. Stay in touch. And when you've got some deep thoughts on this case, come on in and brainstorm them with me and some other cavemen."

"Cavemen? Given the scene of the crime, I guess that's a joke. Will call again soon."

Office of the "Comité Champagne" (CIVC, 11:03 a.m.
The phone rang at the grand, red-brick headquarters of the Comité Interprofessionnel du Vin de Champagne at 5 rue Henri Martin in Épernay. Familiar CIVC name: *le Comité Champagne*. Its director, Jean-Jacques Denoirjean, took the call from a *L'Union* journalist. Repentigny being the CIVC's co-president for the merchants' side, this news was of tectonic proportions.

Denoirjean cursed, then immediately rang Repentigny's vice-president for the merchants, Jean-Jacques Lieuvrain. Then he called the growers' co-president, Jérôme Larquay. Each side was supposed to work out inevitable short-term conflicts of interest with the other and to seek a shared long-term interest. Sublimation of differences allowed the two parties to act in tandem, and to give the industry a single, fully representative voice.

Director Denoirjean quickly organized a conference call with Lieuvrain at the merchants' *Union des Maisons de Champagne* and Larquay at the growers' *Syndicat des Vignerons.*

By now, the news was on radio and TV. The growers' remaining president and the merchants' acting co-president had already flashed the news officially to their people through their internal networks.

When Denoirjean had the call set up, the wires burned.

"What a shocker," said Larquay. "I hope it wasn't one of our guys who tried to kill him. Repentigny bullied a lot of our people, and plenty of these hate him, I'm sorry to say."

Lieuvrain, cool and contemptuous, retorted:

"His business practices, *cher collègue*, are a matter of perspective. And maybe we shouldn't dwell on his supposed faults even as he lies bleeding in a hospital bed. Instead of attacking him, let's brief the Permanent Commission, then call an emergency meeting of the executive committee."

"I agree. Let's get going on that right away." Larquay urged. Each went off to alert his half of CIVC centers of decision. Then they put out an extraordinary joint statement as follows:

"The CIVC, representing the entire champagne industry, deplores the cowardly and dastardly attack on our distinguished colleague and co-president, Hubert Repentigny. We offer our solidarity to him and his family, and encourage the authorities to track down the culprit as soon as possible. The CIVC executive committee will meet tomorrow in emergency session. Meanwhile, we shall issue no further statements on this tragic matter."

The news had hit the entire champagne region like a deep-digging bunker bomb. Every producer, every blending and marketing *maison* – and many suppliers, politicians, tourist and media people -- not only knew of Repentigny. Nearly everyone had either personally dealt with him or had a brush with him. He had a few friends at the top, in his role as the *maisons'* co-president of the Comité Champagne.

The emergency meeting would happen a day later, with the state's local representative presiding. This was both local and national business.

Élysée Palace, Paris... 11:17 a.m.

News of the attack stunned the President of the Republic, Roland Guérin. He and Repentigny were close friends, old warriors in the ruling Mouvement des Français (MDF) party. Classifiable as moderate rightwing, MDF had deep roots in Champagne-Ardenne.

"My God, Monsieur le Président," said Élysée secretary-general Jean de la Ribière, "could one of our enemies have done this?"

"Or one of our allies. Hubert has not just made friends on our side. Get the Interior Minister going on this. Tell him to monitor not only the Reims police but to alert the DCRI."

Interior Minister Dominique Morel's *Direction centrale du renseignement intérieur* (DCRI) – part of the Police nationale – is renowned for preventing terrorist acts in France. It's effective too in countering foreign espionage, including theft of industrial secrets. Skeptics sometimes suspect it of spying on the government's political enemies. These sometimes allegedly include the President's political enemies.

"Do you suspect business or local political enemies?" asked the secretary-general.

"Who knows? Hubert ran roughshod over much of the champagne industry. And he ran the

Conseil régional like Brezhnev – with brutality and secrecy."

Repentigny had been President of Champagne-Ardenne for three years, dominating its 48 other regional councilors. He was also the eyes and ears of Guérin in Champagne-land. As such, he often slipped into the palace for late-night scheming with the president. The two men shared many things besides politics. Including a taste for creative arrangements and exotic women.

One of these women was Ma Chuntao, a charming 28-year-old currency officer at the Chinese Trade Mission's Paris office. Intimates knew that Chuntao meant "Spring Peach" in Mandarin. Professionals knew that Ma was the family name of a respected expert on central bank liquidity swaps.

The president needed to stay close to central-bank currency issues, especially since the euro was fragile – and China might become its savior.

Repentigny, who had met Ma in Beijing with his *chef de cave* during a business trip, needed Ma's advice on opening the vast Chinese market for his champagne.

This was a trio of multilateral advantages. For Ma, the payoff was top-level political and commercial information for her real master – Tsaï Yongkang, chief of Department 2 of Beijing's Ministry of State Security (commonly called *Guoanbu*). Department 2 conducted "reconnaissance abroad." Areas of interest were broad economic intelligence, weapons systems and, above all, industrial espionage. Such as stealing French economic and technological resources. Ma's immediate mission: to plan a gradual takeover of France's champagne industry.

Classic techniques of Chinese economic penetration: manipulation of Chinese student organizations in the West, strategic computer break-ins, investment in technology-stealing joint ventures, setting up dummy companies in the West to spy on local firms, and compromising of Western politicians, businessmen and journalists in "honeypot" entrapment.

This standard Soviet-era technique infiltrated NATO by placing female agents termed "swallows" near Western bases. Trawling women as bait before men is a system as reliable as the world supply of testosterone. And as old as the Bible's Judith and Holofernes – the Assyrian general who literally lost his head to his Hebrew paramour-spy.

France's well-known 1986 Bernard Boursicot case should have lingered in Palace minds. Bouriscot, a French diplomat, got sucked into spying for the Chinese by dallying with a beautiful Peking Opera singer called Shi Pei Pu. Shi, alas, turned out to be a man – making the scandal even more titillating when it blew up. Guérin and Repentigny, like so many powerful men, could occasionally be made to forget security risks simply by a shapely thigh – in this case, slipping out of a high-slit *cheongsam*.

Ma was bright, informed on world affairs, and full of witty, cosmopolitan conversation. She was a graduate of China's top foreign language school, the Beijing Foreign Studies University. Her French was flawless, a point that could easily make people forget she wasn't French.

"She has skills far beyond banking," gloated the goatish Guérin about Ma. "With her, I have the impression that the East invented sex," concurred Repentigny. Both men – as stupid as men can be when rutting – had broken an elementary security rule. Each man, at his summit, tended to believe that power confers impunity. And that no enemy could possibly be as clever as they.

Guérin at first felt confident seeing Ma. DCRI had warned him she was a Chinese spy – industrial for sure, but maybe even military. Quickly, he phased Ma out of his pleasures. She really wasn't worth the risk. Besides, the supply of women available to a French President – amply documented in a 2006 book called *Sexus politicus* – was as generous as Henry Kissinger's dictum claimed: "Power is the ultimate aphrodisiac."

Guérin also cautioned Repentigny about Ma. "Watch out, Hubert," he joked. "She might be plotting to steal your champagne secrets." Repentigny cracked a tight smile. "Well, to make real champagne, she would have to ship the vineyards of Champagne-Ardenne all the way to China."

Centre Hospitalier Universitaire (CHU) de Reims...
11:29 a.m.

Caron walked quickly to the familiar trauma ward.

"I'm so sorry, Madame," she said, placing a hand on Madame Repentigny's shoulder. "Thank you, Commissaire," replied Madame, before bursting into tears. She had heard the news only minutes ago, just after her morning Mass.

Caron saw Painteaux on the bench beside Madame. He had brought her a coffee.

"*Bonjour Commissaire*," he said. As you requested, I'm at your disposal."

Caron turned back to the victim's wife. "Please forgive me, Madame, I must ask monsieur Painteaux a few questions. Are you all right sitting here? I must interview him in my office."

"Yes, of course."

Monsieur Painteaux, would you mind meeting me at the outside door, then following me in your car?"

"Gladly, Commissaire."

"Just allow me a few minutes first to talk with the surgeons."

"Yes."

Operating room, CHU... 11:37 a.m.

Caron, dressed in hygienic hospital gown, briefly watched the surgeons at work. Repentigny was fighting for his life. His bandaged face twisted in agony, he moaned sporadically.

"In order to treat him, said the chief surgeon, "we're going to sedate him – what laymen call inducing an artificial coma."

"I understand."

"This will be a carefully calibrated sedation with anesthetics, pain-killers and anti-anxiety drugs. Dosages will change in synchronization with heart and brain monitors while a respirator helps sustain life."

"What's the prognosis?"

"Not good. His head is dreadfully smashed. All we can hope is that the sedation may give the patient's wounded brain a long-shot chance of survival, dodging between clots and bleeding. With great luck, it might also help him swim his way back painlessly to some shred of lucidity – for now an unlikely prospect."

"Any chance he will ever be able to help identify his aggressor?"

"That's totally uncertain, though miracles occur. The aggressor's back-of-the-head blow has deeply damaged the patient's parietal lobe -- the brain sector affecting recognition, orientation and perception of stimuli. He may not even be able to identify his wife and family."

At flickering intervals before the sedation took hold, Repentigny caught visions of himself suspended from the hospital-room ceiling. He watched as doctors and nurses hovered over his body below. Vaguely, he recalled that such imaginings often preceded death.

A spark of anger and curiosity fleetingly aroused his determination to defeat death. And to punish his aggressor? But soon, brain-fatigue effaced both illusion and query. Unable to grapple with more speculation, he could only face his fate. Then slip into nothingness.

"We've lost him for now," said the surgeon. "God knows if he will ever come back."

"I would be grateful if our *police scientifique* could liaise with you and share information on the crime and the patient's outlook."

"Of course. We're always happy to work with your specialists."

Hôtel de Police, Caron's office, 2:30 p.m.

Alerted by Caron's call, *Identité judiciaire* chief Louis Trumaut had a detailed file on Painteaux sitting on her desk before she got back. It noted his eye for the ladies, but also his high professionalism at work, in spite of a volatile temper and soaring ambition – justified by numerous prizes.

After a sandwich and coffee, Caron greeted the two police officers she wanted to monitor the Painteaux interview. After routine ID preliminaries, she began:

"Tell me again when and how you found Monsieur Repentigny."

"It was at about 8:40 a.m. this morning. As I told you, I discovered him on my early walk from our blending area down to the underground storage area."

"Why were you going to the storage area at that time? You're the *chef de cave*, responsible for quality-control, blending and production, I believe. What took you from your normal lab work early in the morning to go inspecting the caves?"

"Sometimes I also do a little public relations."

"Underground? How is that?"

"Well, we try to craft vintages for specific customer niches. So to convey the image of a carefully tailored artisan approach, it occasionally makes sense to trot out the chief craftsman to meet major clients."

"I see. That's reasonable – like bringing out the chef at a top restaurant. Now who were your guests this morning? I expect an attempted murder under their noses didn't make a very reassuring impression."

"I had some Chinese customers coming this afternoon, and I wanted to make sure that a special display for them in the caves was ready. China is a huge growth market for champagne, as it is for fine Bordeaux and Burgundy wines."

"Impressive. But let's get back to the crime. What did Monsieur Repentigny's wound look like?"

"The back of his skull was a sickening red mush of blood, bones and hair. Pieces of bone lay hanging like pieces of a broken-up jigsaw puzzle. It looked as though somebody had clubbed him from behind.'

"Did you first think he was dead?"

"Yes. I couldn't see how anyone could survive such a blow. Then I saw that, miraculously, he was breathing. I could plainly do nothing for him. And I knew that once police were alerted, medical help would come quickly.

"What did you do next?"

"I immediately called the police, using a nearby wall-phone. My cell-phone wouldn't work so far underground. I think I made the call just after 8:40 a.m."

"At 8:43, to be precise." Then what did you do?"

"I ordered two of our cave workers to mount guard over the scene without disturbing it."

"Good."

"Once you had supervised removal of Monsieur Repentigny to the ambulance upstairs, I drove Madame here to the *Maison Blanche* facility of the CHU Reims. Emergency traumatology, as you know, is a major specialty here."

"First, Monsieur Painteaux, a practical question: How many people have keys or easy access to the caves, and who are these people?"

"About a dozen people have keys and authorization to go down to the caves – obviously, Monsieur and Madame Repentigny, myself, three of my assistants, the chief visitors' guide, and the chief of marketing. Oh, and two maintenance staff and two watchmen. The last four are trusted, longstanding employees. Everyone except the owners must sign in and out, leaving their keys in a protected alarm-box."

"Is the alarm-box regularly checked?"

"Every evening at closing."

"When is that?"

"For the guides, around 6 p.m. For the blending and marketing staff, sometime between then and 9 p.m."

"I presume that the maintenance staff and watchmen might need to visit the caves at any time, even overnight?"

"Yes, of course, especially to watch for fires. But we have smoke-detectors as well. As for routine moving of bottles, we try to do that during daylight hours – for both safety and union reasons."

"Why do you think Monsieur Repentigny was down in the caves last night?" she asked.

"I've no idea. Except that as owner of our company, he had an elevator key and often visited the caves at odd hours, sometimes with guests."

"What kind of guests?"

"Some were VIPs, others business partners or family. A few others were special friends."

"Special?"

"Well... forgive me. Despite my great loyalty to him, it's not a state secret that Monsieur Repentigny sometimes brought a lady or two here for a personal tour."

"I have heard hints to that effect. He is known as a very charming man. Could you make a guess at which category of guest he might have had with him last night?"

"No. I haven't the slightest idea. But the brutal blow to his head doesn't suggest to me that his guest was a woman."

"Monsieur Painteaux, some women illustrate well enough the old saying that 'hell hath no fury like a woman scorned.' But I take your point. Now think hard: Who *really* could have committed this crime? Taking account of motive, means and opportunity, who most *likely* might have committed the crime?"

"I still have no idea. I was at a movie with my wife last evening, and went to bed before midnight."

"Can you prove those two points? What was the movie?"

"Oh, I see I'm a suspect."

"As are many people."

"The movie was...by coincidence, a police biography called *J. Edgar* by Clint Eastwood with Leonardo DiCaprio. It was playing at the Gaumont-Pathé on the Place Drouet-d'Erlon."

"I hear it's pretty good."

"Yes, it left us guessing a lot – like a real thriller. You might like it."

"For how many years have you worked at the *maison Repentigny* as *chef de cave*?"

"Eight years."

"Well, perhaps, as M. Repentigny's key man, running the whole technical and quality side of this operation, you would have some idea of his business rivals, or even enemies? Might any of these be angry enough to attack him like this?"

"He did... I'm sorry, he does... have a number of people in the champagne community who have complained about his robust business practices."

"Robust?"

"Some say brutal."

"How so?"

"Some competitors have accused him of bankrupting their businesses by dodgy practices, including disinformation, manipulative press campaigns, and stealing valued staff."

"Nasty stuff."

"Oh yes, and financial collusion, marketing tricks, price-fixing, even being less-than-impeccable about where our grapes come from."

"That's quite a catalogue of grievances. Are the complainants mainly *grandes marques* or little firms as well?"

"They come from all sectors of the industry. Monsieur Repentigny knows the industry inside and out, in all its manifestations. Unfortunately, he made enemies far and wide. In my view, most of these were just jealous of his success. He was not unethical; he just had sharp elbows."

"Could you supply me with a list of his most unhappy competitors? In all categories of the industry, big and small?"

"I think I could -- but may I do this confidentially?"

"Of course. Just write the names on this paper."

Painteaux took fifteen minutes to denounce possible enemies, blushing and looking strained.

"One more thing, monsieur Painteaux. Our officers will go with you to obtain copies of the hard disks in all your computers, both business and personal. They will also want the disks from the guide group and senior administration."

"Understood."

"I may have still more questions for you. Like this time, we will meet in my office with police witnesses and a colleague filming our interview. We need such documents to constitute a complete 'album' or presentation for the tribunal. Meanwhile, I'm asking you now to restrict your travels to the Department of the Marne. And to Paris."

"You have my full cooperation."

Conseil   régional,   Hôtel   de   Région...
Châlons-en-Champagne

The afternoon after the crime, Jean-Philippe Gueilliot, the Conseil's first vice-president, opened the session for the 42 councilors present with a tribute to their president:

"Mesdames, Messieurs, we are all in a state of shock at this morning's tragic news. Our esteemed president, Hubert Repentigny, has brilliantly served this region as our leader, and we hope with all our hearts that he will recover to lead us again after this horrific crime. Kindly raise your hands for a unanimous vote of solidarity with both him and his family."

All hands went up. Some faster than others.

As president of the Champagne-Ardenne region, Repentigny had executive power over all decisions approved by the councilors. He controlled well over half a billion euros a year to fund an astonishing range of activities – economic development, infrastructure, secondary and university education, professional training, research, agriculture, culture, sports and territorial development – even European and international affairs.

As in France's twenty-one other Metropolitan and four overseas regions, some of this money seemed to find its way into private pockets – allegedly including the regional president's. Repentigny served himself generously for pet projects. But he also starved political adversaries of funding whenever he could. Under his iron gavel, his moderate right-wing MDF (*Mouvement des Français*) majority

had made him equally devoted friends and enemies. Several of the latter would gladly send him
even deeper underground than his caves.

Hôtel de Police, Reims...
Caron's chief fan and protector, Commissaire
divisionnaire Georges Baraquant rushed home
from Lyon to back her up. He planned to give her
maximum latitude. But he would be constantly at
hand as a sounding-board and adviser.

"You're off to a good start," he assured Caron.
"But this is going to be a dangerous, even explosive,
investigation no matter what we do. Repentigny
has his finger in a lot of pies. And he has more enemies than the Borgias."

I'll be making specific assignments tomorrow
morning. I propose to break up our investigation
into several logical segments."

"Sounds good. Just fly the list past me first."

"I'll e-mail you a tentative list of assignments
tonight."

Painteaux's list of Repentigny enemies showed
that the P.J. had just just gained scores of new suspects.
Caron went over them with Baraquant and Duroselle,
who approved her plan to categorize her suspects as
follows: family and friends, industry rivals and enemies (subdivided), politics, personal, other.

Next morning, she subdivided the industry investigations among four team-leaders. Each had a
clear mandate and all an urgent mission. Each was
to suggest a second, or even third, comrade to work
with him.

"Bailly, you check out the growers. I hear that quite a few of these 15,000 entrepreneurs have collided with Repentigny's often rough negotiating methods. Oh, by the way: Don't be too influenced by David-and-Goliath stories about so-called helpless 'small' growers versus big, bad merchant houses. Over the past twenty years, the average grower has become quite prosperous. The *grandes maisons* don't have them over a barrel anymore. More often than not, growers can squeeze the merchants by threatening to withhold grapes."

"Good to know that. I will try not to see the growers as martyrs."

"Jeanson, you dig into anti-Repentigny grudges among the major champagne brands and houses. There are theoretically about a hundred worth looking at – but in this case, maybe the top twelve to fifteen. Don't forget to check with the *Service d'Information Générale*"

"Millet, you get the industry organizations, especially their umbrella group -- the Comité Champagne, aka the *Comité Interprofessionnel du Vin de Champagne* (CIVC). They're a huge font of information about everything and everybody in the business, as well as about industry economic trends. Watch especially for tricks on the key issue of pricing. These champagne guys all virtuously trumpet that they defend top prices for champagne as a luxury product. But even the average newspaper reader thinks some of them cheat and chisel. Thirteen bottles in a dozen, and so on."

"Remember: Repentigny is CIVC's respected – and feared -- co-president. This has made him known to everybody in the champagne community. And it has given him privileged access to global market figures, as well as the strengths and vulnerabilities of all the major houses."

"Rousseaux, you get a really tough one, a long shot. You can look into the *Institut national de l'origine et de la qualité (INAO)* – the body charged with making rules on protected product origins or *appellations d'origine.* They're supposed to defend ferociously the exact borders of the fields officially listed as "champagne" areas. But pressures to enlarge official areas continue. Naturally, this being France, some people suspect skullduggery. They run a pretty mysterious operation. Try looking for evidence of bribery aimed at snagging the official champagne designation."

"Can I organize a sting?"

"No, Rousseaux, this is not the FBI," Caron laughed. Just sniff around. We have quite enough complications as things stand."

Investigating all four categories of players would give Caron a quick and multi-faceted overview of the whole industry. And, with luck, it could identify individuals with serious grudges against the victim.

Much of the information sought could come from published documents of companies and organizations. And "even," noted Caron, "from our local daily, *L'Union.* We all know it has a team of reporters monitoring the champagne industry. And it's a useful source of gossip – possibly kept quiet for fear of advertising reprisals. The champagne world is a small village. People know far more than they say. They close ranks to protect their own. They know bad PR of any kind can harm the whole local economy."

Relations between the Hôtel de Police and *L'Union* had not always been friendly, especially concerning the Police judiciaire. It was tricky to make allies of journalists for anything. Only must-cover civic good news, humanitarian or human-interest stories earned ready cooperation. Corralling news people to share gossip that might instead serve as scoops made herding cats look easy.

Later that evening, Caron turned to another document that had just come in: the first medical-legal report of the Ministry's *Institut National de Police Scientifique*, which coordinated France's six crime-related laboratories. It combined both the CHU-Reims hospital and *police scientifique* analyses. It was graphic, and sickening.

MINISTÈRE DE L'INTÉRIEUR

Direction Générale de la Police Nationale
Direction Centrale de la Police judiciaire
D.I.P.J Strasbourg
Sous-direction de la police technique et
scientifique (SDPTS)
REIMS, le 7 octobre 2011

RAPPORT TECHNIQUE D'INTERVENTION
Le Commissaire Jean-Noël Virissel
Directeur, Institut National de Police scientifique
Écully – Lyon (-69-)

à

Le Commissaire Denise Caron,
Chef des Divisions Opérationnelles
Police Judiciaire de Reims (-51-)

S/C via normal hierarchy

OBJET: Preliminary crime scene report

AFFAIRE: Repentigny / Flochard / Caron

VICTIME: ATTEMPTED MURDER

RÉFÉRENCE Hubert Repentigny, attacked October
2, 2011 Your instructions.

In sending this document, I have the honor of reporting the following facts:

On October 1, 2011, under the direction of Commissaire Denise Caron, and with colleagues from Identité judiciaire, our team visited the Repentigny champagne caves. All data gleaned at the crime site over two days went to the Institut national de police scientifique for laboratory analysis.

This report includes findings from all the Institute's lab specialties, as well as comparison with medical reports from the CHU de Reims.

DESCRIPTION OF CRIME:
Medical analysis estimates the time of the attack as roughly between 20h:00 and 23h:00 in the evening of September 30, 2011. The victim fell forward from a violent blow to the back of his head, delivered from behind by a right-handed assailant. The aggressor's blow with a heavy blunt object deeply damaged the victim's parietal lobe -- the brain sector affecting recognition, orientation and perception of stimuli. Severe damage there risks making the patient useless in identifying the perpetrator. The attack weapon was a 75 cl. full bottle of champagne, left on the floor near the victim. It showed no fingerprints (supposing gloves), but its bottom carried blood samples and hair, both the latter identified as belonging to the victim. A bloody black head-scarf lay nearby.

The wall immediately beside the attack site contained a splash of the victim's blood, along with spattering also confirmed as his blood. In the wall's splash of blood was drawn, with an abandoned stick, the well-known company logo-letter "R" for Repentigny. A top-to-bottom line crossed out the letter – presumably proclaiming murder.

The victim had other wounds apparently caused by a sudden fall forward on his face. His nose was broken, his right cheek was badly bruised, but his forehead was surprisingly untouched -- his thrown-forward hands seem to have broken his collapse. Shards from his shattered glasses entered his eye-sockets and eyebrows.

There was no sign of reciprocal combat, thus indicating a surprise attack from behind. But there was disturbed dust indicating agitation around where the victim was found. The only identifiable shoe-prints near the victim were his own. But other shoe-prints, in a running-away pattern, turned up in dust twelve meters away. Assuming these to be the aggressor's, he appears to have been wearing large (size 46) flat deck-type shoes with no tread – or possibly treaded shoes wrapped in some cloth-like material. This size of shoe, and the indentations in earth found nearby, would normally suggest a man at least 183 cm. tall.

A search for footprints extending 100 meters into adjoining corridors revealed only fragmentary and inconclusive traces of a similar footprint. In a scouring of a 25-meter radius outward from the wall beside the attack site, no other human evidence turned up.

FOLLOW-UP:
The P.J. of Reims (Police scientifique and ID) will build profiles of potential aggressors from the above categories. This should facilitate questioning of suspects in order of plausibility.

SDPTS remains at the disposal of the P.J. of Reims for further investigations of either suspects or the scene of the crime.

Fait à Écully (Rhône), October 7, 2011

Le Directeur,
Jean-Noël Virissel
Commissaire de police

31, avenue Franklin Roosevelt
69134 Écully Cedex

That same Friday evening, Caron sent her first report to the Ministry. It added in appendix a preliminary list of suspects, by category: family and friends; employees; major champagne houses; smaller growers; political enemies.

MINISTÈRE DE L'INTÉRIEUR

REIMS, October 7, 2011
Direction Générale de la Police Nationale
Direction Centrale de la Police judiciaire
D.I.P.J. Strasbourg / Service Régional
de P.J. de Reims
40, boulevard Roederer
51100 Reims

Le Commissaire de Police Denise CARON
Chef des Divisions Opérationnelles
Police Judiciaire de Reims

à

Monsieur le Commissaire Divisionnaire
Georges BARAQUANT
Directeur du Service Régional
de Police Judiciaire de Reims

OBJET: Attempted murder committed against monsieur Hubert Repentigny, of French nationality, owner and president of the maison de champagne Repentigny à Reims. Crime committed in the night of September 30-October 1, 2011.

AFFAIRE: X – assailant unknown.

RÉFÉRENCE: Instructions of Messieurs Rodolphe Tournier and Jacques Chanoir, assistant magistrates under mission from Maître Philippe Machet, investigating judge at REIMS.

ATTACHMENTS:
Report of Institut National de Police (Écully) on nearly lethal attack on monsieur
Hubert Repentigny
Rogatory mission to investigate this flagrant crime.

I have the honor of informing you of the first results of the above-authorized investigation.

1. <u>The attacker was almost certainly a tall, powerful male familiar with the Repentigny caves.</u> He might either be
   a) an employee or relative with access to a key to the caves.

b) a friend or enemy (business, political or personal) who had infiltrated a tourist line and stayed behind in a well-planned attempt at assassination. Note: Given the victim's well-known business, political and extramarital activities, these most plausible suspects will require wide and simultaneous enquiries.

c) a random murderer angry at the wealth or notoriety of the victim and determined to strike a blow for reasons either of ideology or personal satisfaction.

2. SRPJ-Reims is pursuing all the above tracks, and is mobilizing a special task force of 22 officers for this case. Reports will follow as significant evidence appears. We shall inform the media only as this is useful to the investigation.

Service Régional de Police judiciaire de Reims-Champagne-Ardenne

Le Chef des Divisions Opérationnelles
Denise Caron
Commissaire de police

Department 2, Ministry of State Security, Beijing

Within 24 hours of the crime, the news had reached Tsaï Yong-kang at the *Guoanbu* overseas secret services offices at 14 East Chang'an Street. First, Tsaï had received a flash from his special Paris agent, Ma Chuntao, friend of Repentigny and the President. It simply said "Friend gravely injured." Then a source at the French exporters' Champagne Bureau at No. 16 Xinyuanli in Beijing had rung him. It confirmed the wounding, but could add nothing.

Tsaï, a former student and worker in Paris, like statesmen Zhou En-lai and Deng Xiaoping, took a strong personal interest in France. Working with overseas secret services of the People's Liberation Army and the Ministry of Commerce, he had put in place a remarkable spy network covering the country and its industries woven as tightly as Beijing's bird's-nest Olympic Stadium.

His department used professional agents under diplomatic or commercial cover. It set up dummy companies to buy trade secrets, especially high technology. It recruited overseas Chinese professionals and students – some volunteering, others bullied. And it blackmailed weak politicians and businessmen to extract information via KGB-style "swallows" like Ma Chuntao.

Tsaï demanded further information from Ma, especially on how the crime might affect penetration of the Élysée Palace. And how, if at all, this might harm the bold champagne market strategy that he and Ma had been developing.

La Basilique Saint-Remi, Reims...
The news stunned both priests and faithful at the famous old church where Hubert and Sophie-Charlotte were parishioners. It was a blow especially to those close to Madame. Her gifts and

commitments had made her a rampart of orthodoxy both theological and historical. Most shaken was the family priest, the thin, elderly Vladimir Farfelan. He heard weekly Confession from Madame, who normally had nothing serious to confess. Her husband, who had rather more to confess, always walked briskly past the four dark carved confessionals, two on either side of the soaring nave.

The Repentigny Caves, three days later...
As a student, Caron had visited these caves a couple of times over the years. Now with a possible murder on her hands, she decided to go down again alone with her boss Baraquant and Painteaux to refresh her memory.

She checked again where Painteaux had allegedly found Repentigny's body behind a rack of dark, dusty bottles. The chest-level display sat in the half-darkness among millions of bottles awaiting maturation or sale. Racks lined the cave's maze-like corridor-tunnels.

She stared at the splash of Repentigny's blood on the wall. The would-be killer must have acted in a fury to sign his crime with the crossed-out Repentigny "R."

"You know the numbers," offered Painteaux. "Reims alone boasts 250 kilometers of caves; its rival 'champagne capital' Épernay claims 110 kilometers. The Reims caves even stretched at one time into the spider-web *caves* of Saint-Remi" -- the venerable 5th-6th-century bishop of Reims famous for baptizing France's first king, Clovis I.

"Right now," he went on as they approached a walled-in section, "there's a group of amateur archeologists trying to locate links to the two Benedictine abbeys of Saint-Remi and Saint-Nicaise. They stumbled on ancient documents mentioning a gold treasure left by Saint-Remi. That may be legend – as it probably is."

"A pretty good story," observed Caron. I did see a newspaper piece on that. But I've never heard of any serious, well-funded follow-up."

"I've met some of the archeologists, and they seem to be working from a credible lead. And they're totally dedicated."

"If I believed in Saint-Remi, I might be after the treasure myself. But I think I'll stick to my own kind of police work."

Tightly packed, endless arrays of bottles filled deep, rounded, stone storage-rooms dedicated to black-stenciled export destinations: Barcelona, London, Berlin, Moscow, Shanghai, Rio de Janeiro. New York. They also stood, arrayed for tourists, beneath huge, twenty-meter-high ceilings in the massive white rooms that Roman slaves had carved out two thousand years ago. Their quarried chalk had built ancient houses. Now it guaranteed the 11-degree Celsius temperature that preserved champagne for optimum integrity and taste.

A few racks even lined the startling art-gallery *salles* installed by the owner's beautiful blonde wife, Sophie-Charlotte. Mixing Bacchus with abstract expressionism, her *salles* displayed eye-opening sculptures and frescos to incongruous but often spectacular effect.

"Monsieur Painteaux, while I think of it, could you give us a little more background on the Chinese guests you had coming through here just after the crime? I gather our bubbles are catching on in China?"

"It's been a long, hard sell. The Chinese have no tradition of either cold or fizzy drinks. But we've found the lever: snobbery. Well-off, even upper middle-class, Chinese, are starting to buy champagne because it's a luxury product. For twenty euros, they can announce to compatriots that they're rich and worldly. It's conspicuous consumption. Think of Louis Vuitton luggage -- but cheaper and in a bottle."

"So who's pushing the Chinese market?"

"Nearly everybody would like to, but Repentigny is definitely leading the chase. Some major Chinese investors are also sniffing around."

"Interesting."

"Well, Moët has marketed in China since 1843. They've long had a profile there. And now, with Scarlett Johansson as their ambassador, they're dazzling the Chinese."

"That's good for France, isn't?"

"Of course, but on top of that, Moët is planting a new vineyard in northwestern China to produce a bubbly drink that – who knows? -- may come close to real champagne."

"This, at the same time as the Chinese are buying vineyards in Champagne?"

"Yes, they have bought a few properties. They're doing the same with Bordeaux wines."

"What do your think the Chinese strategy is – normal investment, or something else? At this stage, we're not dismissing any hypotheses. And just conceivably, there might be a lead here somewhere."

"Personally, and I'm no expert, I think it's a little like their high-tech strategy. They buy and invest in high-end western products on some co-production basis – then undercut us in some of our other markets with made-in-China products."

"As with Airbus?"

"Exactly, western firms ache to sell to the huge China market, and pester the French government to back them. As it always does. President Guérin rarely visits China without trying to sell French airplanes, TGV fast trains, nuclear reactors and other expensive toys."

"Then we might expect that in five or ten years our world market will find an aggressive Chinese competitor?"

"Indeed. But for now, our company just wants to sell them our champagne. Although... there were unfounded rumors that M. Repentigny might one day be tempted by more original arrangements."

"Really? I take note. Some people in the Comité Champagne, the CIVC, must be getting extremely edgy about that."

Baraquant, impatient, dismissed the colorful digressions. "Let's not waste time on treasures, art-galleries and hypothetical Chinese trade strategies. We're here to investigate attempted murder – which may very soon become murder."

He stepped away from Painteaux to whisper a few words to Caron. Then he said to both: "We need to get back to the office to look at our growing mountain of reports. Goodbye, Monsieur Painteaux."

As the three of them had strolled through the grand art gallery, Painteaux's mind wandered back to an incident with Sophie-Charlotte that he certainly wasn't going to mention to Caron.

About a year before, in Repentigny's absence on a foreign trip, Painteaux had agreed to lead a VIP tour of the caves with Sophie-Charlotte. A lean, blond 51-year-old, Painteaux was meticulously respectful around his boss's wife. And she, a very bourgeois Catholic matron (very well-preserved nonetheless), held her rank.

After the ritual glass of champagne in the upstairs bar, Sophie-Charlotte approached him: "Sébastien, I am thinking of expanding my art-gallery down in the caves. Could you possibly spare a little time to advise me on the best space and layout?"

Sophie-Charlotte had already expanded the extravagant art gallery she and her predecessors had started in a few of the *grandes salles* below. The VIPs and upstairs staff leaving, Painteaux asked: "Do you have anything specific in mind?"

"Why don't we take the elevator down and have a look," she said.

"Of course, just give me a couple of minutes to make a call."

"Fine, I'll change my heels for more reasonable shoes at the guides' counter."

They got on the small elevator, suddenly aware that their bodies were very close. After the end-of-day champagne they had just drunk with their guests, they felt relaxed and talkative. Reaching the bottom quickly, they entered the dark *caves* and started walking along the alternating cobblestones and cement. Distant lights came and went. The ancient mystery of the caves made them speak softly to avoid echoes.

The cool, dank air added to the caves' eeriness. The round glass bottoms of millions of tightly racked, fermenting bottles faced them on either side, seeming to spy on them like wide, vigilant eyes. Painteaux and Sophie-Charlotte walked side by side, softly exchanging occasional small-talk. Sometimes their voices seemed a little strained, as though each was trying to pretend that this unusual stroll was perfectly normal.

For fifteen minutes or so, they meandered toward the huge high-ceilinged gallery-rooms. Finally, when they reached the first gallery, their voices began to echo, heightening the artificiality of their chat, which they tried hard to keep level, slow and clear.

Sophie-Charlotte commented on the weirdly beautiful frescos that an earlier baron's wife had sponsored. "I doubt that these damp walls will keep them safe for many generations."

"I'm sure you're right," agreed Painteaux.

Then she turned to the heavy stone statues of animals. They stopped beside a multi-ton three-meter-long statue of a bull. Sophie-Charlotte sat up on one side of its back to survey her realm. Painteaux joined her a little further along its back. They continued whispering about the room's grandeur. And some possible changes.

Sophie-Charlotte slipped down off the bull's back, risking a twisted ankle or heel, Painteaux caught her hand and helped her down. This was the first time they had ever touched, and each took fleeting note.

They walked on and on through the high chamber, corner lights barely lighting their way. The shadows grew longer, and the racks of bottles continued to watch them like secret sentinels. Between the great chambers, the light almost disappeared. Once, missing a small trough in the cobbled floor, Sophie-Charlotte slipped again, almost to one knee. Painteaux lifted her up with both hands, asking her if she was OK. She was, but seemed a little shaken. Her thank-you sounded strangely hoarse.

They walked carefully to the next tunnel. There was a broken stone stairway down about fifteen steps. Painteaux said: "I'll go ahead, so if you slip again, I can stop you."

Tentatively, with Painteaux a step or two below her, Sophie-Charlotte stepped downward, cautiously turning her feet sideways on each step. Three steps from the bottom, she shrieked and fell forward. Painteaux whirled around. He caught her full on, her body slamming against his so that he had to put his arms around her. She slithered down his body, both of them aware – glad? -- that their instinctive cat-and-mouse game had ended with her arms around his neck. And his around her waist. Then, as she jerked to recover upwards, his hands found themselves for a split, undeniable, thrilling second, gripping her buttocks.

Blushing, they instantly disengaged, pretending that nothing had happened.

Ministry of the Interior, Paris... Repentigny's national notoriety and connections drew government interest outside the Élysée Palace. Minister of the Interior Dominique Morel had got the President's signal to dig widely. Morel himself read the SDPTS and SRPJ-Reims reports and told his senior staff: "Digging into all these hypotheses will demand extraordinarily diverse investigative skills. Run thorough files on all the suspects identified by P.J. Reims. As well as key political allies and enemies of the victim."

Morel also asked for a report on Caron to make sure she was up to the job. Her profile showed a colorful, fast-rising police star with an unusual profile – a woman able to tie the Reims and Paris strands together?

MINISTÈRE DE L'INTÉRIEUR

Direction Centrale de la Police judiciaire
Dossier no. R-2011-6/11
Service des Ressources Humaines

Parcours et Profil de la CP Denise Caron

ÉTAT-CIVIL:
Name: CARON
Given names : Denise Ambroisine
Birth date : August 2, 1979

Place of birth : Biscarrosse, Landes (40)
Family status : Single

STUDIES:

Elementary and secondary studies in Biscarrosse and Arcachon (40)
Advanced Academic:
* University of Reims – medieval studies: Licence, mention Histoire (Reims and Troyes)
* Conservatoire à rayonnement régional (Reims) : Diploma in classical music (opera-singing)

POLICE TRAINING:
* École Nationale de Police de Reims (graduated 1st in class)
* École Nationale Supérieure de la Police at Saint-Cyr-du-Mont-d'Or (graduated 2nd in class)

POSITIONS HELD:
* Préfecture de Police de Paris: National Division for Repression of Attacks on Individuals – assistant to director for three years
* Six-month study at Interpol, Lyon
* Service régional de Police judiciaire de Reims (four years in all specialties)
* Regular upgrading of management and investigative skills in yearly seminars

NOTABLE SKILLS:
* Languages: facility in Latin, basic English, some German
* Singing: amateur opera (mezzo-soprano)
* Sports: black belt in karate

OBSERVATIONS:

Caron is a strong, sophisticated, top-of-class Commissaire de Police. She appears destined for rapid promotion and is a potential candidate for very senior service. Her work with the director of the National Division for Repression of Attacks on Individuals makes her a specialist in tracking down killers in complex cases.

Her unusual qualifications in medieval history, Latin and music give her an intellectual discipline, poise and original approach that may prove of value in cases culturally broader than most.

Leadership qualities: Caron is clear-headed, steady, decisive, and a good communicator. She carries a natural authority, though she might show a little more tact in gaining acceptance of her leadership. She is popular with most colleagues, though a few older ones resent her high level of cultural accomplishment, as well as her place as a possible rival for promotions. She can also display a prickly personality: one senior colleague at the Paris Prefecture termed her *la Rosse* [the ill-tempered horse] as a play on her red hair [la Rousse].

Conclusion: Marked for close attention as candidate for future senior HQ position.

Caron's personnel assessment reassured Morel. He passed it up to the President, scribbling this margin comment: "We're in good hands..."

A woman Commissaire de police was no longer folkloric. First allowed to compete for this senior rank only in 1975, women soon proved among the strongest, sharpest Préfecture officers. Since the legendary Martine Monteil in the 1970s and '80s, top policewomen shone as crime-busting and anti-terrorist strategists. Even among the famous ones, Caron stood out as anything but a mere *fliquette*.

Putting her in charge of this extraordinary investigation gave the crime even more profile. The daily *Aujourd'hui en France* teased about a "Maigret in high heels," and leftwing *Libération* trumpeted tritely: "Morel: Cherchez la femme!" But Caron didn't need their silly sobriquets and jokey headlines to make her reputation. She had a much more richly textured life. A wall-full of commendations and advanced university diplomas. A solid culture.

And a handy, discreet, uncomplicated lover.

Her secret was Stéphane, a handsome, hard-bodied 27-year-old carpenter with curly black hair. A few speculated about his being her alleged "cousin from Grenoble." But only her cat Mendès knew her secret. Stéphane's job: to make sure Denise glowed with primal confidence, vital to keeping the boys downtown in thrall. Denise and Stéphane wasted no time on cop-talk or any other talk. They just collided each time as man and woman. That's all she – or he -- wanted. And Stéphane, remembering the cry of many a cop-baiting crowd, could only chuckle at his good luck in – to put it politely – bedding the police.

Caron's lusts, we've seen, went far beyond the boudoir. "Even before the École Nationale de Police," glowed *L'Union*, the local daily, in her first hometown profile, "she had acquired a university *licence* in medieval history and Latin, her thesis focusing on the Champagne-Ardennes region. Church history is rich around here. Of course, it has often intersected with the reputation and marketing of champagne."

L'Union also marveled at Caron's musical skills. "She knows opera from Bizet to Wagner -- scores, conductors, major singers. She has even sung opera semi-professionally. 'In the middle of a tricky case,' confided an amused former Paris colleague, 'she sometimes startled us by letting loose a phrase or two from *Cosi Fan Tutte* or the *Ring*. These little bursts, or the lingering hum of a favorite aria, often happened when she was nosing her way to a conclusion.' Naturally, her cop nickname is 'the diva.'"

Hebdo Vendredi, the Reims give-away weekly, echoed the praise. But true to its quick-info style, it gave her a less lyrical welcome. It packed in her background details, played up her University and police studies in Reims, and ran a small feast of photos of her in its central picture section. Showing the judgment that won her grudging loyalty from most of the old P.J. warriors, she insisted on posing nearly always with her police colleagues. "We invariably operate as a team," she told the paper on her appointment as head of operations. "There is no single 'Maigret' here," she purred. "We are all Maigrets."

Perhaps the most telling point about Caron was her veneration for Olympe de Gouges – the French revolutionary decapitated by male revolutionaries Robespierre & Co. for daring, among other things, to publish a Declaration of the Rights of Woman and the Woman-Citizen. This was, in macho eyes, a sacrilegious parody of their Declaration of the Rights of Man and the Citizen. Framing it on her office wall led a few yahoo policemen to say she must be a lesbian – the very concept of equality, for some of them of course, constituting a form of castration.

Caron, like de Gouge, was a formidable woman. Though not at all favorable to castration.

Within a few days, almost anybody in Reims – and even in upper-class, political Paris – knew about Caron. And the list of suspects quickly expanded. Caron had assigned twenty-two of her thirty officers to blitz the industry. To untangle possible financial crookedness in Repentigny's personal and company affairs, she had also borrowed two top accounting sleuths -- Riquet and Bardy -- from the Paris sub-directorate of financial investigations. For possible leads to the victim's regional and national MDF party links, she assigned two specialists in political skullduggery, Dossereaux and Braillard.

Three experts from the *police technique et scientifique* would build on their initial report as new evidence appeared. Two of these, like their immediate boss, were women: Lemoine and Lévesque. Caron, playing off their churchy names, promptly dubbed them "my nuns."

Now Caron would handle interrogation of family and friends herself – with shoe-leather help from a couple of young local-born cops, Jenneret and Marcambault.

CHAPTER TWO
A Most Respectable Family

With her two eager investigators in tow, Caron turned for her first, classic suspect to Hubert Repentigny's wife, Sophie-Charlotte. Today would be mainly a courtesy call to a traumatized widow-in-waiting. Future meetings would be in Caron's office.

The Family Estate: Madame Repentigny...
Preliminary research had turned up a reassuring profile of Madame, and a hint or two of eccentricity. As with most people, Caron knew, a first look rarely told the essentials.

What did Caron learn, and not learn, before interviewing Hubert's wife? Her team had quickly pulled together some press clippings and talked to enough media and industry observers to form a rough impression.

By all accounts, Sophie-Charlotte defended supremely well her status as a pillar of society. "She graces everything she touches," gushed *Bulles d'Or*, a glossy 'people' magazine covering the industry. "She is a generous *animatrice* of charity events. She visits and donates to homes for the elderly. She leads her city's artistic life, personally funding exhibitions and sponsoring artists."

"Madame Repentigny," went on the magazine, "enhances her husband's image at every turn – both the man and his *maison*, just by standing beside him.

Sophie-Charlotte also drew praise for her commitment to fitness. As a board member of the Club de Tennis de Reims, she displayed a redoubtable backhand in both singles and mixed doubles.

Sophie-Charlotte also appeared as a prominent Reims figure in the elegant Helsinki-based quarterly *Fine Magazine Champagne*, distributed worldwide. The local daily *L'Union* and even the industry technical organ *La Champagne Viticole* praised her for promoting the region's signature product.

Part of Sophie-Charlotte's image, said industry colleagues, was her conscientious upbringing of her four children: Marie-Laure, 27; Laurent, 24; Christian, 21; and the vivacious, hormonal 19-year-old Christelle. Marie-Laure, a dynamic business graduate and junior executive gaining experience at high-end champagne house Billecart-Salmon, had her sights on a senior role at her father's firm. So did the two boys. Still completing their studies, they were apprenticing in-house with their father. Primed for rivalry, each had already mapped out tentative long-term strategies to see which one would take over the empire from *papa*.

Christelle, noted neighbors, was far more interested in boys than bubbles. In time, her mother hoped she might become a sleeper candidate for business glory. For now, she was mainly getting practice for monkey business.

Madame's public image also rested on her remarkable devotion to her Church. "She attends Mass each morning," said her vivacious friend Sylvie, wife of another champagne *baron*. "She gives unstintingly to Catholic causes - including minor repairs to our Notre-Dame Cathedral. She even arranged from her own purse a small supplementary pension for Notre-Dame's veteran janitor, 90-year-old Claude." Stooped and twinkle-eyed proud, Claude bragged to tourists that "I have had only two mistresses: my wife, and this beautiful cathedral."

A discreet few knew that Madame even supported with her own money repairs to the Basilique Saint-Remi, where she often walked for an hour or two in the beautiful, high-arched Déambulatoire. She convinced Hubert to let his company join seven other *grandes maisons* as a financial patron of the great Bertrand Cattiaux Franco-Flemish organ – a masterpiece for J.S. Bach's sublime polyphony. She had even chaired the restoration backers' group, the *Association Renaissance des Grandes-Orgues de la Basilique Saint Remi.*

Many, including her, thought that Saint-Remi himself was buried behind the altar. She also personally financed special protection for St-Remi's reliquary and the annual *Fêtes de Saint Remi* (in Reims alone, written without the accented é.)."

That was the public sketch of Madame Repentigny. With these few vignettes in mind, Caron and her two sidekicks arrived to visit the lady herself. To dig behind the image. This was barely a day and a half after the crime. It would be partly a get-acquainted courtesy call to a likely widow before her hard interrogation began a day later.

Caron and her two investigators arrived at the family's private residence in a modest, unmarked police Peugeot 308 SW. The house sat far back behind the elaborate black iron gates bearing the firm's name and huge gold "R" for Repentigny.

Elegant and imposing, the house flew French and European Union flags – for it also served as venue for formal greetings and receptions. Through the gilt-tipped grill, about 150 meters at the end of a large lawn, spread five 19th-century buildings in different styles: the owners' residence, two wide round towers bracketing a yawning warehouse, and a two-storey stone office building-cum-visitors' center.

The likely widow-to-be, forewarned, was waiting on the steps in a simple black dress. Caron thought her anticipation a trifle eager for a woman still in shock. But Madame Repentigny displayed dark circles under her eyes, and looked truly distressed. She wore minimal makeup, and simple gold earrings and a gold pendant shaped in what was plainly the Repentigny "R."

First impression: Madame Repentigny was a youthful 49 of medium height, a convincing blonde, bourgeois variety. Her long hair held up in a bun, ready to cascade downward -- for a favored lover? Tasteful black heels encased small, delicate feet. An aristocrat in the incestuous village of *grandes familles du champagne*, she looked solid, settled and soignée. Proper and poised, she was a strikingly attractive woman *dans la fleur de l'âge*.

Caron greeted her hostess. "Good morning, Madame Repentigny. My apologies for disturbing you so soon after this appalling crime. First, allow me to present my colleagues, Commissaires Alain Marcambault and Georges Jenneret."

"Good morning, Commissaire, good morning gentlemen. Please don't apologize. I appreciate your promptness, and your willingness to meet me here. Kindly sit down and join me for tea – or coffee?"

They all went up the steps, down a long corridor. They entered a magnificently decorated, high-ceiled room full of glowing Jean Lurçat tapestries, gold drapes and Second Empire furniture.

"We are all, alas, addicted to coffee, Madame – a hazard of police work. To spare your time, may I begin by laying out how we would like to proceed?"

"Of course, I am in your hands, Commissaire."

"To begin, I would like to ask you a couple of routine questions related to the crime. Then a few basic questions about you, your background, life and duties, the family enterprise, and of course your husband. I am glad, by the way, that he is getting the best of care. I understand that the Reims medical team have brought in an eminent specialist in brain trauma from Paris's Hôpital Pitié-Salpétrière, Dr. Raymond Aurillac. "

"That's the hospital, I know, where Princess Diana died," noted Madame.

"And I'm told Aurillac is the best of the best in his field," added Caron.

"Thank you for your encouragement, Commissaire. We can only pray now."

"If I may start with you, Madame. For the record, could you please tell us where you were and what you did the day and evening before the attack took place? And where you were during the night of the crime?"

"On the morning before this horror happened, I was engaged in philanthropic work for the aged. I go to visit the elderly twice a month at *Ma Maison*, a residence of the Petites Soeurs des Pauvres. You may know it: it's at 38 rue de Bétheny."

"Yes, I've driven past it."

"Then after a light lunch with two lady friends downtown, I went home for my usual nap. When I awoke, I spent a couple of hours planning fund-raising for the Centre Culturel Saint-Éxupéry."

"Would you mind writing down the names of any people you met that day or evening? Your lunch companions and others?"

"Of course. I should say that monsieur Painteaux – such a kind man – dropped off a new book he had found on Saint-Remi. By an impressive young female scholar from Lyon."

"What time did he stop by and leave? He came at about 5:30 p.m. and left shortly after."

"How did he appear?"

"Elegant, as always."

"I mean his demeanor. Was he calm, tense, or agitated, or anything else that struck you?"

"I could only say that he seemed extremely eager to please, as he always is."

Caron pressed: "Now where were you that evening and during the night of the murder?"

"I was simply at home. I went to bed and slept all night."

"Another question related to the attack. Did you ever notice anything at all in your private family quarters that might give us a clue to the crime?"

"None I can think of, Commissaire. But I am not a police person, and would not know what to look for."

"Any unusual placement of objects, any sign of precipitation? A note or phone message indicating worry or trouble? Or even mentioning a person, place or time for an imminent meeting?"

"Well, Hubert did leave a phone message about being called for an urgent meeting. But he didn't add any details."

"May we record your previous phone messages, Madame, to look for a revealing detail?"

"Of course, but much of it will be boring personal matters. Including quite a lot about religious activities."

"We understand that you are a devoted believer and philanthropist."

"A passionate believer, but truly just a modest philanthropist."

"Since searching is our professional business, Madame, do you mind allowing us to scour your family's entire living quarters? This will take most of a day, even more. The *police technique et scientifique* can go much farther than the naked eye."

"Please do whatever you need to. Here is a key to the entire building. Also some keys to private drawers and cupboards. Please take your time."

"Thank you, Madame. That is extremely helpful. We would like to start immediately and spend the rest of the day here. Maybe part of tomorrow too."

"I shall pack a small suitcase so I can vacate the premises and stay with a friend as long as you need."

"Splendid. Jenneret, please alert Dominique Flochard to come as soon as possible with her team. You and Marcambault can stay behind to lead the visual research."

"Now, turning to your background, Madame. Is the following information correct? You were born 49 years ago in the Prefecture town of Châlons-en-Champagne (then Châlons-sur-Marne) as Sophie-Charlotte Battonnier. You came from a very Catholic upper-bourgeoisie family: father Jean Battonnier, mother Dorothée Heucq. Your families were parishioners at the Collégiale Church of Notre-Dame en Vaux, famous for its onetime relic of Christ's navel."

"Yes, those are my roots."

"You met your future husband when you were twenty years old and you were both attending the arrival of the BOC-Challenge round-the-world solo sailing race. Wasn't that the ancestor of today's Vendée Globe race?"

"Yes, it was."

"Monsieur Repentigny, I believe, was there as a sailing instructor. He was twelve years your senior, a rather dashing older man who swept you away to become the wife of a future champagne baron..."

"That's a romantic but fair description. Ah, I see your coffee has arrived." A costumed maid served it to the three police, while Madame took more tea.

"Merci, Madame," said Caron. "Now about your family here. The children?"

"Four, as you must know. Marie-Laure, the eldest at 27, is quite a modern young woman, with business ambitions taking her to Sciences Po, then INSEAD, the international MBA school at Fontainebleau. Strong and determined, she has visions of becoming a Veuve Clicquot -- but perhaps without becoming a widow first to echo that famous brand."

"And she has a sister, I think."

"Does she ever. Nineteen-year-old sister Christelle is just emerging from her teenage years. And has the preoccupations you might expect."

"Boys, beauty and fashion."

"Alas, yes. Studies run a poor fourth."

"And your sons?"

"Laurent is twenty-four and looking for his way. He too has done Sciences Po, but hesitates between the family business and a political career – both fields his father loves. Christian at twenty-one is for the moment specializing in girls. He tells them he might become an astronaut, a poet or a famous scientist. We are all waiting with anticipation to find out which. So, I hear, are the many girls he impresses."

"We might be able to use such a versatile brain in the police. But tell me, do you notice any budding rivalry as to one day taking over this famous champagne house?"

"It's far too soon to say. But in such families, the potential always exists. Often the children are reasonable enough to work out some kind of understanding, of playing different roles. In other cases, some children decide to make totally unrelated careers, outside the champagne culture."

"And if they don't do either?"

"In a few cases, a passionate ambition can lead to jealousy, jockeying and harm to the house. In such cases, there are usually larger houses willing to absorb a divided house. Such a threat can sometimes help bring an arguing family to pull together. Or bring in a respected family friend as mediator."

"So no incipient or simmering rivalries?"

"As a pure hypothesis, I could only imagine Marie-Laure and Laurent colliding. But they love each other very much and would surely collaborate. We are indeed a very loving family."

"On that theme, Madame, I would like to leave you to recover a little from this shock. We need to ask you quite a few more questions of possible interest in this crime. Could you possibly come to my office at the Hôtel de Police tomorrow morning at 10 a.m? You should anticipate spending most of the day with us."

"Of course, Commissaire. I shall be there."

"Thank you, Madame, for your time and generous welcome today."

Hôtel de Police...interrogation of Mme Repentigny

Madame had her chauffeur drive her white Peugeot 3008 HYbrid4 to the interview with Caron. She arrived just before 10 a.m. and parked in the big police parking-lot. She climbed the stone steps and entered the large main lobby full of lost souls of all conditions. Facing a high desk of three security women, she spotted Jenneret waiting. He called out to her in friendly voice, waived off security, and led her to the elevator on the left.

Enquiring how she was, he took her up to Caron's wide office on the fourth floor. Caron got up to shake her hand, again introducing Jenneret and Arcambault. She offered a chair facing her. Then she sat down with the window-light behind her.

"Thank you for coming, Madame. May I offer you a coffee?"

"Please. *Un crème* if you can."

"No problem" Jenneret brought coffee for both women – a double espresso for Caron.

"Madame, we are now officially questioning you. We are taking careful notes on your testimony, as well recording you. I would be grateful if you could be as frank as possible, even though some of our questions must be extremely personal, indeed intimate. This is, after all, a potential murder case. We need to get to the truth – all the truth – as quickly as possible."

"I understand, Commissaire. I shall do my best, even though I am a rather shy person, little given to confessions – except with my priest."

"Thank you for your cooperation. I also know that the world of champagne, especially at the top, is an extremely discreet, even closed society."

"Indeed. That is a matter of tradition, taste, business secrets, indeed security."

"I know and respect that, Madame. But I am mainly interested in your personal observations. Not so much on the champagne world, but on your husband, his life with you and your family. Also, his friends and possible enemies -- known or presumed. Unfortunately, this will become quite intrusive."

"I shall try not to take offence. Your must do your duty."

I'm afraid there is no other way. I hate to ask certain questions, but I'm grateful that you accept that these are only a vital part of any such police investigation.

"I appreciate your delicacy, Commissaire, and will do my best to be open with you. But I am still in a state of shock."

"I can see that, Madame. But since you are kind enough to see me so soon, may we go straight to the point. I wish to touch on your husband and your life with him."

"Of course." She lowered he eyes, touching and turning her wedding ring.

"How did your marriage evolve over the past nearly thirty years? Though not married myself, I am well aware that love can change its colors many times, for better or worse. And that even in the best of marriages, there can be clouds. How did love between you and your husband develop over the years? Did you manage to keep the love in your marriage?"

Madame Repentigny blushed, slowly went white, then fell silent. After a long delay, she said: "That is a terribly, terribly personal question. But I believe we have had a good marriage. Obviously love has redefined itself more as respect and partnership."

"I understand. I realize that my question reaches into the deepest recesses of your heart. And of your husband's. But knowing more just might cast some light on this tragedy, if only indirectly?"

"Does that mean I am a suspect?"

"Forgive me, but yes, you are a suspect. As is automatically anyone as close to Hubert as you would be. You are not the only suspect. But unavoidably, you are a suspect. I will have to probe quite intimately into your relations with your husband and many other people. That includes any men or women you or he are close to. This is just long-tested, textbook police procedure. I beg you not to take offence. We are not insinuating anything. We are investigating."

"First, Madame, were both your families happy you married?"

"Naturally. It was plainly a love match. Few quibbled over its May-December aspect, because the age gap was not enormous. And Hubert, a wealthy, handsome businessman and sportsman, plainly had the means necessary to give me a very comfortable, secure life. For the young girl I was, this was a dream. My family fully supported the marriage. And Hubert's family thought I was quite a catch too. I was beautiful, intelligent and well-raised, even if a rather naïve and traditional girl. Potentially, I'm sure his family saw me as an ideal wife and mother."

"Part of your traditionalism, I believe, came from a strong religious upbringing."

"Yes, it did. We were a family of believers, and very close to the Church. One might say that we were even a leading Catholic family of Châlons-sur-Marne, now of course Châlons-en-Champagne."

"I did learn of your family's position there."

"I went to religious schools at both primary and secondary levels. My father was active in fund-raising for repairs to the stained-glass windows of the Cathédrale Saint-Étienne. And my mother devoted herself to helping isolated elderly people at our family parish – as you noted, 12th-century Notre-Dame en Vaux. When a teenager, I dreamt of becoming a *carillonneur* there. The bell-tower has 56 bells – one of the largest outside of Belgium. I also loved walking in the crypts. It was so moving and mystical to walk among the tombs, to ponder ancient lives and events of church life."

"You will no doubt hear that we will be talking with your former teachers at the École Privée Sainte-Thérèse Verbeau and the Collège Notre-Dame-Perrier."

"*Mon Dieu*, you are very thorough. They may not remember me. I was just a quiet, problem-free girl."

"I'm sure you were. But even that is good information. We shall just do our job and add any new information to our file."

"Then your family moved to Reims when you were sixteen, I believe," said Caron. "Did that make much of a change in your life?"

"It certainly did. That's when I discovered first-hand the incredible history of the early church in Reims. I was stunned to learn that, even before Christianity came, the town was the second largest of the Roman Empire. At that time a tribe called the Rèmes allied itself with Rome, and gained favor. Hence, later, the name of Reims."

"You are quite the historian."

"No. Everybody knows these things. I also found peace and sanctity in the Basilica of Saint-Remi – after the Cathedral of Reims, the city's greatest sanctuary." Hubert and I often attend major ceremonies there, though I go to Mass much more often than he does. I also love strolling in the Basilica's grand *Déambulatoire*, the lovely convent-like gallery running from behind the choir. It gives me such peace. And it helps me think about my life and those I love."

"How did the arrival of four children affect your life and marriage?"

"As a well-raised Catholic, I devoted myself to the children's upbringing while Hubert took on increasing duties at the *Maison*. I tried also to be a supporting 'champagne wife.' I did whatever Hubert wanted me to do, to reflect well on our brand and business. This meant quite a few social responsibilities. These were of the *noblesse oblige* variety: the arts, the less fortunate, young people and the elderly."

"Commendable."

"But my spiritual side also came to the fore. Combined with unstinting devotion to the Church, I became increasingly aware of the intersection of faith and history. In Reims, that's what the stones and statues whisper to us every day."

"But did any of this affect your marriage? Did it bring you closer to your husband? Or take you away from him?

A small cough and long silence answered the question. "As marriage matures, the magic and mystery can fade a little."

"I understand. That must be almost universal. Please go on."

"After about eight years, I noticed that Hubert didn't look at me quite as before. Superficially, little seemed different. But over time I became a living ghost – no, that is too strong. I just didn't seem to be the center of his life any more."

She blushed.

"I fear," said Caron, "that may be a condition of the institution itself. Sad, even tragic for many. But it is, I hate to say, classic."

"It was so painful. He wasn't nasty. He just came to look through me. I was becoming a stranger. In public, he still treated me with respect and apparent affection. But when we were alone, we became partners without a partnership. I had become an invisible woman. "

"I'm so sorry. What happened then?"

"After a dozen years of this, it became clear to me that Hubert must have other interests. I mean interests outside of champagne. And outside of our marriage. He was discreet, but watching more carefully, I could catch tell-tale signs: a suddenly cancelled appointment, a mysterious business trip, a vagueness about names, times and places, more attention to his appearance. Watching his weight. I came to presume a mistress. Or mistresses."

"Do you have any idea who she or they might be?"

"I have very strong suspicions. Mainly from watching certain women, but also his reaction to them."

"A name? Or names?"

"Reluctantly, I believe Hubert had an adventure with our chief tourist guide, Frédérique Pommier. A few years ago, she was, as her name suggests,

Eve with her apple in the Garden of Eden. She was his first known conquest, at least within the company. I believe she got over the affair, and has since married a nice teacher from Épernay."

"There were others within the firm?"

"You might say that he did a thorough survey of all the young candidates for guiding jobs. They were all in their twenties, he was their handsome, energetic boss, and I understand that most got very personal tours of the caves with Hubert."

"He considered these girls a kind of personal harem?"

"You might say that."

"Did any of these girls stand out as longer-lasting favorites?"

"An English girl called Jenny comes to mind. A fresh-faced school-girl type with charming braids. She taught Hubert English, often strolling with him in the caves – of course so he could explain to her the champagne industry."

"I once stumbled on a note from her telling Hubert how thrilling it was for her to pursue their English lessons on the back of the big stone bull in my underground art-gallery."

"On the back of a bull?"

Jenneret and Arcambault struggled to suppress a smile.

"I can't imagine what they did, or how they did it, but apparently Jenny found it exciting. I guess a bull in itself might have teased her tender mind, never mind any Minoan echoes."

"Where is Jenny now?"

"Safely back in England. Doubtless as a milk-maid with a herd of cows and a prize bull." Sophie-Charlotte smiled a contemptuous smile that dissolved into fatalism.

"Besides the harem of guides, can you think of any other dalliances?"

"Alas, yes, far too many. Hubert was also friendly with a few of the wives of the *barons du champagne*."

"How do you know that?"

"Unfortunately, that kind of gossip reaches many ears. The champagne world at our level is a big private family. We all know each other pretty well. And I have become adept at recognizing a smirk, pity or condescension. Or effusive greetings that last a trifle too long."

"I've heard how hermetic your champagne high society can be. But surely some people talk more openly."

"Not really. First, there is a sense of duty toward the group. In an industry where taste, elegance and joy are the product itself, people are reticent about tarnishing the community's image. To shift metaphors, I don't want to rock the boat – we are all too close. Our children intermarry, dynasties emerge, and we cherish many common rituals."

"You might say an image associated also with culture, charities and a certain religious ostentation."

"I'm sorry you call it ostentation. Many of us are sincere believers. If people happen to observe our faith, it doesn't mean we're parading our devotion."

"Forgive me, Madame. That was not my intention. There was a second reason?"

"The second reason is that most of us at our level are particularly attached to our families. We have a horror of divorce, even though that happens."

"And it does, as I see in *L'Union*."

"We don't appreciate their coverage at all. At least for such voyeurism."

"Any other suspicions about mistresses?"

"To simplify, why don't we just say that Hubert is something of a skirt-chaser. He has a compulsion to seduce every woman he meets. We have seen several men in the news recently – national and international figures – who have the same problem. Some of them are violent. Others just crude. They are basically vulgar, though at first somewhat charming. Hubert is a non-violent charmer."

"Love affairs don't always end well. Some lovers – men as much as women – can't forgive being abandoned. In our experience, some of these people commit crimes of passion."

"I've read about that."

"But can you think of any specific abandoned women who might hate your husband enough to want to kill him?"

"A few who might *want* to kill him. But none that I know would really try. Their anger is more rhetorical, I suspect, than real in the sense of acting on a feeling of betrayal."

"Could you not come up with a plausible candidate or two? Forgive me for insisting, but we need to dig hard."

"All right – but bear in mind that I am not accusing such women, only noting their apparent onetime passion for Hubert and their deep dismay about 'losing' him."

"Who then? Reims has almost 190,000 people, but it's still a small town. You must have had suspicions about the lady."

"Or ladies."

"Yes. Now think hard, and bear in mind that we need to establish means and opportunity, as well as motive."

Madame paused, looking down. Then, lips tight, she slowly expelled a name:

"Anne Varendal – wife of Roger Varendal, a major *grande marque* competitor. She may be the only one. I know she is still furious at Hubert's dumping her about three years ago. She had hoped to supplant me. She has the anger. She also has the financial means – if I were to wildly imagine -- to hire a killer. But her opportunity of a free run of the caves is next to impossible."

"Really? Might she not have kept a key? Or given a copy to someone else? How well do you control the numbers of tourists who visit the caves? Might not a really clever killer hide among them, lurk in the caves for a few nights with food and water, then strike when he spied your husband?"

"That seems awfully far-fetched."

"We are in the business of the far-fetched, Madame. And very often reality, as the saying goes, is far wilder than fiction."

"I have to cede to your experience in these matters. But I still think something like that could never happen. Besides, once the crime was discovered, how could the killer escape from the caves?"

"Good question. But believe me, anything is possible with a brilliant, well-paid assassin. A big pay-off can induce criminals to put up with plenty of danger and discomfort."

"So, suspecting a mistress, what did you do?"

"Nothing. As a good Catholic wife, and aware of the world, I considered marriage sacred and unbreakable. I knew that men had other needs, and other opportunities. My priest also told me that such dalliances often burn themselves out. And the husband returns to his holy bonds."

"I can see that a little stoicism could help."

"I also had children to consider. And the Caesar's-wife reputation of the whole family, which was now mine as much as Hubert's."

"Ah, I see. Did you do nothing at all to try to win him back?"

"By the time I realized what was going on, it was almost impossible to seduce him again. I was starting to show a wrinkle or two. And I was not raised to know how to compete in the bedroom with his no doubt freer women."

"So did you just give up and play public wife? Did it ever occur to you to take a lover?"

"Absolutely never. I am a believer, and parallel lovers seemed no way to reunite a couple."

"Some people believe it can."

"Not me."

"Not even tempted? Ever?"

"Never, never!" Blushing angrily, she spat out the words

"So where did you find solace? Friends? Family – the Church?"

"Essentially in the Church. I was far too ashamed to confide in family or friends."

"Maybe you should have."

"Maybe. But that's not me."

"So – just guessing, in light of your up-bringing – you turned more to the Church?"

"Yes, very much. It was the only refuge for my grief, the only relief from my pain."

"How did this deepening of your religious life express itself?"

"By an even more intensive faith. By constant prayer. By a deepening, as you say, of my spiritual life. And, in that regard, I would say that the marvels of church history in the architecture of this city greatly facilitated my spiritual quests."

"How so?"

"Well, of course I read a great deal about the saints and bishops of this place. I explored the crypts and secret places of our churches. I visited old or abandoned convents and nunneries – especially the vestiges of the *Couvent des Cordeliers*, a place so stark, so evocative, so open to God's blue sky."

"What thoughts did these old sites stir in you?"

" A deeper and deeper yearning for saintliness. I often saw myself as a nun. As the so-called 'bride of Christ'. Or even – and this is blasphemy – of some saintly man."

"The link between human love and love of God is an old story, as you know."

"That is what Christianity tells us over and over."

"To bring this even closer to earthly marriage, with its pleasures, do you recall seeing Bernini's famous Vatican statue of the Ecstasy of Saint Theresa? Eyes lost in radiant vision, and apparently swept away by passion, her face conveys either beatitude or orgasmic agony. Really, as many have observed, both at once."

"Is that a police question?"

Caron smiled. "Anything that explains psychology can be a police question."

"I have seen this statue in person, of course. It spoke to me intimately. And it still does." Fleetingly, eyes lowered, she let her finger brush over her family pendant.

"Do such reflections bring you shame or pleasure?"

"Both, I admit. When in the grip of such thoughts, I feel I am in a state of joyful sin. Of indescribable strength and weakness. Of commanding my obedience to a higher power or person. Does that sound ridiculous to you?"

"Not at all. Sexual and spiritual passions, as we just said, are often Siamese twins. Especially when a person feels lost, or crushed by inescapable pressures. If you dig a little into the history of comparative religion, such affinities seem commonplace. I think of the Temples of Khajuraho or certain African dances."

"But those are obscene! They have nothing to do with me. My passions are chaste. I cannot be a lady in the drawing-room and a whore in the bedroom, as a vulgar saying has it."

"Are you sure? I ask this bluntly, for if I may say, a too-chaste wife, as even you hinted, cannot easily compete with unchaste mistresses. I am trying to determine to what extent your passionate spiritual life may have crowded out an earthier life with your husband."

"Are you accusing me of making no effort to keep my husband? Or of being frigid? I'm beginning to resent this."

"Of course not. I am only trying to understand why your husband might have sought the greener fields you mentioned."

"This is very, *very* hard for me, Commissaire. It is all so intimate. Had you been a man, I would have walked out long ago. But as a woman, I admit you have given me much to think about. I am actually grateful that you spoke to me like this. I can't imagine my priest expressing himself so frankly and sympathetically."

Jenneret and Arcambault remained statues. But discreetly, they took notes.

"In conclusion, Madame, I can see that your spiritual life is vital to you. I will need to ponder this more myself. To try to imagine how, if at all, such forces may have shaped events. I will also review some points of our discussion with other colleagues. We do that every day to bring into play the judgments of our entire investigative team."

"I hope that my intimate revelations will not leave this building?"

"I assure you they will not, Madame. But we need to compare notes and pool perspectives freely within our investigative team."

"Of course."

"Now, Madame, may we get on with a few more practical questions?"

"Of course."

"Financial matters, to begin. Did you and your husband have a pre-nuptial agreement? You know, *en séparation de biens*? Or was it agreed that you would share equally in all wealth acquired during the marriage?"

"We had a pre-nuptial agreement. This was because our families brought very unequal financial means to the marriage. And because Hubert wished to preserve the main body of his heritage for his children."

"Perfectly understandable, and perfectly in conformity with the *Code Civil*. Now do you have separate bank accounts?"

"Yes, he puts a generous allowance in my account for personal spending every month. He also gives me access to an adequate joint account to handle common expenses – household, vacations, and so on. And of course he has his own personal account, which I have no reason to see."

"Most women would likely be very happy with that."

"I think so."

"Now is there anything unusual in his Will, as far as you know? Has he shown you his Will? Do you know the *notaire* who will handle it?"

"As I said, we have a s*éparation de biens* pre-nuptial agreement. So, under the *Code Civil*, as you say, everything is automatic. To ensure the main body of their inheritance, the four children each hold large blocks of shares – in equal parts. Our family notary is Maître Alexandre Gueillot. He comes from a long line of distinguished Reims notaries, and is well regarded."

"We shall naturally have to talk with him, as well as with your family bankers."

"We do our personal banking at the BNP branch at 89 rue Gambetta -- not too far from here. The current branch manager is Mr. Félix Corzelius – with no acute accent on the "e.""

"We shall subpoena all your accounts and holdings there. Do you have any other accounts or holdings?"

"No, and besides my current account at the Gambetta branch, I keep there only an *assurance-vie* savings and investment policy of about two million euros. That is a long-term nest-egg that Hubert helped me establish."

"And your husband's accounts?"

"I am not privy to my husband's banking and investment activities. All that is his personal affair."

"If all this proves to be as simple as it sounds in your case, Madame, I don't think our investigations will become embarrassing for you. But we must still study movements of capital in your accounts, as well as your spending. Including gifts and donations."

"Do you need any other information?"

"Yes, we need to know who owns this beautiful house, and whether you have any other houses or assets."

"This house belongs to the company, for we use it frequently for business entertainment. But we have a splendid small château near Grézan in the Bas Languedoc. Just half an hour from the Mediterranean. One day, I may retire there. It has memories of the Knights Templar, and the climate is warm and sunny. It's surrounded by fields producing a delightful little Merlot."

"An enviable prospect."

"The castle is in both our names. Hubert insisted on that so that it would automatically go to me on his death. Oh, we also have a chalet in Gstaad. We are all rather ardent skiers. That is owned by the company – again for business as well as personal use."

"Are there any more significant aspects to your financial life, Madame?"

"Nothing that I can think of. Really nothing at all."

"Well then, I think that will be enough for today. May I simply ask you not to leave France until we complete our investigation? It would be ideal if you could remain within a day of Reims – say, no further than Paris. That is only a request, but we would appreciate your cooperation. Do you foresee any problems with that?"

"No, Commissaire, of course not. I wish to help you, and will do everything I can do to assist in catching the horrible person who attacked my husband."

"Thank you so much, Madame. Goodbye. Oh yes, one last thing. Could you please send to me at the Hôtel de Police a full list of all the people – including you and your family, I presume – who hold keys to the caves, and especially to the elevator? In theory, any visitor might have hidden during a tour and stayed behind to commit the attack. But the list of key-holders may narrow the list of suspects and speed our enquiries. We already have a tentative list. I want to confirm it."

"Immediately, Madame la Commissaire. There should not be more than a dozen or so people. We have to guard our caves scrupulously."

All hands shaken, Caron led the way out. Madame Repentigny accompanied her ahead of the two policemen. She kept one hand over her heart, the family "R" pendant now a kind of totem of grief.

Noting Madame's comment about careful surveillance of the caves, Caron decided to keep her two police guards there. One would watch the upstairs tourist and office area, the other the downstairs tourist meeting-point.

She also decided to install a remote video link to the Hôtel de Police from the surveillance cameras already monitoring the caves' entrances and exits. These would show – and record for police -- the long stairway, the elevator, and key galleries below. Twenty-four hours a day. No one would now be able to enter or leave the caves secretly. Perhaps, in a classic return to the crime-scene, the actual culprit might even appear.

Le Grand Café, 92 Place Drouet d'Erlon...
To digest her interview with Madame Repentigny, Caron took her two sidekicks to a late lunch of *moules frites* at the popular Grand Café. Specializing in mussels and pasta, it draws bargain-conscious students and employees to the city's long, wide pedestrian thoroughfare and meeting-place. Big, cheerful, and open non-stop seven days a week, it makes a handy cop hang-out as well.

Caron would not eat here all the time. When alone, she often splurged at the trendier *L'Apostrophe* down the street, her secret *cantine*. She saw its cozy back-room as a useful antenna for local gossip, especially from intellectuals, artists and other trouble-makers. Its shielded noise and half-secluded dark-brown leather chairs, she thought, protected sensitive conversations.

"What did you gentlemen make of Madame Repentigny," Caron asked her colleagues quietly over their mussels. "She just seemed like a grief-stricken wife with lots of money," said Marcambault, never obsessed with nuances. "I suspect," differed Jenneret, "that a women of her background might have a rich and perhaps surprising life, quite apart from the money. But at this stage – taking account of the shock she is under – it's too soon to speculate."

"Yes," agreed Caron. For now, we have only appearances and quick impressions. We should not take this one meeting with a woman under heavy immediate stress as definitive."

"Exactly," the two policemen said almost together.

"My own first impression of Madame Repentigny," went on Caron, "is that of a typically controlled, properly raised *bourgeoise*. I saw eyes etched in genuine pain – from the assault on her husband, of course. But also, perhaps, from illness? Or indeed from her unhappy marriage? The lady's eyes held a stoic gaze, never darting away, except to look down at her pendant a lot. Touching this icon of the Repentigny family identity is clearly a comforting reflex. A totem."

"Yes, said Jenneret, "I was beginning to think it might even be a borderline obsessive-compulsive tic."

"But there was one other thing," added Caron. "Just as I turned away, I thought for instant that I caught in Madame's eyes a kind of fierce intensity. Terror? Hysteria? Guilt? Crushing grief?"

Before she left Jenneret and Marcambault late that afternoon, Caron shared a final impression. "I sensed behind the impeccably correct bourgeois champagne aristocrat a hint of something else. Some kind of passion? A failing about which she's uncomfortable – and is eager to hide?"

"I didn't notice exactly that," said Jenneret. "But I agree she was very tense and controlled. As though she might either explode, or burst into tears."

"Of course, all this could just be the understand-able strain of learning your husband may have been assassinated – then having to face the embarrassing probing of three police officers."

"We'll need to dig a lot more into this lady," Caron said. "There's much more to her than we've seen or heard. For one thing, she protests her virtue a little too much. I want to find out what her secrets are. And what they might make her do. I want to dig seriously into her love life, if she has one. Something tells me she has a wild side. It may be a man, a woman, a fantasy – or even money or power."

Love life? For the wife of a champagne baron, indiscretions were tricky, if far from unknown. The champagne corridor from Reims to Épernay allowed lots of innocent cover – friends, shopping, business, culture. For a handful, it was a veritable highway to sin – as was the TGV train to Paris. But illicit shenanigans, most people believed, held no interest for a lady of Madame Repentigny's status and profile.

For one thing, the risks were enormous. Her reputation in society and at the Basilica. And perhaps more frighteningly, the certain fury of a humiliated Hubert. He had crushed competitors and employers for much less than a *galipette*, a little escapade on the side.

But all things considered, the lady's moral convictions were stronger than any of these dangers. And they prevailed. If she had any sensual fantasies at all, society largely presumed that these would be at the level of harmless day-dreaming.

Sophie-Charlotte, thought indeed most people, undoubtedly had a highly moral mind as well as pure heart.

After lunch, the three sleuths went back to the Hôtel de Police – an imposing five-storey, white-gray-and glass building. The building supplied office space and communications for almost a thousand people: several types of police, and many kinds of support staff.

For convenience, visiting police from both Paris and Écully (near Lyon) stayed at the Grand Hôtel du Nord at 75 Place Drouet d'Erlon, a handy four-minute walk from both the SNCF train station and the Hôtel de Police. Built in the 1920s but recently renovated, it was noisy and slightly seedy, with impeccable Soviet-style housekeeping.

Caron had rented her own large, bright apartment at the other end of the esplanade. But sometimes, to favor closer-to-work punctuality, she would hold small meetings at the Grand Hôtel du Nord. These were usually to discuss renovations with her personal carpenter.

CHAPTER THREE

Leads, Lies and Lust

After four days, the case remained wide open. Not for lack of suspects. But for too many. Caron and her P.J. team started moving systematically through them in a gradually expanding circle of plausibility. Caron had sized up Madame Repentigny in two interviews – one, to get acquainted, at the lady's residence the day after the crime; the second, formal, in Caron's office.

The Commissaire's team was checking the backgrounds and observations of family servants. They would quickly turn to company employees. But before seeing these herself, Caron wanted to check further into Sophie-Charlotte, Hubert's uptight, rather strange spouse. Caron remained haunted by the lady's eyes, and even some of her reflexes.

If Hubert's wife had secrets, likely they would be known to Madame's best woman-friend, Ludovine Pfaffenzeller. Routine enquiries about Repentigny family friends had quickly put Ludovine near the top of Caron's list of interview candidates.

Hôtel de Police – best friends forever...

Ludovine, a fellow champagne baroness, had known Sophie-Charlotte since early-married years. They were universally seen as close confidants – a little unusual, for the Pfaffenzellers, unlike the Repentignys, ran one of the great 'Protestant' champagne houses. Ludovine was a descendant of one of the old German Protestant families long present in Champagne-Ardenne. Major champagne houses called Deutz, Piper Heidsieck. Krug, Bollinger, Taittinger, Roederer and Vranken – though thoroughly French now -- ran through Champagne-Ardenne like a distant tributary of the Rhine.

Caron, as always out of uniform, welcomed Ludovine to her office, showed her a chair, offered a coffee, and shut the door.

Arcambault and Jenneret took notes. The visitor, in dark-brown heels, autumn-toned wool suit, discreet gold brooch, and matching watch and bracelets, looked true to her age and upper-bourgeoisie status.

"We know you are very close to Madame Repentigny, Madame. We need your help. We need you to help us understand in more detail Madame Repentigny's interests and aspirations. We also need to learn about any friends or relationships of hers that may or may not be known to family, friends or the public."

"So you're asking me to betray my best friend?"

"No. I'm asking you to help us find the truth. To better understand your friend. We have a pretty good skeleton of basic information about her. Now we need to put flesh on it, to grasp her real hopes, fears and motivations."

"You may think of that as understanding Sophie-Charlotte's personality. To me, it still sounds a lot like betrayal."

"Police terminology and procedures often scare ordinary citizens. But I assure you we want you to feel at ease with these necessary and routine questions."

"You want me to feel at ease as I tell you of some so-called secret life of Sophie-Charlotte."

"I didn't say that at all. Why did *you*? *Does* she have a secret life?"

Ludovine laughed.

"If she does, it must be pretty tame. The only mildly amusing episodes she confided to me were utterly innocent. Well, two of the three were; the third was borderline."

"How so?"

"Well, the first two were just tingly, I suspect one-sided, infatuations with her dentist and ophthalmologist. By definition, you might say, close relationships."

Caron cracked a rare smile.

"This is kind of absurd, just day-dreamy stuff, but she once did avow that her young black dentist from Guadeloupe had briefly stirred unchurchly thoughts. Jean-Baptiste and Sophie-Charlotte often came close to touching faces as he probed, each quarter, for early signs of periodontal disease."

"Very romantic." Caron dismissed this trivia as the silly gossip of a well-meaning friend. She thought the same of the second day-dream. Either Ludovine was mocking the investigation, or she was hopelessly stupid.

"Ah, and Dr. Philippe Peverell, her ophthalmologist, played the frisky, silver-haired devil. He stared into her eyes with such tireless intensity that Sophie-Charlotte decided he must be looking for love -- instead of, as he claimed, evidence of hyperthyroidism or autoimmune disease. Both afflictions, he had warned, were serious risks for middle-aged women."

"Charming fantasies," said Caron, now accrediting the stupidity option.

"But charming fantasies of neglected wives," picked up Ludovine. "Hubert had long found his closeness elsewhere. For many years, he had abandoned his spouse to the clergy and other medicine men."

"You say there was a third event?"

"Even that was just a one-off, possibly accidental hug that got a little out of hand. Though not out of the man's hands."

"The man being?"

"If you have to know, it was Sébastien Painteaux. Commissaire, as a Rémoise, you must know that it's not entirely unknown to hear of an attraction between a champagne owner's wife and his *chef de cave* – especially if the latter is fairly young, handsome and vigorous."

"Classic – indeed a bit of a cliché."

"Well, Sébastien, at 51, is an athletic, sensitive man a little taller than Sophie-Charlotte. His job, you know, is to direct the choice and purchase of grapes, and the blending of grapes and *vin tranquille* wines, to create each vintage. Once a year, surrounded by a small committee of cellar experts, he makes the final decision on the taste, texture, mixing and qualities of each yearly vintage."

"Absolutely key to a *maison*'s success."

"Yes. And he has to craft special vintages, often including a *Brut rosé* or a new "prestige" blend named after an 'Augustine' or 'Albertine,' or some other historic female family member with a marketable archaic name. If Repentigny is the king of his cellar, Painteaux is his prime minister – the day-to-day, year-to-year decider on growth (or not) of the Repentigny fortunes."

"So I understand. A *chef de maison* and his *chef de cave* might as well be married. But marriages have mishaps, especially with best friends. What happened between Painteaux and Madame Repentigny? Are they lovers? Do they have a long-standing or ongoing relationship?"

"Not at all. And that's why I'm so relaxed telling you even this."

Relaxed? Caron saw a woman whose cheeks were turning pink. And whose eyes started to avoid hers.

Ludovine gave a slightly censored account of the inconclusive but thrilling hands-on cave incident involving Sophie-Charlotte and Painteaux. No reference to full-body collisions or hands on buttocks. But, noted Caron, Ludovine's blush and uneasy eyes while telling it suggested that the innocent slip on the stone stairs might also have entailed at least a bit of groping. Just enough to suggest a little more probing into Painteaux's game.

Had he made a pass at the absent boss's wife? Could Caron take this as a sign of a possible later motive to kill the boss and (after a decent interval) seduce his widow?

Or was Painteaux up to something quite different? Some unimagined scheme? Or nothing? Where does he go in his spare time?

"Madame Pfaffenzeller, you have been quite helpful. Just one last question: How would you describe Madame Repentigny's religious devotion?"

"It is commendable. It is sincere. It is generous and totally committed. It is passionate. This evil world we live in needs more women like her."

"Thank you so much, Madame. You have indeed fleshed out our portrait of your friend quite a bit. And, if I may say, I don't think you have betrayed her by any definition."

Caron's visitor smiled and shook hands with her, nodded her head slightly, then departed, head high. She had done her duty. But to whom?

Caron turned to her two assistants.

"Marcambault, tell the Hôtel to put a 24-hour tail on Painteaux for the next week. I want to know where he goes in his spare time, whom he sees, and what he does. I want regular reports. Daily."

"Jenneret, you can work with Arcambault to brainstorm all plausible options for Painteaux's motives and private life. Might anything he did suggest he tried to kill his boss? Hoping, maybe, after a while, to win his widow and take over the *maison* Repentigny?"

Both men nodded agreement.

Caron had divided up the investigative pie, and launched her officers on plausible – even a few implausible -- leads. She adjourned to brood alone at *l'Apostrophe* over pâté de campagne, a glass of red, and a Panter Mignon Deluxe cigarrillo. Later tonight, she smiled, she would take another carpentry lesson.

That evening, at the all-hands briefing, Caron summarized everything learned so far with her whole team. She drew a chart on the fourth-floor white-board to summarize how she was splitting up her team. Assistant director Duroselle sat to the side and raised a few additional or clarifying points.

"Denise, two questions. You've now met Madame Repentigny twice. What's your gut feeling about her as a possible suspect?"

"She's a classy lady who seems shy, but is open to prompting. Obviously, we need to do a lot more probing – not just with her, but with still others who know her. I have started with her best friend, who was very protective. We still need more. It's far too soon to suggest anything firm. For now, I wouldn't rule her in or out. The Painteaux link is interesting, but far from conclusive. I would have to say that this lady so far shows little ability to commit such a crime – though just conceivably she might have commissioned it."

"Really?"

"That's pure conjecture. I just want to keep doors open. She doesn't come off as a sophisticated scheming type – though who knows? Just two alarm-bells: a flash of fierceness or terror (or just grief?) in her eyes; and a mite-too-cloying show of playing Mother Teresa."

"A second question: Have you got enough manpower to cover all the categories of suspects you need to look into? Do we need to import extra investigators from Strasbourg or even Paris?"

"For now, I think we can handle it all. In principle, I'm not eager to bring in people with no knowledge of the champagne world. This is a huge story for Champagne-Ardenne, as we are all aware. We know this region and society pretty well."

"I agree," said Duroselle. Outsiders always come with the superior air of brilliant rescuers, and they end up being a pain in the neck. Or they need constant baby-sitting."

Caron wrapped up the briefing:

"Any more questions? No? OK, let's get some sleep and hit the deck on the run tomorrow morning. Goodnight everybody."

She was pleased to adjourn. With ever-ready Stéphane, applauded by her feline friend Mendès, she faced a very good night indeed. *Mens sana in corpore sano.*

Comité Champagne (CIVC), Épernay – emergency meeting

Cynics outside the industry often dismiss the CIVC as a price-fixing cartel. As a cozy Mafia, a lovable OPEC, whose only goal is to fleece the public at home and abroad. Its perennial strategy: to wrap its bubbles in an aura of magic, romance and prestige – all to keep the world price of champagne ridiculously high, and as stable as possible.

Price-gouging? Far too rude a word. The CIVC – firmly backed by the French government – sees itself as merely defending a valued and beloved national glory. And doing so as legitimately as the French might promote Airbus, Chanel No. 5 or (an unforgivable analogy) soft-drink Orangina.

A fairer view would emphasize the intelligent, admirably balanced and democratic CIVC structure. It rallies all the champagne players to defend common goals: quality, reputation, prosperity. Members, in the end, usually agree. With courtesy and reason.

But in a tense situation (and this crime was certainly one), they could disagree more testily. Emotional sequels – anger, or strained friendships -- are not unknown here. It's not unheard-of for resentments generated by grandfathers to cast a cloud on a relationship today.

Things were not always even ostensibly collaborative. In 1911, the government sent the army to quell violence in Champagne between growers and merchants. In 1927, bitter arguments broke out over delimitation of fields considered as authentic champagne areas. Ironically, today's two-headed cooperative CIVC came to fruition only in 1941 – during the German Occupation.

In the days following the assault on Repentigny, the CIVC board was in almost permanent session. Who committed the crime? For what motive? What might be the impact on the industry?

In the genteel upper reaches of *les grandes familles*, well represented on the CIVC board and senior staff, people trembled. Could the attempted killer be one of their own? Or an aggrieved grower, perhaps even one selling his own labeled bottles? Any such outcome would shake the CIVC to its foundations. And instead of projecting a public image of charm and celebration, champagne might end up as a running joke – a "killer drink" or some such stupidity.

At CIVC headquarters, the executive committee and governing Permanent Commission sit behind second-floor windows atop an imposing white stone façade. It displays three art-déco panels of carved iconic images related to champagne. Above the windows, in black metal capital letters, are the words: MAISON DE LA CHAMPAGNE.

On the morning of the emergency meeting, the whole building was abuzz. Staff dashed about. Delegates frowned. Waiting journalists discreetly smirked at each other – a great story awaited.

Promptly at 8:45 a.m. on the appointed day, Regional Prefect François Guizot arrived. A lean, gray-haired top civil servant, he had driven in from the Châlons-en-Champagne *Préfecture* in his large black Citroën C5 to open the emergency meeting. In this role as chairman, he was legally acting as Commissaire du Gouvernement – special representative of the State.

Guizot shook hands all round. Then he sat down at the head of the table, folded his hands, and spoke in his low gravelly voice:

"Mesdames et Messieurs, we meet to discuss a tragedy that grieves and affects us all. We meet to assess its impact on our industry. But more importantly, we meet to confirm our compassion for the victim and his family. And to support the police in finding the aggressor."

"First, I ask our acting co-president for the merchants to give his views both on the impact of the crime and his suspicions about possible culprits. Then I will turn to the co-president for the growers."

Why the CIVC co-presidents? The CIVC is designed under national law to govern the champagne world collegially. All its structures, from Permanent Commission. -- a kind of parliament -- to specialized technical commissions, are *paritaires*. That means growers and sellers have an equal voice in virtually anything affecting champagne.

Lieuvrain, representing the *négociants* or merchants, spoke first.

"Obviously, this is a matter for the police. But given today's stressful market conditions, we cannot exclude the possibility that this might be the mad act of a disgruntled grower. Rightly or wrongly, some of these have become increasingly angry at their economic plight. A few have even publicly blamed Monsieur Repentigny for allegedly pushing them to the wall. He, like many of us, saw how slumping world champagne prices were demanding more discipline on costs – notably the cost of buying grapes from our 15,000 growers."

Larquay, the growers' co-president, exploded.

"But that's a gratuitous calumny. The crime only happened a couple of days ago, and monsieur Lieuvrain has already found the culprit, even ahead of the police."

"*Cher collègue*, I realize you're upset. But maybe you should just help the police with a list of a few angry growers who are known to have cursed or even publicly threatened the victim."

The tension was testing customary CIVC civilities.

"Ah, so now our esteemed acting co-president is inviting me to play police spy against my own members. And here we were just talking of solidarity. He would do better to look for some of the victim's defeated, even destroyed, competitors among the *grandes maisons*. To lay bare some of the dirty tricks we know some big-boys play."

"Fairy tales. In your case, I don't think solidarity means covering up for possible criminals."

"You were skating close to the edge of insult, *mon ami*, and now you have just crossed it."

Guizot briskly stepped in.

"Gentlemen, this conversation is also going over the edge. I invite you both to remember that our meetings, while open to free and even vigorous debate, traditionally never violate the courtesies of our corporate solidarity. I am giving the floor now to our ten other members – equal time to the five on each side."

Chastened, committee members from both grower and merchant camps offered more measured views. But the basic split remained.

"It's true, noted a small grower from near Chouilly, that several modest growers blamed Repentigny for squeezing them to death. And they vowed to send him to hell. But there's a huge difference between cursing a predatory merchant – and there are a few – and trying to kill him."

"Predatory? Aren't we smearing again?" replied a representative of a *grande marque*. I could cite some pretty nasty games played by growers."

"Gentlemen, ladies, order again. Exchanging recriminations is unworthy of our committee. And it will get us nowhere."

The argument went on between the two camps. The growers admitted that many of their fellows had denounced Repentigny virulently, occasionally even muttering about violence. But they refused to accept that the most likely suspects were growers. Far more plausible suspects, they argued, were furious Repentigny competitors – some taken over, others ruined, one even committing suicide.

Both sides, still bristling, remained at daggers drawn. After two hours, Guizot decided to cut to the chase.

"I think we have aired this as much as we can," he said. "And alas, not all that fruitfully. I am declaring this meeting over. But I wish any of you, on either side, who may entertain specific suspicions to communicate these to me in the next two days. And I ask you to pass along this invitation to all your members."

"People can mail me any suspects' names and motives confidentially – or even anonymously. We simply must assist the police to narrow down its list of suspects. And, painful for us as it is, they cannot ignore the whole economic milieu in which M. Repentigny has lived and worked."

Members murmured assent.

"Send me in complete trust what you really think – forgetting your loyalty to either growers or merchants. And let me remind you as we depart that the CIVC is a uniquely fair and balanced organization. It demands that we all rise above ego, personalities and temporary interests. It can only assure the prosperity of our region if we never forget the complementary roles of both your groups, each vital to the other. We succeed only because of two attitudes: realism and goodwill."

Spoken in the name of the Republic, his master, and the common interest of Champagne-Ardenne, Guizot's words echoed like a *Nunc dimittis*, the priestly farewell. The quarreling parties could now serenely go back to their quarrels.

Hôtel de la Police: Understanding Hubert

The prompt interrogations of Madame Repentigny and her best friend Ludovine opened the door to family secrets. But much more remained to discover. Especially about Hubert. Over the next days, Caron dug further into his family. She asked them all to come to her office.

First – to flesh out Repentigny's character and temperament, she saw his brothers and sister. First, she met his younger brothers Charles and Antoine; then later his older sister Adeline. All three emphasized Hubert's brilliance and drive. But, reluctantly, they also referred to his moods, his "dark zones." They cited a childhood squeeze between an admirable but absent father and a secretly domineering – or smotheringly affectionate? -- mother.

His father, Alphonse, they said, was a rough, ambitious man. He was determined to drive his sagging *Lamartine* champagne brand to the top. He didn't manage that, but he did the next-best thing: he turned his son Hubert, the eldest of four, into a driven entrepreneur. Neither Charles nor Antoine cared to join the family business. Charles, a pinched and dour sociologist, was a disciple of Bourdieu, high priest of class resentment. Antoine, a jolly cherub of a man, was harpsichordist in a small baroque orchestra. Both brothers chose fields far outside the family business. It was clear to them from an early age that Alphonse wanted to anoint Hubert as his successor.

"Did that," asked Caron of the young men, "leave any scars on you?"

"Not at all," said Charles with rather forced nonchalance. "I was never predisposed to enter the world of capitalism. I was happy to let Hubert follow his star. He chose a stressful life I would never have wanted. Also, I don't relate well to business people."

"I feel the same – in Technicolor," added Antoine.

"To his great credit," said Charles, "Hubert unilaterally gave Adeline and us some guaranteed revenues from his success – five percent each from the net profits of his holding company, Repentigny-Reims S.A. He didn't have to do that. And we didn't have to work to earn our shares. This was simply a very generous *ex gratia* arrangement. A remarkable proof of solidarity toward us all."

"In principle," said Caron, "that would seem to limit the possibility of sibling rivalry as a motive in this crime."

"It's reassuring to hear that," replied Antoine. "But even without this remarkable financial sharing, we were all raised to love each other. And to help each other – however diverse our paths might become."

"Just one key point. Could you possibly set aside, just briefly, your gratitude toward Hubert? I would ask you to be totally frank, even blunt, about the business style he has demonstrated in achieving his great success."

"We can try," said Charles. "What are you alleging?"

Caron fixed each sibling in turn with her Putin stare. "I allege nothing. But many people paint a rather harsh picture of his methods. They say Hubert resolved to achieve by almost any means what his father couldn't. He elbowed aside weak competitors with practices bordering on brutality. He took the Repentigny brand into new and grander territories. Proud Alphonse, your father, egged him on as long as he lived. When your father died," say some, "Hubert became even more ruthless. He allegedly bullied and tricked competitors," say many, "as well as associates. So that now, he has almost more enemies than allies."

The brothers looked at each other, hesitated for almost half a minute. Then they gently nodded accord. "Well, you put it pretty bluntly," offered Charles. "But I guess there is some truth in what you say. Your words don't define the whole man, by any means, of course. He also has a shining public record for generosity to the less fortunate. He has a powerful and creative sense of public service, as evidenced by his political, cultural and humanitarian activities. But if you just stick to business – yes, he is a robust, even very rough, customer."

"Thank you very much for this honest delineation of your brother. I take careful note that his business style is not the whole man. But since we are now looking for enemies -- thus suspects -- the business dimension is vital."

"We all understand, I believe."

"Gentlemen, you have already told me that you revered your dear mother. I have a rather vivid picture of the dutiful country spouse you have all described. I know she was born Sarah Pimpernet in the tiny village of Chouilly near Épernay, and I may go there. I think we can now let you go. You both have busy calendars today. So I'll now ask Adeline to come in for a while. It may be useful to get a further, female, view of your mother."

The sons left. Caron opened the door to greet Adeline. She was an earnest, sixtyish brunette in gray skirt, rimless glasses, and a gray sweater-set with pearls. She looked like a pharmacist you could trust to cure a cold, a stomach ache or a mild depression. "Now Adeline, you called me aside just before the meeting with your brothers. You wanted to add some personal impressions."

"Yes, I would like to flesh out a little what you have already probably heard. I think my observations – unknown to my brothers – may cast some new light."

"Please go ahead."

"Mother raised all of us in exemplary fashion, as all witnesses could attest."

"All witnesses but one?"

Adeline nodded sadly.

"In addition to raising and educating Hubert like the others, mother also raised him in the shadows. When other family members were present, she seemed just a normal, nurturing mother. But when she was alone with her little Hubert, I fear she retreated into her own deep dissatisfactions. Frustration with her life, and especially with her inattentive husband. Inattentive, I suspect, in every way."

"I understand. How did she make up for this? A lover? Extravagance? Bitterness? A change in personality?"

"No," said Adeline softly. "I wish she had done any of those things. Unfortunately, she focused her attention on Hubert. Intimately, obsessively -- unhealthily."

"What exactly did she do?"

"When Hubert was three and onward, she gave him two identities. You might say she injected him with a split personality. Sometimes, she would encourage little Hubert to pretend he was her *petit ami* or boy-friend. At other times, she would call him girlish names, like Hubertine, after a 19th-century suffragette."

"How do you explain this?"

"Mother had dreamt of having another girl. She found the boys rambunctious and hard to understand. When Hubert turned out not to be her passionately wished-for girl – well, you can guess..."

"I can imagine your mother's disappointment," sympathized Caron, "as long as it stayed within limits."

Adeline blushed. She paused, then added: "I'm afraid I can't go further."

She hesitated, lowered her voice, and stuttered.

"As Hubert grew into adolescence, he asserted his masculinity, as he had to. Mommy withdrew into a shell. She looked sullen, defeated, and old."

"How sad."

"Soon enough, Hubert discovered girls his own age. But he found that he bore them – and all girls – a deep fear and suspicion. He came to believe that all women are predators, just biding their time. Their smooth, irresistible seductions," he reasoned, "are mere traps. Prisons of all-commanding, all-annihilating love. Of a selfish treachery just aching to reveal itself. Of scheming to capture and cage a male."

"Almost a textbook case of male terror of women. Have you read much Simone de Beauvoir? Or Benoîte Groult's *Ainsi soit-elle*?

"Of course I know de Beauvoir and Groult, replied Adeline. I've read lots of articles on this theme too. But few such texts – usually written by feminists with other agendas -- dwell as honestly as they might have on mothers as a source of misogyny."

"How," asked Caron, "did this strange mother-son relationship affect Hubert's apparently happy marriage to Sophie-Charlotte."

"It wasn't happy, never was, and still isn't," said Adeline. "After the big love-show of the wedding, marriage rapidly became a social mask, a charade hiding indifference. It sublimated love into a kind of psychological master-slave relationship that allowed Hubert to take out on Sophie-Charlotte his revenge on his mother. His anger led him not only to turn his back on his wife, but also to betray her routinely. After the babies in quick succession, you could say he abandoned Sophie-Charlotte, even while according her all the external honors of marriage."

"That's a lead we suspected, and will have to follow," said Caron.

"Clearly, his youthful fear of women marked all his adult relationships," added Adeline. "In each parallel or successive relationship, Hubert was a Jekyll and Hyde. The more intensely he craved and expressed his love, the more desperately he ran away when each hapless woman responded with love. In spite of his womanizing reputation, he spent more time fleeing women than chasing them. Love and terror were constantly at war in his heart. As if on some programmed signal – such as a woman's open claim or presumption of 'owning' him – fear would engulf his heart. He would freeze in terror."

"This was far more than classic male fear of commitment, wasn't it?"

"It was downright pathological. My brother has left an endless trail of broken hearts behind him. All his life, he was a wounded animal. Running to each woman, then dashing away. If suddenly he felt trapped, he would turn to stone and end all contact. He ached for intimacy, but panicked at the first hint of suffocation – for him a synonym of dreaded commitment. He was never violent. That is, unless you consider sudden abandonment violent."

"How did you come to these conclusions?"

Adeline looked down, white-faced. Her lips trembled. She spoke slowly, almost inaudibly. She seemed to pull each word up from some deep, dark place.

"First, as a child, I was perplexed, then a little scared, by Hubert's ambiguous treatment. There may be more. In fact, maybe I was a bit jealous. But... I fear false memories."

"How distressing for a young girl!"

"It was. And it still is. Anchoring my impression of Hubert's underlying terror of women is our continuing dialogue as adults. Gradually, he and

I have been able to dig into his fears and analyze them as we couldn't as children."

"That's lucky for both of you. It may help you both."

"It does, at least it helps me. I fear Hubert is permanently harmed, even if he understands more. But Commissaire, let me emphasize again: I am confused – conflicted -- about our mother. I don't want to portray her as an evil or twisted person. Throughout our childhood, she was a kind, loving and supportive mother."

"I'm sure she was."

"In her generation, there was great ignorance about sex. And certainly about its psychological effects. People never talked about it. Today, every popular magazine carries articles about pedophilia, child psychology, gender roles, gay marriage, and sexual abuse. The rape of thousands of little boys by Catholic priests makes a mother's gender foibles seem harmless."

"Indeed. We're drowning in such information – or speculation. We live in a very different world."

"I could easily argue," went on Adeline, "that *maman* was just a good-hearted, sexually rather innocent woman. An average woman of her time. A kind, generous mother who – perhaps in part because of an inattentive husband – poured her affection into us. Just maybe a bit too much into Hubert."

Adeline broke down and sobbed. "Commissaire, I don't wish to blacken my mother's memory. I want to give you a balanced, fair and realistic view."

"You are right to try. And you're being extremely fair to your mother. Not all adults can be as perceptive and nuanced in judging their parents."

"I don't know about that," said Adeline, dabbing her eyes with her handkerchief. "But my purpose in opening up to you is neither to discredit my mother nor to excuse her. It is only to try to explain what I saw happening in Hubert over his formative years – and perhaps to help him now."

"I can see that. This is very valuable. Please go on."

"As I said, in my twenties and thirties, I was able to draw closer to Hubert. Surprisingly, with *maman* gone, we were able to confide much more. He came to see me not as one of the threatening women, but just his sweet, loyal sister. He told me things he would tell no one."

"As I said, he was fortunate to have you."

"And I him. But behind his hyper-confident exterior, he's a seriously damaged man. A man with a cheerful face but a melancholy soul. He's not a 'bad' man. He's... He's just... my little brother." Tears rolled down her cheeks.

"I'm so very sorry to see your anguish," said Caron. "Do you think that Hubert, as a driven entrepreneur, was again running away from these early nightmares?"

"I am absolutely certain of that. The early sexual confusion led to terrors of pursuit, betrayal and entrapment. To a claustrophobia constantly urging him to escape. To self-programming that made him risk adventure instead of security, freedom instead of stability. This mindset added fuel and desperation to his basic energetic disposition. They added more than desperation – they added real paranoia. But a little paranoia drives every entrepreneur, doesn't it?"

"It would all seem to fit. And maybe the end-result in business was his reputation for – shall we say, robust – competitive methods?"

"Probably," agreed Adeline. "But one last point. Of course our father prepared Hubert to salvage and expand his own lost business reputation. This was an additional burden – perhaps the cruelest one, a kind of compensatory expectation. A duty to save what Hubert saw as his family's honor."

"Summing it all up," proposed Caron, "Hubert was under pressure from both parents. From a mother who, with whatever kind impulses, and however inadvertently, laid a certain sexual burden on him. And from a father who – also no doubt impelled by his personal dreams or demons – laid on him a duty to repair his own inadequacies. Result: Hubert carried within himself a double duty: to play out both his mother's and father's needs. Parental thirsts that he could never quench only pursue. Sisyphus twinned."

"Put that way, Commissaire, I can see with even greater clarity – and pity -- what was driving my poor brother."

"None of us is an angel, Adeline. And probably fewer than we think are really born devils. God knows what burdens a little probing would find within all of us. And what strange motivations might push us to good or harm. Push us to success, failure or folly. Let me end this with a compliment: Your first-hand perceptions strike me as extraordinarily observant and sensitive. I'm only sorry to learn how both Hubert and you have suffered all these years – he as a victim, you as a witness and, in a sense, thereby also a victim."

"Thank you for your compassion, Commissaire. You have made it much easier for me to open up. I almost forgot that we are really Commissaire and suspect – as I presume I still am, along with others."

"Inevitably, you count among the growing list of suspects. But I must say I've been much impressed by the spontaneity and nuance of your words. Your explanations have the ring of truth."

"Thank you, Commissaire. Did you elicit useful information from my brothers?"

"Not nearly as much as I have from you. But I did learn some things, even from their reluctance to unburden themselves on intimate family matters. My guess is that even if they had some inkling of what your mother was doing with Hubert, they preferred not to analyze it too much. Perhaps they thought the gender ambiguity a harmless passing phase. Perhaps too their silence aimed at protecting your late mother's memory."

"Again, do count on me, Commissaire, to assist in any way I can to find the culprit. He mustn't be allowed to get away with this horror."

"We'll do our best, Adeline. And with that, I say goodbye and thank you very much indeed for your help. We shall no doubt be tracking down several of the ladies that Monsieur Repentigny allegedly had liaisons with."

"Ah yes, there are quite a few."

"If you could possibly supply me with a confidential list of ladies you have known about, we shall get on more quickly with that phase of our work. And be assured that your list will remain totally confidential, as will our conversation."

"I know. That's a good thing, for a few of these ladies are very well-known. Some are even my friends."

"Friends make excellent sources for us. I'll await your list in the next day or two."

"I'll mail it to you promptly at the *Hôtel de Police*. Or drop it off."

"Thank you, Madame, and *au revoir*."

Caron would turn now to Hubert's children. She grabbed a fast-food lunch of a tuna-and-tomato *panini* and a glass of red. Then, mind and tummy content with her day, she returned to the *Hôtel de Police*. The victim's grown-up children would meet her there, an hour apart.

First Christelle. Just emerging from her teenage years, she was tall, lean, and ricocheting between gawky and slinky. Civility range: sweet to bratty. She wore heels rivaling the Eiffel Tower. Her eyes were still red from crying, and showed dark circles. Mostly, she looked lost and scared. Caron put her at ease.

"Please sit down, young lady. I know you've been terribly shocked by what has happened."

In a high, tiny voice, the young Amazon sniffled: "I'm just so sad about daddy. Why would anybody want to hurt him? He's such a good father."

"I'm glad to know that, Christelle. Now I must ask you a few questions that you will find hard to hear, and maybe harder to answer. First, can you think of any persons who might resent your father in his business, political or personal life? He has been active in many arenas."

"How would I know? I'm just a kid."

"But a kid entering maturity, and with eyes and ears."

Christelle said nothing, and furrowed her brow. "Let me try, but I really can't think of anybody. We never talked much about his life except for family matters, including my schooling and friends."

"You never heard echoes of disgruntled employees or business partners? Or political rivals?"

"Are you joking? Do you seriously think I'd know stuff like that?"

"Will you allow me to probe into more personal and family matters? Forgive me, I have to pursue such things as part of my job. Oh, and by the way, would you mind putting down your iPhone – you can play with Facebook after we talk."

Christelle scowled, and rolled her eyes.

"Whatever!"

"First – and I'm getting straight to a classic question – how would you describe your father's relations with your mother?"

"Well, I guess they're OK."

"You guess? But you've observed them up close for all your life."

"We never pay much attention to them. We just figure they get along."

"But there are different ways of getting along. Who's the one who really seems in charge?"

"Daddy, of course. But on a day-to-day basis, he's not always there. Mommy is."

"That sounds pretty normal. Now have you any idea of how your parents spend their spare time – when they're not with you and your brothers?"

"My father of course devotes most of his time to our champagne business. And a few times a year, he and *maman* go out as a couple to public events."

"But he's also very active in politics, as you probably know."

"Yes, I know. He's an important man in party politics. And, if I may say, in champagne industry politics – as in the Comité Champagne, of which he's a co- president. And I hear he's influential behind the scenes."

"Have you also heard that his CIVC or his business practices have made him enemies?"

"He never shared such things with us. But I've heard rumors. And sometimes I see things in *L'Union*, our local daily. I don't read it all the time, but when it's lying around, I may glance at it."

"What kind of things have you read there?

"Obviously, a lot about the champagne industry, its ups and downs."

"And I suppose about its key players, including your father."

"Yes. But it's normally respectful stuff. Either business-related, or social and cultural events. *L'Union* can sometimes be nasty."

"You can't recall your father being at the centre of any...so-called scandals?"

"Only grumbling about his influence. – commercial, of course, but also political. Being ambitious, he has risen high. And that always attracts jealousy, doesn't it?"

"Indeed. But may I get back to family and personal matters. Your father is a very handsome, dynamic man. Inevitably, such men attract the attention of admiring women. Surely, as a young woman yourself, you must have seen other women besides your mother finding him to their taste."

"It's not for a daughter to observe such things. Apart from being proud that he's a handsome man, I have not gone around looking for mistresses. I expect that's the point of your question."

"Would it surprise you if a mistress -- or mistresses – turned up in our investigation?"

"What do you think, Commissaire? Why do you have to ask a daughter such silly and insulting questions?"

"I'm sorry if I upset you, Christelle. But in a complicated investigation like this, we have to pursue every dimension, however remote. However banal. However embarrassing."

"In the end, Commissaire, even if I did know of a mistress, I certainly wouldn't tell *you*."

"Spoken like a loyal daughter, Christelle! And on that, I think we can end our interview. Now I have to meet your brothers."

Ah, one last question about your parents. To the extent that a perceptive child might measure such things, do you think your mother and father are still in love with each other?"

Christelle exploded.

"Now you're just being totally rude. I take their love for granted. And I have no reason to think otherwise. Goodbye!"

Christelle tried to stomp out, mustering as much dignity as her Eiffel Tower heels would allow. She came close to slamming the door, but held back for fear of falling flat on her face.

Next up: the brothers, starting with 24-year-old Laurent, the elder son.

Tall, dark and stereotypically handsome, Laurent entered Caron's Hôtel de Police office, looking like what he was: a young man trying to find his way. Caron extended her hand. His handshake was confident, but not crushing.

"*Bonjour, Monsieur Repentigny.* I just have a few questions."

"Please ask them. I am at your disposal."

"The basics, first. My job is to understand your father and his life – and, if I may be so direct – to investigate all possible suspects."

"That includes me?"

"Sadly, and inevitably. But don't draw any conclusions about our suspicions. We're just following the routine of leaving no stone unturned."

"I understand."

"You are the first-born son. You've done Sciences Po – a prestigious first degree for entering government. Are you tempted by politics, like your father? Or do you see yourself perhaps one day taking over the family business?"

"Frankly, Commissaire, it's a little early to ask such questions."

"But not too soon to think about them. Young men of your age do dream, don't they?"

"Of course. But there are fantasies, idle dreams, and systematic plans."

"Well, where, on this scale, would you situate your attitude to one day becoming a champagne baron?

"Let's say, I'm somewhere between fantasies and idle dreams."

"Fair enough. But– if I may be so direct – now that your father may be dying, can you see the idle dreams becoming a determined plan sooner than you would have wished?"

"You realize that such speculation is heartbreaking for me. It's ghoulish."

"Again, my apologies. But I have to get to the bottom of this awful crime as soon as I can."

"All right. To the extent that I've had even a little time to ponder my future, I would expect that the board of *Repentigny-Reims S.A* would quickly put in place some kind of interim administration, perhaps with a board member temporarily taking the helm."

"Which board member would you think the best qualified – and/or the most motivated – to take on the task of stabilizing and developing operations? Is there a member that your father manifestly trusts?"

"My father does not trust many people. He even jokes that that includes him. But if you wanted a safe pair of hands, a clearly unambitious placeholder or expediter of current affairs, I would risk saying "Claude Saclet."

"Thank you. That's very helpful. Now to get a little more personal, as I must: Do you admire your father? Do you *like* him? Has he been a good father – present, guiding and supportive?"

"Yes. Even though his devotion to work and politics often takes him away, he is kind to us when he's here – and generous with his time and advice. We love him and are proud of him, even though his somewhat bossy side often gets on our nerves."

"What are your father's strengths and weaknesses?"

"As I said – and sticking only to family matters – he's a powerful, sometimes overwhelming, role model. As for his weaknesses, or faults – well, as with all of us, they're the flip-side of his qualities. His energy could be draining, his convictions crushing, his heartiness grating, his moods disturbing. We sometimes suspected, I might add, that his strength sometimes hid some dark doubt or fear or wound. But I'm not a psychiatrist, just a son."

"But a pretty perceptive one, if only half of what you say proves true."

Christian, the fit, well-tanned 21-year old younger son, came in next. Caron greeted him warmly:

"*Bonjour, monsieur.* Kindly take a seat." She shook hands, then pointed toward a chair. Still a student in mind and demeanor, Christian slouched down in his jeans, bomber-jacket, and open collar.

"Are you accusing me of trying to kill my father?" he asked with nervous defiance.

"Of course not, we're not accusing anybody at this stage. We're just questioning everyone close to the victim. That's standard police procedure, as you probably know. And it always includes family. Don't let this upset you. Just try to answer directly and honestly."

"All right, but this is still a bit scary."

"I know. Please just listen carefully, and answer as best you can."

"OK."

"Where were you when your father was attacked?"

"If it happened after midnight, I was sleeping."

"All night?"

"Until 9 a.m."

"And before midnight?"

"I was visiting a girl. At her house."

"Her name? And will she vouch for that? We'll have to call her right away, if you could give me her phone number."

"Her name is Marguerite Petitglou, and her cell number is 06.23.23.57.99."

"Thank you. Jenneret. Will you please check that out?"

"Will do, boss."

"Now, Monsieur Repentigny, you see how we have to operate – if only to get our facts right."

"I see that when you make a show of checking things out immediately in front of a witness, you quickly warn him not to stray from the truth."

"Very observant, monsieur," smiled Caron. "You would make a good cop."

"That isn't in my life plan."

"What is in your life plan?"

"For now, girls, fun, and a few books."

"What kind of books do you like?"

"History and biography -- plus, to relax, the odd railway-station mystery. A *roman de gare*."

"Decidedly," smiled Caron, "you sound like a perfect candidate for police work."

"I'll let you know if the urge seizes me."

"Back to what brings us here. Can you think of any person with whatever motive who might have wanted to kill your father?"

"If my father's own words were taken at face value, that might cover quite a range of jealous rivals."

"Of what sort?"

"Business, political...maybe even romantic. I'm not unaware that my father has had a colorful life on all those levels."

"But names? Even family names?"

"Nobody in our family should interest you at all. Even with the usual asperities of temperament, we all love each other."

"I'm sure that includes your mother."

"I don't like that insinuation at all. *Maman* is devastated by this news. And she has always loved *papa* with utter devotion."

"I'm not insinuating anything. But given the historical pattern of murders, I have to probe into any sign of dissatisfaction or anger. Many spouses, alas, do end up killing each other. Intimacy sometimes generates repressed passions."

"Neither dissatisfaction nor anger is in play here. And they never have been. As for repressed passions, I'm not a shrink."

"Names outside the family?"

"Truly, off the top, I couldn't pick out one or another. But if I think of any, you'll be the first to know."

"Thank you. I can't ask for more, at least at this stage. Good luck in your own life -- which with girls and books sounds a good mix of the colorful and serious."

Christian departed, relieved at being let off so easily. For now. "No doubt the cops are already digging into my background," he thought. "And into the background of everybody in the family. What should I worry about?"

Marie-Laure, the eldest sibling, came to Caron's Hôtel de Police office later that afternoon. Caron's first impression: a svelte blonde soon in sight of 30, with sad but alert eyes. A black silk blouse with a strand of pearls under a well-tailored pepper-and-salt wool skirt and jacket. Class.

"*Bonjour, Madame.* My condolences for this awful crime."

"Thank you, Commissaire. Please ask me whatever you want. I understand you have already done some research on me."

"Yes, a little. What I'm after today is your personal view of things – of your father, of course, but also of your whole family. Also, your perceptions and aspirations concerning your father's firm."

"I'll help as much as I can. But we are on sensitive ground, especially on family issues."

"Since you are a mature woman, and the eldest child, could you hazard a frank description of your parents' marriage? Please excuse this blunt question at the outset. But we're trying at this stage to cast light on all the relationships involving your father."

Marie-Laure hesitated, and took a deep breath. "The easy answer is that our parents have been living the kind of busy, multi-faceted life that families here usually live: hard work, civic and cultural contributions, meetings, family duties, friends, personal interests. Many of their activities are both business and social obligations -- and in a broad sense, probably good for our family."

"But would you say your parents are close?"

"As for their intimate relationship – how much do children ever really know? Their marriage has appeared steady and without drama. I must say, however, that mother has increasingly seemed withdrawn, and indeed a little mysterious in recent years. She is a Catholic of passionate conviction, for better or worse. Perhaps partly because of that, my impression is that their relationship is not as intimate as it could be– they definitely have different emotional wavelengths."

"And the harder answer?"

"Father was – is – a driven man with admirable qualities and a few significant faults.

"Significant?"

"Painful, for those who oppose him, especially in business or politics."

"Examples?"

"He has a tendency to crush opponents if he can't win them over. He will only compromise at the edges. Most of the time, he wants a big win, with neither concessions nor prisoners."

"How is he seen within the champagne industry?"

"I just told you."

"But hasn't he sometimes played a statesman-like role, such as getting elected co-president of the CIVC, the key industry grouping?"

"Of course he's clever enough to navigate the shoals of electoral politics. And it's his shrewdness and adroitness, plus his strong personality, that help him win. But I would have to admit that he hasn't just made friends among his peers. There are a few people who really seem to hate him. People who are jealous of him, or angry for having lost to him in a disagreeable way."

"Could you help us by supplying some names?"

"Of course, but confidentially."

"This interview is confidential. Just write down all the names of people you know who seriously dislike him."

Marie-Laure took the outstretched ballpoint pen. She wrinkled her forehead, looked out Caron's misty window to nowhere. She jotted down three names. She paused, wrote again. And again and again, shaking her head with dismay.

"These are the only ones that come to mind – thirteen in all. But I imagine there are others."

Glancing at the list, Caron lifted an eyebrow. Several names were well-known.

"Now about your personal ambitions. Several people have told us that you might one day make a good leader for your father's company. Setting aside your grief of today, is such a prospect appealing to you?"

"I think it's macabre and disrespectful to ask that just now. Can't that sort of questioning wait?"

"I'm afraid it's a routine and necessary question."

Marie-Laure hesitated.

"If you insist. It's no secret that some people have speculated that I might one day end up as president of my father's company. I would, it's true, like to play an important role in future years. Many women in the industry think they might imitate the legendary Veuve Clicquot. I'm one of them."

"In the tragic event that your father does not come out of his coma, would you be ready for the top job now?"

"Maybe, if the board could help surround me with good, experienced advisers."

"Including your brothers?"

"In time, yes. But for now I think both are too young."

"Thank you, Madame. That gives us a helpful start. My colleagues and I will be in touch with you again."

Marie-Laure left, leaving Caron with new speculations.

CHAPTER FOUR
Eastern Exposure

Everyone knows that only the French can make real champagne. Throughout the world, the French government fights bottle by bottle to uphold this belief. And the name "champagne."

However...

Chinese Trade Mission, Paris...

Ma Chuntao sat that morning in her modest office in the Chinese Trade Mission. A nondescript seven-storey office block, the Mission made little impression in Paris's shady, upscale 8th *arrondissement*.

Ma's day job – her cover – was that of a central-bank currency-swaps consultant. She monitored, and sometimes facilitated, the Frankfurt-based European Central Bank's currency dealings with the Bank of China. (The Bank of France kept only some residual payments duties that she watched). The "swaps" were agreements allowing each bank to provide liquidity in the other's currency to facilitate trade deals. Intricate, fast-moving work. French associates praised her expertise.

Like almost everybody in the building, Ma had Chinese government links as well as commercial duties. In her case, economic spying was her primary activity, and her real boss was Tsaï at the *Guoanbu* in Beijing. He was not happy today.

Reading a coded overnight message from him, Ma felt his impatience. "You signaled that your key target was gravely wounded. But why, by whom, and with what impact on your mission? Give me details."

It was tricky for Ma to research Tsaï's queries. She suspected that, like many Chinese trade people, she was being bugged and watched. Media stories about a "Chinese economic invasion" and a "Chinese industrial takeover" turned up almost daily. An all-too-typical example: a December 2011 cover-story in the respected economic monthly *L'Expansion* warned "Pourquoi la Chine fait peur – "Why China frightens." As the euro trembled, anti-Chinese paranoia took hold everywhere in Europe.

Ma's best source in Reims was probably under suspicion already. But she had to risk a fairly safe, coded Blackberry message to him, asking to meet later that afternoon. Her message said: "Too busy to meet." Translation: "Bring info urgently to the Librairie Chapitre Guerlin, 70/77, place Drouet d'Erlon. Leave note in *Petit Robert* dictionary

ASAP." Ma could hop the 45-minute TGV from the Gare de l'Est and be there shortly after.

The Librairie rendezvous point was Reims's largest and best-situated bookstore. Hidden notes in certain books made quick consultations and passing information extremely easy. Notes used codewords such as "busy," "hello," "soon," "weather" and "love." These pointed to specific dangers or to other places and times in Paris or in Champagne-Ardenne. Ma and her source switched code-words regularly to signal other venues and hours. They preferred hidden notes, and would only whisper in the busy Librairie if the coast were clear, then very briefly.

Ma's cover-story for visiting the bookstore from time to time was her pretending to write a guidebook to champagne country for the Chinese public. Cheerfully, she told this to the bookstore cashier. "It's my hobby," she joked, "and I have to do lots of liquid, as well as documentary, research." Of course this dovetailed with her goal of acquiring strategic information on the "bubbles" industry.

To cover her tracks, Ma wrote up a few innocuous, touristy pages on Reims. She carried these with her just in case somebody contested her story. They never did, and she and her source used the hidden notes whenever security demanded.

This time, Ma and her source needed more time to chat.

Reaching the bookstore, she retrieved the hidden note. It told her in code to meet immediately at the less frequented Musée du Vieux Reims, Place du Forum. The gabled 16th-century landmark allowed lengthier, more discreet conversation while standing side by side in front of artifacts.

Within fifteen minutes, the source briefed Ma on the crime, people's reactions, suspects, and his assessment of the attack's impact on Chinese plans.

Pondering all this in her office that evening, Ma drafted a short message to Tsaï. She took it to the Mission's cryptographer for coding and transmission. The cryptographer, Lin Yi, had played an ancillary role in finding a weakness in the vital U.S. National Security Agency algorithm SHA-1. He was fast, brilliant, and incidentally a handsome older man whom Ma enjoyed flirting with.

Ma's reply to Tsaï:

"Target attacked by unknown assailant, linked to our key source. In deep coma, death almost certain. Our friends in Paris, Reims and Épernay still willing to help us, although our key ally feels his position shaky. Many suspects – industrial, political, personal. Am feeling heightened surveillance as result of target's friendship with our source. Propose pause to reassess focus, timing and pace of our actions."

Next morning, Ma got a call from an acquaintance at the Banque de France, Jean-Baptiste Capelle, a senior macro-economist. He invited her to breakfast two days later at the elegant Café de la Paix beside the Opéra. She had already met him socially. Now what was he after?

"I would like to update my knowledge of Chinese investment and trade strategies," he said.

"I know you're a currency specialist. I would also like to better understand how you see swaps affecting trade and investment at a time when the euro is still shaky."

"I see."

"Could we do a brief *tour d'horizon* some morning?"

Ma quickly thought that meeting Capelle, a thin, 50ish technician with a brush-cut, might prove useful in checking how firmly France really remained behind the euro. And what kind of help Paris hoped to extract from Beijing to save it.

"OK. Next Monday at 7 a.m., Café de la Paix, under the big skylights?"

"Ideal – lots of light, and splendid coffee and croissants. See you there."

"Agreed. See you there and then."

Ma suspected another agenda. A gallant one? She was used to Frenchmen fantasizing about 'submissive' Oriental girls – from Madame Butterfly to geishas to Indochinese teenagers. But that brush-cut? How boring that so many DCRI agents signaled their game that way...

Basilique Saint-Remi...

In days following the crime, good Father Farfelan, in deep shock, brooded on Sophie-Charlotte.

Majestic, gray, and illuminated within by a blaze of stained-glass windows, the Basilique-Abbey is a sister shrine to Reims's Notre-Dame Cathedral. Together they form a UNESCO Heritage site. And Saint-Remi is the world pilgrimage-place for the adoration of the sixth-century saint. Born in 433 and living to a Methusalahian 96, Remigius (Remi) is renowned for baptizing Clovis, France's first king. This led to the conversion to Christianity of the entire Frankish people.

This is where Sophie-Charlotte attended daily Mass. It's where she participated eagerly in activities venerating Saint-Remi. She took her children each year to the grand October 1 Saint-Remi Procession here beneath a blazing chandelier with ninety-six candles. Hubert mocked her devotion as "pathetic superstition." This wounded Sophie-Charlotte very much, but she didn't complain or insist. She just retreated into her private, burning convent of faith.

At Confession here, Sophie-Charlotte weekly met bony, white-haired old Monsignor Vladimir Farfelan. "I know many passionate devotees of Saint-Remi," Farfelan would tell his fellow-priests, "but none whose soul is as inhabited by our saint as is Madame Repentigny. I know her well. I am probably her only male confidant, clerical or not."

Under Farfelan's guidance, Sophie-Charlotte had delved into ancient texts about her beloved saint. Over the years, she had asked her priest to help her deepen her commitment to Saint-Remi. "She has studied both of Remi's testaments," Farfelan marveled: "the apocryphal 'long' one, and the better-confirmed 'short' one."

Such was Madame's passion to believe in her saint, he recalled, she came to insist that even the contested 'long' version was true. Hauntingly, it hinted at treasure. And it hurled a curse that rang down through the ages:

If one day this royal race that I have so many times consecrated to the Lord, rendered evil for good, became hostile to Him, invaded His churches, destroyed them and devastated them – May the guilty man be warned a first time by all the bishops of the diocese of Reims that... If, after a seventh warning, the rebel persists, he will be separated from the body of the Church – no more indulgence! Make room for threats! He will become a Judas the traitor! ... May his days be numbered and another receive his position...

"You will find all this and more," Farfelan told doubters, in the compendium of Flodoard, *Historia Remensis Ecclesia.*

Farfelan knew his church history. But confronted by troubled older women, he drifted, as many aging clerics do, into a kind of amused, seen-it-all skepticism.

He knew what drew Madame Repentigny every day to the city's patron-saint Basilica. Her Catholic upbringing alone could explain it. So could her unhappy marriage. So might her highly unusual devotion to Saint-Remi. So even – most improbably – might a human love affair for which the church was part of the cover? Wasn't there a man sometimes spotted on a chair in sight of the choir where she knelt?

Father Farfelan, for sure, rejected such fleeting suspicions. The reverent cleric, untutored in ecstasies beyond the Elevation of the Host, saw Madame as a secular saint. At Confession, he couldn't fully grasp Sophie-Charlotte's anguish. He saw a normally disappointed wife burying her slowly-drying lusts in godly consolations. From the Church's viewpoint, such women were its core believers. He had to tread gently.

"At this stage in your life, Madame," he told her, "it is natural for earthly joys to give way more and more to spiritual ones."

After this counsel of cold-shower fatalism, he had risked a little empathy. Even flattery. But Sophie-Charlotte had resisted. She had held back a deeper secret.

"I understand your pain," he had piously reassured Madame Repentigny long before the crime. "But it is a holy anguish, enriched by your awe of the story and relics of Saint-Remi."

"But Father," she had shamefully admitted, "it is so much more than that. I am seething with conflicting, often barely controllable emotions. It is no doubt sacrilegious to say this – but I often dream about being... about being... the *mistress* or lover of Saint-Remi himself! Just as nuns see Christ as their husband, I see Saint-Remi as my man – in spirit, mind, and even body. This shocks and frightens me. But I cannot help myself. Please, please forgive me, please guide me!"

The good Father gasped. This was fantasy close to hallucination.

"That is horrible, my daughter. Indeed it's sacrilegious, an outrage. Such emotions and thoughts go infinitely beyond adoration of God's saints.

Your dreams are deeply sinful. You must pray to overcome them."

"I pray all the time, Father. But I usually just end up talking with Saint-Remi. These wild visions will not go away. I am sometimes gnawed by a hunger that I can't define. My body, as well as my soul, is on fire with a passion for holy union."

The old priest, appalled, was close to collapse. He tried to sympathize with Sophie-Charlotte's sufferings.

"Only great faith and time and reflection on purity can bring you peace," he nodded, improvising as she burbled on.

After weeks and months of such exchanges, he began to yawn behind the confessional grill. He decided that Sophie-Charlotte was just another menopausal woman floating restlessly between religious ecstasy and its scruffy cousin, runaway sexual fantasy. It was probably harmless. And almost inevitable in extremely devout middle-aged women saying a long, reluctant goodbye to the conjugal bed. Religion and sex, he and the Church knew in so many ways -- with men, women and little boys -- were very old friends.

Hôtel de Police, Reims... sibling rivalry and gossip?
Five days after the crime, Caron met her team to summarize findings and issue new instructions.

Jenneret and Marcambault, the two officers from her Sophie-Charlotte interview, had already doubled back to dig deeper into Repentigny family affairs.

"Our first inklings," said Jenneret, "gleaned from widening interviews, is that financial rivalry between Hubert and his three siblings may be much sharper than his two brothers had let on. All of them, including sister Adeline, seemed to be angling for a bigger piece of the family inheritance: their current five percent cut, albeit *ex gratia* from Hubert, they consider far too little."

Added Marcambault: "A cousin and friends told us that rivalry is also starting to blossom between Hubert's daughter Marie-Laure and her macho brother Laurent. The ambitious young man doesn't at all like the idea that a woman might one day elbow him out of the top family job."

"Anything new on Madame Repentigny herself?"

"Nothing astonishing," added Jenneret. "Just confirmation that Madame is a *very* rigid Catholic. She lives and breathes her faith, attends Mass every day (as we knew), and has a special attachment to the Basilique Saint-Remi. Two or three times a week, she takes long walks in the high-vaulted *Déambulatoire*. She often prays beneath Saint-Remi's reliquary and his presumed burial place near the altar. Many believe that Saint-Remi was buried in a small chapel beneath it. A detail: Madame Repentigny is a confidante of a respected old cleric of the Basilique, a Father... what is it?... Farfelan, as I recall."

"Just one other point," added Marcambault, "a weird one. Yesterday at the Basilique we also spotted Painteaux, the *chef de cave*. He appeared to be praying about fifteen rows back while Madame was kneeling up at the choir, near Saint-Remi's presumed tomb. He looked up at her several times. This could be a coincidence. Or he might have been praying for the victim. But that's highly implausible. *Chefs de cave* may sometimes be devout. But their daily work doesn't allow much time off for God-bothering."

"I agree," said Caron. "He bears watching. As you know, I have put a full-time tail on him. I've also asked the state prosecutor about monitoring his email, text-messages and telephones."

"Oh, and here's another point that's not really news," chimed in Jenneret, "we're finding that the list of suspects among ex-mistresses and jealous husband-competitors may be even longer than we thought. We know Repentigny annoyed rivals first by his brittle, domineering personality. Then, he earned distrust through a reputation for ruthless competition."

"And the mistresses?" asked Caron.

"The victim had a love life picturesque even for these champagne-family 'aristocrats.' Not a few gentlemen found their wives fascinated by Repentigny's wit and dynamism. To their fury, he had a nose for women's availability as infallible as his nose for vintage champagne. Result: he has cut a swath through scowling or oblivious husbands to routinely delighted prey. His slogan, we hear, was *mari lourd, cuisse légère*. Boring husband, easy wife."

"I can just imagine how the husbands would enjoy hearing that," smiled Caron. "Well, let's narrow down our lists, and focus mainly on our most plausible suspects. We shouldn't be chasing a hundred suspects without some filtering."

"Right," confirmed Duroselle. "Twenty good, well-checked ones would be more useful. And to get to that, we're going to have to separate chit-chat from credible leads. Let's chase down all the rumors and keep an eye out for wild cards. But we should be leery of unproven or vengeful gossip and – if I may say – mere sour grapes. The trick, as always, is to recognize the impossible that just might be possible."

Caron assembled the whole team later that evening. Precisely to discuss the difference between possible and impossible.

Champagnes Repentigny headquarters – staff
The P.J. team split up over most of three days to question other high-priority suspects – especially among company staff. First, the cave staff managing storage and shipments; then blending experts; marketing staff; the tour guides; and household servants who mingled with the owner's family every day.

"We have all visited various caves over the years," Caron told her team. "Now I want us to refresh our knowledge of champagne-making as well as of these particular caves. This may give more context to some of our discoveries and witnesses. Probably the fastest way to do that is to ask the professional tour-guides to run us through the processes. For your patience, you may get a free glass of bubbles at the end of the tour."

"That's the kind of orders we like," joked one cop.

As an afterthought, Caron said: "Those who think they are already experts at making champagne don't really need to come. There's lots of fascinating paperwork at the office."

"Are we doing this just to learn how to make champagne? I'm not sure that will help us solve this case," said a skeptic.

"I have ulterior motives. First, the tour will make you follow many of the steps the victim took, perhaps suggesting a new lead or even motive. Second, it's conceivable that the attacker didn't have a key to the caves at all. He could have joined a tour, then hid in the caves to commit the crime. He might somehow have escaped by hiding under a tarpaulin during a shipment."

"Pretty crafty, chère Commissaire," said Duroselle.

Caron chose four officers to accompany her on the standard 90-minute Repentigny tour. They walked down the long stairway to the caves, and gathered at the bottom in the brightly lit departure room.

"I realize that most of you are already pretty well informed about champagne," said Julie Cossiez, 28, a senior guide born in Reims. "I'll try not to talk down to you. Feel free to interrupt me at any time."

"Thanks," said Caron. "You can talk down to me all you want. I've probably forgotten the little I knew."

"OK, here we go. We'll run through all the main stages of production from picking grapes to storing and shipping fully fermented vintages. Most of the grapes we buy come from well-chosen growers among the thousands out there. These are often quite small growers. But people sometimes forget that even a medium-sized champagne house may hire several hundred grape-pickers each fall to bring in grapes from its own fields."

"Are most of the harvesters from around here?" asked one officer.

"That varies greatly from area to area, even from year to year. But many Rémois take a healthy outdoor holiday each year to work in the fields.

"Are grapes the only raw material for champagne?" asked another. "Forgive a stupid question."

"That's not stupid at all. Later in the process, you will see, blenders add what is called *vin tranquille,* wine without bubbles. Both grapes and *vin tranquille* must come from the only three grape varieties allowed in making champagne: Pinot Noir, Chardonnay and Pinot Meunier. Obviously, each house blends these in its own style, which usually include subtle variations each year and for each *cuvée* –each special batch or blend."

"What happens to the grapes when they leave the fields?"

"The next stage is pressing the grapes. This demands great care and delicacy, and we have to do it quickly to avoid oxidation. We have well over twenty presses scattered throughout the fields we draw juice from. Some presses are even here for you to see – they weigh at least eight thousand kilos."

"Impressive," murmured one visitor.

"It certainly is. Tanker-trucks promptly bring the juice (called *must*) from the remote presses to here where our technicians and blenders then begin the wine-making process. Any other questions at this stage?"

"How many full-time employees participate in the entire process?"

"In our case, as a major house, over a hundred, with about fifty in the central wine-making process. Now we can go downstairs to look at the crucial operation: blending. It's downstairs so the *must* will flow downward into the settling tanks. Settling lasts a minimum of a day or two, sometimes longer. After that, the *must* goes to fermentation tanks. There it sits for a so-called "first fermentation" at 16 to 20 degrees Celsius. Some of the fermenting wine enters stainless steel tanks – but some also goes into oak casks for traditional ageing of the main growths or *crus*."

Do you make mainly special prestige wines in the oak casks?"

"Not entirely. But we definitely prefer oak to stainless steel for our top champagnes. Let's look now at the highly guarded blending process. This is the kingdom of the *chef de cave*, the decisive player in shaping out final products."

"That's Monsieur Painteaux?"

The group looked through a thick glass into the blending room, a large laboratory with unfamiliar blending equipment.

"Yes, this is where he works his magic. He leads a small group – often supplemented by our *chef de maison*, Monsieur Repentigny – to taste and debate a variety of possible champagnes for upcoming markets."

"And M. Painteaux makes the final call?"

"Yes, but after canvassing the whole group, and especially the *chef de maison*. The goal here is to design a distinctive taste evoking the company's key values: subtlety, smoothness, elegance."

"And long-lasting, small bubbles?"

"Of course," chuckled Cossiez. "That's one of the obvious virtues of a fine champagne."

"That's what my grandmother always said."

"Grandmothers," smiled Cossiez, "are among the best connoisseurs of bubbles. They have attended many births, fiançailles and marriages. Times when champagne freely flows."

"And don't forget the divorces," rejoined a cynic.

"Let's get on with this," urged Caron. "I see we're entering the bottling-room."

"Yes, this process always delights visitors. But these machines really start rolling in spring each year, several months after first fermentation and ageing. Once they roll, we can produce over 80,000 bottles a day. That's standard bottles, called *champenoises*," but for convenience and specialty uses we produce a dozen other sizes from the tiny *mignonettes* and *piccolos* to the impossibly large *Melchior*, equal to 24 standard bottles. The only large market is for half-bottles, called *demis* or *fillettes*."

"Amazing. Then do you ship and sell those 80,000 every day?"

"Ah no, we aren't even half-way there. We store the bottles by the millions in our caves. They stay there from two to seven years, depending on how the *chef de cave* plans the second, decisive fermentation now occurring."

"A *second* fermentation?"

"Yes, the one that decides the ultimate taste and quality, including the type of bubbles that give champagne its reputation of gaiety. To achieve this, each bottle will in time get a quarter-turn to ensure balance of texture. Machines do nearly all of this, but a few human bottle-turners remain, largely for tourists."

"Is that all?"

"Not quite. After years in the dark, humidity- and temperature-controlled chalk caves, the wine is ready for disgorgement. Watch this little demonstration: You see these impurities in the neck of the bottle? We quick-freeze them into an ice-cube. The pressure in the bottle expels the cube. Then we fill that empty space with a *liqueur* carefully designed to create a specific taste: *brut*, for example, or the sweeter *sec*.

"You also make *extra-brut* and *demi-sec*, don't you?"

"Indeed – from the least sweet to the most sweet. Consumers' tastes vary a lot, although *brut* is probably the most popular now."

"And those complicated wired corks that threaten to hit you in the eye?"

"I think you all know what to do. Point the bottle at the ceiling or wall, or only at your worst enemy. But chances are he or she will not be invited to the celebration."

Cossiez ended the tour with a half-hour stroll through the caves to give her police guests a good feel for the strange, cool tunnels carved out two thousand years before. The dark, dank, winding tunnels and surprise alcoves seemed a fine setting for murder.

"Now," ended Cossiez, "let's go back upstairs to taste the result of all that work we saw. Thank you for your attention."

The police group walked up the long stairway, even the most athletic puffing a little. Gratefully, and satisfied with their new feel for the crime scene, they went to the bar for their free glass of bubbles. This violated police rules, but, winked Caron, this time it was part of their research.

They sat at the small tables, sharing the occasion with several pretty young female guides. This was no time for interrogating, and barely enough for a little flirting. But the visit had been useful for observing and imagining. The Repentigny world and style were now not just police reports. They were locked in investigators' minds -- haunting, realistic and rich in plausibilities.

On the way out, at the surface, they also visited the shipping zone where huge trucks lined up to haul away their liquid gold. Caron and her team were professionals of suspicion and practicality. They wanted to remember every entrance and exit for future reference. These truck docks must be another way in and out of the crime scene.

Caron and her team grabbed a quick lunch at Pizza Pino, then headed back to the nearby Hôtel de Police. They had summoned several key Repentigny employees to help them clarify the crime, its motive and possible author.

First up was the storage and caretaking chief on duty the night of the crime.

Gérard Dehuz, the grizzled, white-haired chief overnight watchman, had thirty-three years in the caves. He knew every itinerary, alcove and storage area by heart. Questioned about his whereabouts on the fatal night, he said:

"I was alone most of the time. But around 10 p.m., just as I started my shift, I greeted Monsieur Repentigny near the largest art gallery. He nodded hello, as did I. It was not my role to ask him why he was there. I just understood that sometimes he came down to walk around. He said it helped him think."

"Was anyone with him?"

"I saw no one. I went my way to do my rounds some distance away."

"Did he sometimes bring guests down to the caves late at night?"

Deluz hesitated, then said softly. "That was his business."

"Were his guests sometimes women, even young women?"

"Once or twice, I did glimpse such guests, but quickly and tactfully I went away."

"You read a description of his head wound in the newspapers. Do you think a woman could have done that?"

"She would have had to be quite strong. Or especially angry and well-coordinated to swing a heavy bottle and actually hit his head. In any case, I read that the attacker wore size 46 shoes – far too large for a woman."

Other officers questioned maintenance and shipping staff. Not one showed real potential for further interrogation. Most, in fact, were not on duty at the late hour of the crime.

Interviews with marketing and publicity staff added information mainly of corporate interest. They touched on positioning (Repentigny champagne is medium high-end), and on national, segmented and foreign markets.

Given Painteaux's first-day reference to Chinese visitors, Caron asked about China. She learned that Repentigny and his *chef de cave* Painteaux had made a joint trip to Shanghai two years earlier.

"They visited our importers, of course," said Anaïs Larmandier, the house's chief of marketing. "They met people from the CIVC's Bureau du Champagne in Beijing. And they met overseas investment people at the Chinese Commerce Ministry."

"What did they report on their return?"

"They said the Chinese market is growing, and has enormous potential, as everybody knows. But growth is occurring mainly among the under '30s, with young people attuned to Western culture. There is also hope that Chinese businessmen will bring back the idea of champagne as a celebratory drink. Instead, for example, of traditional Chinese drinks such as deadly *maotai*."

"Monsieur Painteaux told me you had Chinese visitors the day of the crime. He briefly referred to a Chinese economic offensive aimed at strategic Western markets. Might that include champagne, a virtual synonym of France?"

"I certainly hope not. But we are confident that no one, not even the Chinese, could reinvent real champagne. We have the soil, the traditions, the secrets, the expertise – and an iron-clad guarantee from our government that they will fight any encroachment on the very word champagne."

"Is that monsieur Painteaux's view as well?"

"Of course. Not only is he one of France's reigning experts on champagne; he's a patriot. He would fight tooth and nail to counter the Chinese if they ever tried such a scheme."

Caron wanted to question one other group, stereotypical suspects: the Repentigny's servants. She asked the four household servants – cook, cleaning-lady, valet and personal assistant – to come to her office.

The first three, genteel Rémois and retainers for over thirty years, were all well over sixty. Sweet, a little slow and obsequiously proud to work for their bosses, they did not ring guilty bells. Of course, they might conceivably collude with an outsider against their employers. But given their apparent lack of wit and energy, that possibility struck Caron and her colleagues as unlikely as the *maison* deciding to sell *Coca Cola* as a sideline.

The fourth person was a frail, reassuring forty-five-year-old secretary-factotum handling

Sophie-Charlotte's many personal activities. Not a strong candidate for visiting the caves to club Hubert Repentigny. She was a stronger candidate for a more exciting life. But only somewhat exciting, not too much.

Caron ran her evening briefing with no clear suspects. She adjourned with growing fatigue and perplexity. Were her colleagues beginning to doubt her grip on the case?

Chez Denise – détente above the Place Drouet d'Erlon...

The investigation wasn't advancing. Rather, it was advancing in too many directions. Caron and her team still probably faced a score of plausible assassins. Which one? Where? Why? The tension was fogging her mind.

The Commissaire needed a break. To clear her head, to calm her nerves. That's why she kept Stéphane at hand - a strong, sensitive man who knew what she needed. Her young carpenter lived barely a five-minute walk away on cozy little rue Salin. The lovers sometimes sneaked into the street's only decent restaurant, *L'Antr'Act,* an unpretentious place where she could identify Stéphane – to no one's belief -- as her cousin from Grenoble. Reims being a village, occasionally one of her colleagues would stumble on them. The cousin story made mirthful rounds, assuring the boys on the Boulevard Louis Roederer that their boss was properly looked after.

The love-life of a young female Commissaire supervising thirty investigators was an irresistible topic of conversation at the Hôtel de Police. If she was always seen alone, or only with women, her colleagues might speculate on her belonging to another tribe. If seen with a succession of men, well... not serious.

A semi-regular, handsome young man, however, could elicit smiles, not snickers. Since Denise, in addition to being far too beautiful to be a cop, looked much younger than thirty-two, it was hard to accuse her, with Stéphane, of cradle-robbing.

In any event, Caron made it clear to colleagues that her private life was ferociously private. She would not tolerate jokes or enquiries. The only second-hand details would spin off from the unbelievable "cousin from Grenoble" fiction.

Sometimes, the lovers would slip up to Stéphane's bachelor pad on rue Salin. But when Caron really wanted to unwind, she would summon him to her spectacular apartment, whose floor-to-ceiling windows overlooked the fountain on the long, wide Place Drouet d'Erlon.

Tonight, Stéphane let himself in with his key. He saw Caron in the dark, silhouetted against the windows. She stood with her back to him, in unpolice-like high heels and a long, belted trench coat. She was staring out at the lamp-lit boulevard below, capturing the soul of the city. She drank in the night, the moment.

Neither said a word.

Préfecture régionale, Châlons-en-Champagne...
François Guizot's request to both growers and merchants to send him names of possible suspects,

even anonymously, had borne fruit. He already had in hand four names of seriously aggrieved growers, and two of merchants – one of these a small *maison*, the other one much larger. More names poured in every day. He would send them all over to the P.J. as they came in.

Secret denunciations and poison-pen letters have a long and somber tradition in France. The collaborationist Vichy régime in the Second World War generated thousands of "suspects" this way. Neighbors denounced Jews or supposed *Résistance* members. Thousands of real or imagined *collabos* – or just people with property to steal -- met death or humiliation by vengeful real or fake *résistants* at war's end.

More recently, an attempt to discredit future presidential candidate Nicolas Sarkozy in 2006-07 was the infamous politico-financial Clearstream affair. It came to light via a letter from a *corbeau* or "squealer," a shadowy senior executive living in several professional worlds at once.

Guizot being the region's senior state official, Caron went personally to see him. He could prove a valuable ally in Paris. She took with her two of her senior investigators highly knowledgeable of the champagne world. She received photocopies of the original notes Guizot had received on alleged suspects, and assigned them to her two colleagues for urgent action.

"Thank you very much, Monsieur le Préfet de Région," said Caron.

Turning to her colleagues, she said: "Kilisky, you come from a well-established grower family.

Would you please check out the grower leads and report back to the team?"

"Of course, Commissaire."

"And Hurpeaux, I will leave you the touchy task of tracking down the leads targeting the merchants. This may prove even trickier than looking into possibly guilty growers."

After her two colleagues left, Caron stayed behind to share discreet impressions with Guizot.

"We all know that the world of blending-marketing houses is deeply suspicious of outsiders," said Caron. "They may be polite, and eat with the right fork, but they're a jealously self-protective mafia."

"Mafia?" recoiled Guizot in mock horror. "That's a rather nasty term for these upstanding leaders of society," he observed.

"Well, I didn't call them a cabal," replied Caron. "Let's just call them *les grandes familles*."

"That's more tactful," smiled Guizot. "Many of these people are my personal friends."

"I understand," said Caron soothingly. "Of course they are your personal friends."

The words hung in the air, eliciting brief blushes. Was Caron insulting Guizot? Her sweetly innocent expression allowed him to decide that she wasn't. He thanked Caron for her visit, and showed her out with exquisite courtesy.

Élysée Palace – consulting the spooks...

President Guérin was brooding over his friend Hubert's misfortune. While the Police judiciaire were investigating the attack as a purely domestic crime, the minister of the Interior, Morel, was checking out a possible international dimension. His domestic spies, the Direction Centrale du renseignement intérieur (DCRI), had already warned him -- and the President -- that Ma Chuntao was a likely Chinese industrial spy. Morel now told his Economic Protection service to investigate Ma more closely. What was she up to, and with whom?

Morel had noted that the Chinese were buying high-quality castles near Bordeaux – twenty so far, another thirty under negotiation.

Apart from the castles and large buying delegations, the Chinese were already starting to make internationally competitive wines at home. On December 14, 2011, a blind-tasting in Beijing with five Chinese and five French judges, had awarded first place to a *Chairman's Reserve* from China's Grace Vineyards in the Ningxia region. The top French wine, a *Saga Médoc* 2009 from the Baron de Rothschild Collection, eked out only a fifth place.

The 2011 coup was breathtaking. The Chinese had only started planting Bordeaux-style wines a decade before. With top red-wine coups like this, could a takeover of champagne be far behind? Repentigny had once raised this danger with Guérin. Now the President wanted DCRI to dig deeper – and wider to all of Champagne-Ardenne.

"Champagne and France are indissoluble ideas," he warned Morel. "Step up your digging into this as soon as possible."

For starters, Morel made two moves. First, he told DCRI Reims to walk up two floors in the Hôtel de Police to liaise with the Police judiciaire. Together, could they find a link, even remote, between the attack on Repentigny and a possible Chinese plot to destabilize France in its most prestigious wine market? This worldwide signature of France could not be allowed to end up as a mere competitor to an abomination called 'Chinese champagne.'

Second, Morel wanted a broader report on the accelerating Chinese purchases of Bordeaux estates. By January 2012, Chinese investors had snapped up scores of picturesque castles with lush vineyards and recognized fine wines. That left over 11,000 castles for French and other non-Chinese. But the strong *yuan* (aka *renminbi*) and explosion of well-heeled Chinese investors made a Chinese "invasion" a here-and-now reality. A few Chinese-owned prizes: Château Chenu Lafitte (Bourg), Château Latour Laguens (AOC Bordeaux), Château Richelieu (Fronsac), Château de Viaud (Lalande-de-Pomerol), and Château Laulan Ducos (Médoc) and Château du Grand Mouëys.   .

Morel asked Philippe Rigaud, his chief of the DCRI Economic Protection Branch, to try to monitor strategy meetings of Chinese officials and major investors. The likeliest way to do this would be to keep an eye on all-delegates' meetings.

Bugging such meetings would be hard in China's Paris Trade Commission. Access security there was tight, and there was probably a safe-room cleared of bugs. The deputy was already watching for large

Chinese meetings in one of the many Bordeaux castles owned by Chinese. He could install eavesdropping devices more easily in such places.

But wasn't that war almost over? The Chinese penetration of Bordeaux was not just known. It was happening before France's eyes. The game warming up now appeared to be champagne. Getting inside Chinese official minds was the only hope for countering a Beijing grab for the world champagne market.

Luckily, DCRI Reims had already compiled a short list of castles in Champagne-Ardenne – short, because there weren't many. They had asked castle and large-hotel owners to alert them whenever they had enquiries about renting all or most of their facilities for closed meetings.

Two months before, the Chinese Trade Mission in Paris had enquired about renting the magnificent, and perfectly named, Le Château Fort in Champagne-Ardenne's historic city of Sedan. It was a massive medieval fort with fifty-four colorful rooms, a fine restaurant and meeting rooms. Though eighty-two kilometers from Reims, it was close enough for visitors to explore the champagne areas. The distance also avoided an unwelcome risk: a large group of Chinese in Reims itself would heighten gossip about a so-called "Chinese invasion." From Sedan, the Trade Commission delegates could split up into less obtrusive smaller groups in Reims.

Rigaud was unaware of the Chinese enquiry. He called the hotel to ask if managers had news of a Chinese group. Embarrassed, the hotel manager said: "Didn't you receive our alert ten days ago? A Chinese group of forty is coming in three days from now. They plan to stay two days."

Cursing his luck, Rigaud identified himself and his service. He asked how the group described itself. Answer: Chinese investors. And the contact: the Chinese Trade Mission in Paris. Bingo. Rigaud said DCRI needed immediate, 24-hour access to prepare "surveillance" of this group, which might be hostile to French interests. The hotel, like any hotel in France intimidated by talk of "national defense secrets," had to agree.

Hôtel de Police...linking up with the brothers...

Baraquant, Caron's top-boss Commissaire divisionnaire, got a late-afternoon message from the Director of the Police judiciaire in Paris. "Go and see your DCRI friends to coordinate your efforts. The minister wants you to look into a possible Chinese connection as well as the case at hand." The spooks and cops – DCRI and DCPJ -- would now pool information that might tie the Repentigny attack to a hypothetical Chinese plot.

This will be interesting, thought both of the Reims teams, functionally and culturally worlds apart. Knowing all about inter-service rivalries, they assumed that collaboration would be either a marriage made in Heaven or two scorpions in a bottle.

Caron pulled together all the day's new data at the briefing. She went home at close to 10 p.m. When her mother called to harangue her about settling down with a nice husband, "maybe a young champagne baron," Caron listened dutifully. But looking out over the wide boulevard below, she focused on sipping her cool, blond *Pineau des Charentes* and puffing on her Panter Mignon Deluxe. No room in her life for a husband just now, *maman*.

Stéphane? Fun -- but not tonight.

In the valley of the growers...
The next day, Caron read the first reports on the small producers known to have threatened vengeance on the victim for destroying their businesses. She might interview them formally in her office later, but first she wanted to visit them in their natural habitats. These showed her a universe as exotic as that of the big merchants. And if initiative, courage, hard work and perseverance counted, even more inspiring.

With her two field investigators who had already made a first visit, she jumped in her Peugeot 308 SW and drove to the hamlet of Bouzy, not far from Épernay.

Ma Chuntao at the Café de la Paix, Paris...
Ma spotted Capelle, her Bank of France host, in the huge bright Café de la Paix bar, tea and breakfast room. The high skylights fifteen meters above flooded the elegant small tables with morning sunlight. Under the main *art-déco* chandelier, and punctuated by banks of small shaded lamps, the scene whispered restrained elegance.

Capelle, lean, graying and distinguished, was waiting in a comfortable wing-chair beside a sofa. He looked like a central-casting banker, his slowly wandering eyes hunting down his next prey. He had chosen one of the more discreet little islands of furniture that make everywhere here a cozy private living-room.

Ma didn't exactly slink in, but she came close. Her simple black dress turned eyes with its not-quite-understated gold necklace and her matching heavy gold bracelets. At a glance, she was the quintessence of the *nouveau-riche* Chinese tourist going a shade over the top to impress... other Chinese tourists.

Capelle stood up to greet her, smiling and nodding his head as he walked toward her.

"Good morning, Ms. Ma," he opened. "So good of you to take time."

"Not at all. I'm sure you have much to tell me."

They both ordered the "business breakfast" of fresh-squeezed orange juice, the baker's basket, and coffee.

"I see that both the Shanghai exchange and the Hang Seng are up again today," said Capelle.

"Yes, the trend has been somewhat up, but the world currency crisis still threatens us as it does the West."

"You are terribly busy, Ms. Ma, but let me ask you to sketch out briefly how China sees its investments in French industries developing over coming years. You have seen the scare stories about a so-called 'Chinese invasion,' but, on balance, do you see your growing investment here as strengthening the French economy?"

"Yes, we do – if you include what comes with our capital. In entering certain industries, we hope gradually to bring in – if you will allow me -- better-focused, forward-looking management, and even a work ethic that can only strengthen you."

"Thanks for your bluntness. Neither you nor I can say such things publicly. But between us, you're right."

"We think the media stories about our taking over everything in sight are pretty exaggerated."

"You must admit that what you did with the TGV and Airbus seems to demonstrate a policy of buying high technology, then flinging it back at us as competitors."

"Your governments, especially your presidents, seemed awfully happy to sell us your trains and airplanes. And is there a law, in this globalized world, about learning new technologies in order to compete?"

"Of course not. But what do you say about China's sudden 2011-12 frenzy of purchases of Bordeaux vineyards? This, at a time when you beat our Bordeaux reds in blind-tastings?

Ma laughed. "I realize that nothing can upset the French more than beating their wines."

"Maybe beating them at champagne could. Aren't you right now gearing up for an offensive there too? Buying vineyards here, and getting Moët Hennessy to joint-venture vineyards for sparkling wine with state-owned *Ningxia Nongken*?"

"We didn't exactly twist Moët Hennessy's arm," smiled Ma.

"Still, champagne is an explosively sensitive area. It's intimately tied to France's very identity. An identity based on excellence, elegance and good taste."

"I know nothing of this. I think this fear is a fantasy. Nobody could beat France at real champagne. And I know of nobody in China who even dreams of that."

Ma looked Capelle steadily in the eye. She exuded honesty, transparency and fair dealing.

"Just a word then about currency swaps, your specialty. Without getting too technical, do you envisage that the Bank of China will always stand ready to help Europe-China trade relations in a stable, responsible way?"

"You mean stand ready to bail out the euro, no matter what?"

"That's sounding a bit cocky, if I may say. The day can always come when Europe might need to help China."

"I'm sure you will," she smiled smugly.

"I would guess that if ever that day comes, it will be when your government finds that Deng Xiaoping's policy of economic liberalism and political dictatorship begins to collapse as a new middle class demands more freedom. It's already happening. I give it less than five years before the lid blows off the so-called Communist Party – which forgot Marx and just kept Lenin."

"Now, Monsieur Capelle, you are the blunt one. I'm not offended, but I really must go. I need to make sure that the terrifying Chinese invasion is still on track."

"Let's call that black humor, not a serious threat. Thank you so much for your time. On the currency swaps, I guess we have come to a non-committal draw."

"Something like that."

"Goodbye then, Ms. Ma. Delighted to have met you."

He dropped some bills on the table, and ushered Ma out to the boulevard des Capucines. The pair shook hands briefly before separating on the sidewalk.

Just then, a young female foreign tourist was standing beside the newspaper kiosque across the street. She snapped a fast series of splendid photos of the currency summiteers.

A talented junior DCRI agent, she recognized Ma, and knew by heart her file in *Cristina*, the all-knowing DCRI database. Soon she would learn the identity of her handsome breakfast companion. He didn't resemble any fellow spooks she knew from DCRI HQ at Levallois-Perret. If anything, he just looked like some boring banker.

CHAPTER FIVE
Facing The Maze

Early morning, ten days after the crime. A light autumn rain fell from a cloudy sky. Caron went up to her fourth-floor office, and quickly checked her desk and e-mail for her team's overnight gleanings. These were piling up quickly. But they pointed to no clear direction. She swiveled her chair to look out the window on the nondescript buildings below. As often, she wished she could move her desk into one of the offices down the hall with big windows affording a dazzling view of the town below. She cradled her second double *espresso*, and brooded on her situation.

She had joined the Police judiciaire almost a decade ago. At 21, she had been leaning toward police work or a career as a history teacher. When her father Gilles, a beat policeman, took a paralyzing bullet in his spine during a hold-up, there was no contest: she would be a cop. Everything she did now was in honor of him, a tribute to him. She took every training course she could – in scientific investigation, criminal psychology, leadership, economics and management. She determined to go as high as she could, while keeping his values of courage and decency.

Caron's other inspiration was – as for probably every other P.J. woman – the astonishing Martine Monteil. Granddaughter, daughter and wife of policemen, Monteil had zoomed to the very top as *Directeur central de la Police judiciaire*, step by gritty, cruel step at Maigret's legendary 36 quai des Orfèvres. She earned her way up the hard way, sparing herself no assignment, no challenge, no danger, no nightmarish sight. She showed imagination: she made serial killer Guy Georges walk up a stairway past her whole brigade. She showed humanity, calling the mothers of his seven murdered girls. And even comforting male policemen who sobbed at finding a murdered child.

"Such terrible experiences galvanize us to find the guilty," wrote Monteil in her compelling memoir *Flic*. "In a way, they make us stronger. We should not be ashamed of our tears; they preserve our humanity in the face of the unspeakable."

Like Monteil, Caron saw police work of all kinds as a calling, not a job like postal clerk. Chasing often vicious criminals might not be quite an apostolate. But it was close. It aimed to protect all society by protecting every individual – a mother, a child, a grandparent, a confused and struggling youth. Or a small merchant whose dream of education for his kids a gang of hoodlums stole by beating him senseless into bankruptcy.

Caron loved her work and her colleagues. A few still sniped at her for all the usual reasons – she was a woman, younger, and held the job some had yearned for. But while occasionally wounding, such criticism wasn't personal. Her only challenge, she knew, was to stay on top of her job, and to excel. Happily, after two years of supervising other investigators, she was winning over most colleagues. They recognized her intelligence, her sense of fairness, and her determination.

Determination? The never-give-up P.J. signature. The Police judiciaire, like most French police forces, has its own traditions, customs and rituals. The P.J. grew from *les Brigades du Tigre*, France's first professional, mobile criminal police founded by Premier and Interior Minister Georges Clemenceau in 1907. Its badge still carries the profile of *le Tigre,* a nickname Clemenceau earned for his tough treatment of opponents. *Tigre* implied speed, cunning and resolution.

Caron also drew joy from P.J. camaraderie. You can see and hear it today in the broad hallways of Reims's Hôtel de Police. First names abound, often even for superiors. Colleagues poke noses into offices without formality. Respectful of other's eccentricities, officers also praise colleagues' skills – identification, crime-solving science, marksmanship, foreign languages.

You witness a solidarity that not many professions demonstrate at this level. Apart from covering for each other during investigations, officers keep rituals. When a gunman killed a P.J. colleague in Marseille in December 2011, the entire Reims P.J. staff – officers and support staff – filed out to stand in the courtyard for one minute of silence. Across France, French police of all types joined them. Just as Reims P.J. grieved with *gendarmerie* colleagues when a Riviera thug murdered two young female gendarmes in June 2012.

Next time, it could be one of us, thought every man or woman.

The case at hand exemplified the same solidarity. It was incredibly complex and politically sensitive. Because of the victim's notoriety, the investigation would take place at every stage in the full glare of publicity. Leaks might threaten its integrity, and alert the guilty. Gaffes and misjudgments would draw sarcastic headlines: already, the daily *L'Union* seemed to hold a grudge against certain cops. Any delay could earn a story about police "incompetence" and the continuing danger to the champagne industry's reputation – key to the whole region's prosperity.

Pressure from the industry to wrap up the investigation, and even perhaps the mayor's echo of this skepticism, could add a further burden. Criticism could snowball until the media had created a self-fulfilling prophecy of failure.

Publicity good or bad, of course, would focus on Denise Caron. If she led her team to a fairly prompt, imaginative conclusion, she might grow into a new Martine Monteil. If her search for the culprit dragged endlessly, or even came up blank, the naysayers against the "too young, too inexperienced" Caron could crow victory. And Caron's career might never recover.

All this troubled Caron's mind as she put down her coffee cup, and turned to face the day. She believed she could win. She had to win.

Success might enhance her prestige. But Caron knew viscerally that, in solving crime, there is no such thing as Sherlock Holmes, Hercule Poirot or even Maigret anymore. Catching bad guys is now a collective effort from start to finish. In some ways, 'running' a difficult investigation is like running ahead of a stampede of wild horses, while pretending you're leading them.

One reason was and is the fast-increasing complexity of crime. Technology changes every day. Whole new disciplines of criminology eclipse traditional training. Social, economic and political forces shape mentalities and accepted police behavior. Ethno-cultural diversity of the police itself is a major challenge, as well as an opportunity.

Most of all, senior police realize that these changes demand that teams, not individuals, manage investigations. Curiously enough, thought Caron, maybe this sea-change in the structure of investigations might even favor women. Simplifying the question: men grow up in a hierarchical way, with leaders and followers, chiefs and Indians. Women, by instinct, tend to consult more, and to seek group harmony.

That's enough day-dreaming for this morning, thought Caron. It's 9:15 a.m., and I need to marshal my colleagues for today's pursuits. Pursuits to be carried out within some orderly framework. She chuckled at the word 'orderly.' In this game, order constantly gives way to reality. And discipline needs to relax when improvisation makes more sense.

Caron's first meeting was with her two top bosses, Baraquant and Duroselle. In Duroselle's office, the three met around his small round table.

"So, Denise, where are we at with Repentigny?" asked Baraquant.

"It's moving, as you would expect, simultaneously in several directions. But we're focusing in the first instance on family, friends and the champagne industry at all levels: *grandes maisons*, growers, the CIVC and even the INOQ, the guys who certify wine standards and *appellations*."

"That makes sense. You realize that the champagne *barons* are a touchy and secretive lot. They will not be easy to open up."

"I'm vividly aware of that. But we've developed a couple of – well, I wouldn't quite call them moles – let's say individuals very well plugged in economically and socially with the big guys. Our sources know well the culture of the big merchants. They know their families, relatives, even their mistresses and lovers – although theoretically, none of the latter exist."

Baraquant and Duroselle smiled appreciatively.

"There is one other significant dimension, of course," said Caron. "The political. Repentigny is, as we know, the highly partisan president of the Conseil Général. And if you believe the *Canard enchaîné*, he's a buddy of Roland Guérin."

"Of course, our esteemed satirical weekly loves Guérin and his MPF party."

"I don't wish to be cynical," said Caron, but I'm presuming that any politician at those levels has enemies."

"Really?" said Baraquant in mock horror. "But we prefer you to be cynical rather than naïve, Denise," he smiled, and all three shared a laugh.

"Denise, I've been attending your daily briefings, and have a good idea of your general orientations. But would you risk saying that at this stage, one or another category of suspects is the most promising?"

"I couldn't responsibly say which one at this stage. But the champagne world, taken as a complex whole, leaves us a fertile field to till."

"Prudently put, Denise," complimented Duroselle. "At this stage, it would seem unwise to make too-clear presumptions."

"My instinct is that confronting other top *barons* may tell only part of any story," said Caron. We'll of course question several of the likelier ones. And Guizot, the Regional Prefect, has already given us a few plausible names from both merchant and grower camps."

"Good for you. It was smart politics to bring in Guizot. Depending on how this thing plays out, we may need him on our side in Paris. With either the minister of the interior, the president, or both."

"I do have another *baron* idea up my sleeve, or rather a *baronne* idea."

"Tell us more," advanced Duroselle. "Do you hope to eliminate suspicions against the *baronnes*?"

"Not at all," smiled Caron. "I just want to interrogate a few of these top women who have had business – and conceivably other – relations with Repentigny."

"Ah," teased Baraquant, "all worthy successors of *la Veuve Clicquot*."

"They are indeed, monsieur le Directeur. From what I have already learned, these women have brought a seriousness and management skill that have amazed their employees."

"Names?"

"At a minimum, I hope to see the women running Bollinger, Laurent-Perrier and Duval-Leroy. At Laurent-Perrier, it's in fact the founder's two daughters, Alexandra and Stéphanie, who are taking over. Having scanned media profiles of all these women, I believe they will prove outstanding sources, and offer fresh insights. Often women have a sixth sense about other people."

"How do you think you got *your* job?" teased Baraquant. "Questioning the top women of the *grandes marques* is not a bad idea at all. Many of these women have outstanding character and judgment. Let us know if they come up with better leads than you get from the *barons*."

An exemplary "baronne"-- character is destiny...
Caron wasted no time pursuing her instinct about female champagne bosses. She made an appointment with one of the leading *baronnes du*

champagne Madame Suzanne Piollot-Leytem. Like most of the top women of *grandes maisons*, she took over as widow of a dynamic man who died too young, leaving a house badly in need of fresh leadership. Simultaneously raising three young children while rescuing a complex major firm made her itinerary heroic. Local and national magazines profiled her with unstinting praise. "The new Veuve Clicquot" applied to her (as to so many other female peers) made an irresistible cliché. And like the most famous "veuve," she was tough and determined. She had to be in the macho world she had entered.

As if to make the point that women could also make great champagne, Madame Suzanne Piollot-Leytem gave the three other top posts in her firm to women. One, Jacqueline Grigord-Pacara, held the ultra-sensitive job of *chef de cave.*

In her early sixties, Madame Piollot-Leytem was compact, blonde, and held visitors with steely blue eyes. Among the taller men who usually surrounded her, she cut a redoubtable figure. In a front-page picture in *Sommeliers International,* her blue jeans made the 'suits' around her look like dilettantes.

"I am as shocked as anyone at this monstrous crime," she told Caron. "And I can't even imagine any of our senior colleagues being remotely involved in it."

"But being yourself at the top of the champagne world, you must have heard stories of conflict or resentment touching Monsieur Repentigny."

"I am not in the habit of listening to gossip – and am even less in the habit of repeating it. I also believe in respecting the victim in this story."

"Commendable virtues. But allow me to rephrase my question. Is there anything at all in Monsieur Repentigny's record that might attract antagonism?"

"I would rather call it jealousy. Jealousy at his great success – in business, politics, and society at large. By the standard of business success, many of us who work hard might also be taxed with creating 'antagonism.' Is hard work a crime yet?"

"Not yet, Madame – happily for us hard-workers in the police."

"Of course."

"So, to summarize: You can't suggest a single lead from the business community. May I now ask a less discreet question? What about friends of Monsieur Repentigny? Male... and female?"

"You are testing my patience, Commissaire. You're fishing for mistresses. I told you I have a horror of gossip. And I have no intention of soiling Monsieur Repentigny's name now or at any point."

"You must understand, Madame, that what you call gossip, we in the police consider possible leads. Listening to anything and everything is how we solve crimes."

"Well, I'm sorry but I'm not a 'lead' for you. Just a colleague and friend of Monsieur Repentigny and his wife."

"I can see that this is all we can discuss today, Madame. But if you wish to honor the memory of the victim, and help us solve the crime against him, I ask you to think further about my questions. If even a scrap of information or suspicion comes to you, we would infinitely appreciate your help."

"I guess we can call this a draw, and leave matters at that. But you know my position."

"I do indeed, Madame. Thank you for your trouble."

Fourth floor, Hôtel de Police...

Back at the office, Caron reported her failure to gain Madame Piollot-Leytem's cooperation.

"She's a clam," she told Baraquant and Duroselle. "I couldn't get a whisper out of her. She's one tough lady."

Baraquant laughed. "So much for female intuition. But maybe you can get through to some of the other champagne widows."

"At this point, I'm inclined to believe that the whole caste of the *grandes maisons* will close ranks and not cooperate much. My best hope is the wife of a champagne baron who is close to Sophie-Charlotte."

"I know the one you're referring to. Good luck!!"

Down the hall, two other conversations would soon add small burdens to Caron's day. Just routine human dramas. But dramas intensified by the ceaseless stress of police work. As Caron saw things, listening to colleagues' personal problems that might affect teamwork was part of her job.

In one office, Lieutenant Jacques Ravignaux had tears in his eyes as he reflected on his imminent divorce. His wife could not take any longer the un-predictable, often all-night shifts of her husband. Like so many cops, he was finding that police work was terrible for marriage. He and his wife had talked of divorce for months. They increasingly lived in different worlds. His wife lived in fear that he might get killed or wounded, leaving her a widow with small children. Her commitment was to home and children. His was to children and work, with wife too often forgotten in his passion for saving the world.

Dropping by his office, Caron invited him for coffee and said: "Jacques, your worries from home are beginning to show. You're distracted, and clearly depressed. Try to keep a better perspective on home and work. If you don't look after the home front, you'll end up not being much good here."

He knew that. But he struggled to translate the theory into practice. How can a man stop thinking about his children? But Caron's concern helped a little.

In another office, two officers also debated duty versus home. One saw only duty – he was already divorced, and had no kids. The other took Caron's view: keep your family happy, or at least reassured that they haven't lost you, and you'll be a better cop.

Such debates go on in almost any office. But police culture can make it all a life-and-death matter. Which it is.

"A healthy debate, gentlemen," said Caron when she stopped by. "Just let me know if and when you've found the solution."

Hôtel de Police crime lab...

A colleague probably closer to finding answers was Commandant Dominique Flochard, the sturdy, mid-thirties chief of the crime lab. Caron dropped down to see her every other day. With her trademark oblong designer glasses and round short body, Flochard looked like a jolly elf. Actually, a rather cute one.

This sweet image seemed out of place amid the photo galleries on her walls. No doubt for ambiance, Flochard displayed there hundreds of gory victim photos, as well as terrifying criminals' mugshots. She also kept "albums" of completed investigations. These included a matter-of-fact narrative on the crime, plus maps and usually ghastly photos. These albums would help guide judges and juries to make their decisions – if they had any stomach left to decide anything.

"Any new finds or thoughts, Dominique?"

"I'm doing some research on chemicals found in the chalk caves. This just may come in handy in checking whether a suspect was down in the victim's caves the night of the crime."

"Sounds smart. Any specific progress?"

"Yes, although it may sound a little far-fetched."

"I love the far-fetched," smiled Caron. "Fire away."

"Well, in researching fungi that exist on chalk walls, I found some intriguing reports. The first and seminal one came in 1726 from Sir John Floyer in England. He reported a case of environmental asthma and bronco-spasm in a patient who had just visited a wine cellar. The fungus he found was called Racodium Cellare or Zasmidium. Actually you should think of nasty lichen and spores."

"I'll try. Wow --1726. Now that's what I call digging into the past. What next?"

"When I started thinking about the physical effects of fungi, I started wondering about their mental effects. I clicked on the idea of chemicals and the brain. Including chemicals able to influence behavior. Naturally, that led me to the infamous North Korean and Chinese brainwashing techniques used on U.S. soldiers during the Korean War."

"Naturally? My God, that's an amazing series of free associations! But did this produce any practical ideas for the case at hand?"

"Maybe. In looking into Korea, I found that the CIA and Canada had conducted their own brainwashing experiences from the early '50s on. The program, later declared illegal, was called MKULTRA. Under this, a scientist at McGill University in Montreal developed a concept called 'psychic driving.' It used LSD, mescaline and other hallucinatory drugs to induce zombie-like actions. It heightened this result via sleep deprivation and audio-loop repetition – playing suggestive tapes all night."

"Well, for now, I'm not looking for zombies. I'm concentrating on real, live people. But I'll file your discoveries in the back of my mind just in case."

"Thanks, Denise. I know this info is far out. But if ever we find ourselves grasping at straws, who knows?"

"Right. And believe me, if we have no credible suspects in a couple of weeks, we may very well be grasping at straws. Have a good day, Dominique."

First report on the growers ...

Regional Prefect François Guizot delivered his final combined list of suspects by messenger to the Hôtel de Police. He attached photocopies of each letter in case the crime lab or identity staff wanted to work on them. This might also help decide eventually if some denunciations were based on personal vengeance or commercial trouble-making.

The crop of alleged suspects gave some measure of Repentigny's genius for making enemies. It included two heads of *grandes maisons*, three of medium-sized houses, and no less than seventeen growers.

Plainly, following up on all this was not an Agatha Christie weekend-mansion affair. It would take a few weeks, and perhaps even reinforcements from regional colleagues in Strasbourg.

Caron would have to scour not only Reims itself, but the whole champagne corridor down to Épernay and the administrative capital of the Marne *Département,* Châlons-en-Champagne.

The major houses were mainly concentrated in Reims and Épernay. But to cover the growers, Caron's team would have to visit a score of tiny champagne villages. They would have to try to get into the heads of a group of artisans even more suspicious of outsiders than are the *barons*. The P.J. had to understand intimately what the thousands of small producers as a group might have thought of Repentigny – then try to identify a culprit with a specific grievance. Could there be, somewhere out there, a disgruntled producer bankrupted by Repentigny's hard-ball methods? A person furious enough to try to kill him?

Caron reported all this immediately to Baraquant and Duroselle. Then, with both of them present, she conducted her evening briefing. She had covered the white-board with a large map of the champagne country, with colored pins showing where they would need to go.

Normally, the P.J. would just call in suspects to their offices. But Caron believed in first studying each player on his or her home turf. There you could pick up sights and signals you might miss in a police office. She would also use the on-site visits and questioning to prepare each office interview, allowing her to spot lies or evasions more easily.

First reports on Repentigny's financial and political life...

Early on, Caron had brought in two top accounting sleuths – Roland Riquet and Gustave Bardy -- from the Ministry's sub-directorate of financial investigations. They were hard at work on the victim's company and personal accounts. They had already visited the family notary, Maître Alexandre Gueillot, and taken away relevant files. They did the same at the office of Félix Corzelius. The BNP bank manager."

They quickly concluded that Repentigny had many irons in the fire, some of them rather dodgy-looking ones. They promised a tentative summary of the victim's easily knowable financial life within a week. Knowable, that is, to the extent that he told his Reims advisers his whole story. Offshore accounts were common for wealthy French people. The *fisc* and DCPJ's own financial branches could help. So could a meticulous study of bank transfers. For this, they would need a couple of weeks at a minimum.

Caron's two consultants in political skullduggery, Dossereaux and Braillard, jumped eagerly into the fray. Chain-smoking André Dossereaux, a former journalist at the left-leaning daily *Libération* and the scandal-mongering *Le Canard enchaîné*, was close to drooling over the case's potential for blowing wide open the secretive champagne aristocracy. Jean Braillard, an older, more thoughtful digger, came from newspaper-of-reference *Le Monde* and the fairly new, but scoop-making, website *Mediapart*.

Caron had to be careful about contracting with ex-journalists. They tend to gossip and leak. And scandals had a bad habit of leaving mud on anybody even indirectly involved. But she was astute enough to make informal, oral agreements with these professionals. In return for tips and acting as a sounding-board, she would not be averse to tossing a lead or a hint their way later on.

A shocking conflict of loyalties? No. Real-world, results-oriented police work.

In her initial chats with both bloodhounds, Caron heard echoes of *sub rosa* price-fixing. She heard tales of political alliances and antagonisms that changed major policies at the Conseil Général, or steered big money toward the President's (i.e. Repentigny's) pet projects. She was even obliged to hear gossip of lurid love affairs that might or might not affect the price of grapes...

But most intriguingly, Caron heard reports of a beautiful Chinese woman who seemed close to both Repentigny and the President of the Republic. In these days of rampant anti-Chinese news stories, this was surely just another proof of paranoia. It was just about journalists out to increase circulation or raise TV ratings. If Repentigny happened to believe in multiculturalism, fine, thought Caron. So do I – like cops and carpenters...

La Grillade Gourmande, Épernay...

A warm, sunny autumn day. Guests mingled before the annual board lunch of Champagnes Saint-Eustache, one of France's most beloved *grandes marques*. Inevitably, the probably fatal attack on Repentigny had cast a heavy pall on the normal celebratory mood.

"What a shocker," said one member to another. "This is terrible for Hubert's family. But – and I don't mean to be crass – it's potentially highly harmful to our industry."

"There's no doubt about that," echoed a senior colleague. This incredible crime is focusing world attention on us. And not the kind of attention we want."

"No doubt many foreigners will find this titillating," dared Gilles Honerchick, a junior member.

"And they do say in show business that any publicity is good publicity."

His attempt to sound worldly fell flat. Silence. That murderous silence that follows a gaffe in good French society.

"Frankly, young man, that's not an analogy that I find appropriate on a day like this."

Crestfallen, Honerchick apologized. "I only meant that this crime, however horrible, incidentally makes a lot of people think about champagne."

"Gilles," whispered Delphine Lavertu, the lovely young black PR lady, "I think you might skip any more 'explanations' Have a glass of champagne yourself and think very hard about it," she smiled, trying to rescue him. She knew he had eyes for her. And she hoped he would soon do something about it.

"Thank you, ma belle. You save me from my stupidity."

"Gilles, you're not stupid. Just sometimes a bit hasty – in some things anyway," she added, with a penetrating look into which only an Olympic diver could plunge. She sashayed off on her red Jimmy Choo heels, her nonchalant sway inspiring in Gilles a vision of the Caribbean Sea's slow-rolling waves.

The company president, Georges Ledoyen, seeing all twenty members present, called for attention.

"Mesdames, Messieurs, please raise your glasses to our friend and colleague Hubert Repentigny. May he recover soon and rejoin his family in his normal virile health."

"To Hubert," murmured the group. Flutes clinked, and eyes locked then lowered. Agathe de Boispieux, a happily married matron biblically known to Hubert, shivered a second on hearing the word "virile." Hubert was the second pain in her life. The first was hearing wags deform her family name as Madame de Puispeu – a nasty play on "depuis peu" – insinuating a purchased nobility of mere late 19th-century vintage.

Reverence and niceties observed, the group sat down to a superb meal. Guests sat in red or black high-backed leather chairs. After fresh oysters, they chose between wood-grilled fish or wood-grilled meat. A family-owned and –run restaurant, it served excellent, unpretentious food at affordable prices. A perfect, understated choice for Pol Roger, Winston Churchill's preferred tipple.

Sooner or later, somebody would joke about Churchill and his alleged champagne slogan (echoing Napoleon and countless others): "In victory, I deserve it; in defeat, I need it." This often led to the irresistible topic of Brits and bubbles. Churchill had his Pol Roger; James Bond his Bollinger; Queen Elizabeth II her Mumm's; Lord Keynes had, well, as much as he could get.

Another perennial theme: the insane and unsuccessful attempts by foreigners to produce their own champagne. Italy's Prosecco, Spain's Cava, Germany's Sekt, plus feeble efforts by Portugal and Australia. Not to forget America's too-sugary 'American champagne.' All pale substitutes for our inimitable product." But the group at *La Grillade Gourmande* didn't dwell long on the fact that in 2011, for the first time, Prosecco outsold France's champagne.

These tired jests and stories done, the party wound down. The Repentigny horror hushed all conversations. Whatever their rank, participants in the meal could not refrain from speculating on the act's author and motives. And on the impact of the crime on their common product's luster worldwide.

Media bloodhounds...

It was barely two weeks before the media, or at least its most eager outlets, began to snap at Caron's 6-cm. heels on long black boots. "Investigation dragging," howled the daily *L'Union*'s front-page headline. Sub-heads added: "Young woman Commissaire severely tested" – a first hint that the paper would likely use Caron for target-practice. The story's lead clearly insinuated that Caron might be in over her head.

"Police investigators appear to be making little progress in solving the barbaric crime against Hubert Repentigny, well-known champagne baron and president of the Champagne-Ardenne Regional Council. This is the first major case led by Commissaire Denise Caron. Although it is still early days, some observers remember initial grumbling that at 32, Caron was thought awfully young for her demanding job. Can she manage to focus and inspire her thirty-member investigative team to solve this appalling crime?"

The words hit Caron like a kick in the stomach. Until now, such grumbling was considered routine old-cop bad-mouthing. On the front page of the major local daily, it was a slap in the face – and almost an invitation to her colleagues' gradual insurrection. This was 'wartime' now, not police college. She would have to display total calm and a clear-headed determination to conduct this hydra-headed investigation as she saw fit.

Sometimes in an investigation, the press could help, at least by asking the public to cooperate. They would do that again now, but in following Caron's pursuit, they would do her no favors. She would have skeptical, impatient media on her back at every turn. Suddenly, she felt her job was on the line. It was.

At least the press were not reporting anonymous slurs from her own cops. For now, they were with her. She had to keep them with her all the way. At a minimum, that meant playing up teamwork. It meant avoiding the media's trap of making her the story, instead of Repentigny.

CHAPTER SIX
Eliminations and Illuminations

The *L'Union* story had rattled Caron, but she pretended to ignore its possible implications for her. When the piece appeared, she marched in to see Baraquant and Duroselle just to say, as serenely as she could:

"Of course this kind of stuff is a nuisance," she started. "But they're not giving us a chance. They're nuts to pressure us this way -- before we even get back any of the reports we should get soon from our many lines of enquiry. Some of these may require weeks for results."

"Yes," said Baraquant. "It's unfair, alright. But the paper is probably reflecting the public's own impatience. Or just it's curiosity. Not to mention fear. This is a brutal crime against a famous man. Probably half the kids in Reims are having nightmares about it."

"Right," said Caron. But shouldn't we respond with some facts to counter such hysteria and speculations? Facts about exactly how broad and detailed our investigations have to be? And about the number and variety of our efforts to date? The forensic work, our focus on logical categories of suspects, our early interrogations of people close to the victim, our efforts to get inside the politics, economics and psychology of the whole champagne industry?"

"That may impress some," said Duroselle, "but it might also sound defensive. Like trying to drown public impatience in a multitude of self-justifications."

"I see your points, gentlemen," said Caron, controlling her anger and defensiveness. "But I don't think we should just sit still and let these guys slang away at us. We should get some facts out about how thoroughly we're pursuing this. Gossip loves a vacuum, and I think we should fill the void by feeding the media worthwhile, well-documented stories."

"Nothing wrong with reassuring the public, Denise," said Baraquant. "But I don't want us to be running a full-time propaganda shop."

"That's not what I'm suggesting," countered Caron. "I'm just proposing a well-structured, pro-active media policy. We could, for example, announce a 30-minute press conference every week for wide-open questioning. That could feed the public's and press's hunger to understand. We could also offer frequent 10-minute updates at any time just to show we're moving."

"OK," said Baraquant. Let's try that. It may prove a sensible way to throw some red meat to the mad dogs – forgive me, the lions of the press. Maybe this can keep the news momentum on our side."

"Another thing, gentlemen," added Caron. "I sense that *L'Union* wants to personalize this adventure, and focus on my so-called untraditional background. I suggest we alternate different members of our team as our spokesperson. I'm happy to do my share of this. But I think it would better reflect the collective nature of our work if other officers also had a turn at explaining things. Imagine, for example, our ID man or forensic chief offering specialized briefings. This could prove highly newsworthy – especially when they had something new to report from their fields."

"Excellent idea, Denise. Hey, that might even end the stories about your being too young and too slow to get a grip on this whole thing," offered Duroselle mischievously.

"Oh really, do you think so? I hadn't thought of that," Caron smiled sweetly, but with mock dagger-eyes.

Caron went back to her office to dig through the reports from her field officers. She closed her door and sneaked a soothing *Panter*, blowing the smoke out her window. Those little cigarrillos were her favorite way of breaking the law...

First, the growers. That list of seventeen allegedly aggrieved growers needed trimming, taking care to target the most likely. Caron suggested two approaches, each as a check on the other.

The first approach would be impressionistic: Did any suspects leap out at our visiting officers as hot prospects? Caron made a short list of six from these first impressions.

The second approach was more systematic, though still only rough-and-ready. It would again use the classic filter of motive, means and opportunity. To these, Caron added a fourth category: suspicious behavior during each interview. This could include anything that gave the interviewing officer an uneasy feeling about the "client:" extreme nervousness, shifty eyes, fear, contradictions, spouse's reactions, and even the state of the suspect's home -- and, if relevant, equipment and tools.

Caron asked her expanded group of eight field investigators to draw up a "probability chart." This listed the four criteria in large letters across the top. Down the left margin were the names and village. Then, on a scale of one to five, signifying weak to strong suspicion, all eight officers were to insert a number into each box, then add up the totals.

The weakest totals would be candidates for elimination, though not yet. The highest-total candidates would be for intensified interrogation. This would include a filmed interview in Caron's office with two officers present. Before conducting a formal, filmed interview, Caron would have filtered suspects through four stages: the CIVC co-president's growers' list sent to Guizot; additional independent growers' letters to Guizot – or to Caron; the P.J. field officers' "first-impressions" short-list; and the "probability chart." Caron's personal filmed interviews would be the fifth and decisive police stage.

These interviews – in Caron's office, and more rarely in the field – always included at least one other police officer. "A cop is never alone," Baraquant and Duroselle hammered into young recruits. "Always take your witness and backup with you." Even if an officer volunteered for an outside assignment, he or she had to bring along a partner. This made for stronger evidence. And sometimes it could save an officer's life.

After initial police questioning, a still-suspected person could then face a magistrate for another questioning that could be grueling. This process could dismiss a candidate in a *non-lieu* indicating insufficient evidence; or it could charge him (or her?) – the process of *mise en examen*.

An eventual trial would make the final decision of guilty or innocent. In the Repentigny case, suspects would likely go through Caron's various filters before facing a court.

Caron's procedure left her two credible grower prospects for the guilty suspect. As of 2011, suspects had the right to be attended by a lawyer. The first to face Caron was Henri Lonniaux, a now near-destitute grower and previous modest merchant from near Aÿ – sometimes called Aÿ-Champagne.

Lonniaux, a fiery-eyed black-haired colossus, swore that Repentigny, as Regional President, had gone out of his way to deny him development funds his business critically needed from the regional budget. Why? According to Lonniaux, strictly for partisan reasons. Lonniaux, himself a regional councilor, had consistently voted against Repentigny's sometimes questionable projects. Result: payback time. Repentigny, knowing Lonniaux's financial distress, delayed emergency help he was entitled to after a series of natural disasters. This pushed Lonniaux to bankruptcy.

There was another reason – and it might play against Lonniaux as a suspect. Years before, as a young man learning the ropes, he had worked in the Repentigny caves. His work brought him to explore them regularly as a loading hand. Curious and ambitious, he systematically studied his boss's operations. He tried to soak up any information he could – including on strategies, hiring plans, patented technologies, foreign markets and, crucially, blending secrets.

As a manual worker, Lonniaux stood out for his hard work. He became known as a candidate for promotion to higher things. Then he overplayed his hand. He seduced a sweet young blonde secretary called Agnès Viaire. After courting and bedding her, he convinced her to help him gain access to privileged areas storing cabinets full of sensitive files on blending experiments. Under Lonniaux's direction, she lifted several desk-blotters to look for door codes. Unforgivably, one of the six top blenders had indeed scribbled down several code numbers. Agnès copied them all. Lonniaux tried each code until one worked.

Other codes opened individual cabinets. Lonniaux and Agnès were able to open the files, and even – "just to complete my education," he said – to photograph them. This went on for several weeks.

Late at night, after Lonniaux ended his shift, sometimes they would make love in the caves, laying down clean tarpaulins on the rough floors. At other times, Lonniaux would suggest they take some more educational photos. Then they would rendezvous upstairs, and 'borrow' more ideas from Repentigny.

One night, Agnès lost an earring. In a moment of tenderness, she had let it roll into a liquid-evacuation channel under a blending table. Terrified, she looked forever. With no result.

The lovers concluded that they must have lost the earring in the caves instead.

When, two days later, a cleaning-lady passed a vacuum under the blending table, it sucked up the earring with a noisy click. The cleaning-lady emptied the vacuum, and took the earring to a blending assistant. It went the rounds of all females having supervised access to the blending-rooms. No one claimed it.

When staff told the *chef de cave* (Painteaux's predecessor), he instantly suspected a break-in. He set a trap with light-beams activating cameras. Within a week, they found lovely clear photos of Lonniaux and Agnès.

Both, after questioning, were dismissed on the spot. Repentigny was furious at this collapse of security in his inner sanctum. To protect his commercial and personal reputation, he declined to call in police. All concerned were sworn to secrecy. The guilty were allowed to leave without public stain – again, strictly to protect Repentigny's reputation.

Twelve years later. Lonniaux had built up a promising business as grower-merchant near Chigny-les-Roses, population 520. His young accomplice, Agnès, was now his wife. They had made a decent, though not quite comfortable, start with an inheritance from Agnès's parents.

Caron had all this in the field report from the designated investigator, René Tribouillat, a bushy-mustached no-nonsense former street cop. With camera set to film her interview, she plunged in.

"Monsieur, kindly confirm that you are Henri Lonniaux, now a resident of Chigny-les-Roses."

"That is true."

"You once worked for the *maison* of Hubert Repentigny, mainly as a *cave* assistant."

"That's right."

"You were later fired for illegally entering the company's blending-room to photograph secret reports of current blendings and marketing plans."

"There is no evidence of that. And no public statement to that effect. This is plainly a fiction. I left the firm on my own initiative, and honorably."

"We believe you're lying, Monsieur Lonniaux. We have questioned several witnesses who confirm these acts. And confirm that you were fired discreetly only to protect the firm's commercial reputation. We even have the original videos of your break-in."

"A pure invention. Those tapes, if they ever existed, landed in the garbage years ago. Show me some real evidence."

"You'll be able to confront our witnesses in court when you face a probable murder charge."

"You're bluffing. And trying to intimidate me."

"Intimidation can sometimes be useful – but we're not bluffing. If the court agrees, we can send you to a rather nasty prison for the rest of your life."

"Are you actually suggesting that I would go back and try to kill Repentigny twelve years after I left because of some wildly inflated disagreement?"

"No, that's not all that caught our attention. Over the years, say many people who know you, you have been heard cursing Monsieur Repentigny."

"So cursing is now a crime? I expect that even a few cops could go to the slammer for that."

"Your specific cursing included oaths to murder Monsieur Repentigny. Several witnesses say that, after the Conseil régional turned down your request for emergency disaster funding two years ago, you loudly swore that you would kill him."

"How many times a day do normal people, when exasperated by something, say they would like to kill somebody? Have you ever heard of hyperbole or rhetoric?"

"I've even heard of metaphors –like rotten apples or sour grapes. They teach metaphors all the time at police school."

"Very funny."

"Unfortunately, your rhetoric specifically included shouting that you would love to bash Monsieur Repentigny over the head with one of his champagne bottles."

"Happily, somebody spared me the trouble."

"Happily? So you were capable of doing that?"

"Being capable of something, and actually doing it, are two different things, aren't they?"

"Of course, but in an investigation, being capable may prove the first step to committing the crime."

"All of this is theory, Madame. I thought you cops liked to deal in facts."

"The first fact is that you are here, very strongly suspected of trying to kill a man for two reasons. First, because, as your employer, he fired you. Second, years later, when in a position to deny you financial help, he saw no merit in your case."

"My case for disaster relief was cut-and-dried. Everyone's crops had been devastated by hail, frost and mildew. And nearly everybody got prompt official help from the Conseil. But not me. For reasons I can only describe as personal vengeance disguised by pettifoggery or chicanery, Repentigny made sure I was driven to the wall."

"Those are rich words for a grower. Did you know the law better than the Conseil president and his learned advisers?"

"And you, Madame – or should I say mademoiselle? You mock a professional of champagne like me, but are you really such a genius to remain a mere *fliquette*? Or do you see yourself as one of Molière's *femmes savantes*?

"Very entertaining, monsieur. Just try to answer my questions, and save your cleverness for the court."

"And you're saving your physical evidence of my so-called involvement for the court as well? I don't think you have any."

"We have the evidence of your previous invasion of the victim's property. We have witnesses swearing that you vowed to kill him exactly the way he was attacked. You also have a reputation for violence against neighbors... and, alas, your wife."

"Leave her out of this. Has she been whining to you?"

"Whining is an interesting word for a loving husband to use about his wife."

"I could give you even less flattering descriptions of her."

"You are not improving your case, monsieur. You just keep confirming that you are known as a dangerous, vengeful man. We have even ascertained that you were absent from home for the three days surrounding the attack. Where were you then, in fact?"

"If I told I you a had a mistress in another village, would you be surprised?"

"Not at all, unfortunately. And her name?"

"She doesn't exist. I was just leading you on."

"We'll see about that. I note that you refuse to say where you were. We'll just check further on your whereabouts the night of the crime. And now, with this refusal to answer a central question, monsieur, I think we can end this interview.

Your confession that you are 'just leading us on' will likely color all your testimony when the court views this recorded interview. That is all for today. By the way, I'm asking the prosecutor for an order confining you to Champagne-Ardenne until further notice."

"More bluff, mademoiselle."

"Tell that to the prosecutor."

Caron told Duroselle that Lonniaux was a nasty piece of work. He might well have broken into the cave to attack Repentigny, but the police needed hard evidence. Her team would check with his wife and neighbors about his untimely absence. And Caron, backed by the prosecutor, would send the scientific police to look at Lonniaux's home and operation for traces of the specific dust found near Repentigny's body. And for size 46 shoes.

Caron put two officers on Lonniaux's missing hours. Then, after clearing a new search with the prosecutor, she went downstairs to ask Dominique Flochard, her scientific and technical chief, to have her staff scour Lonniaux's properties. They planned a chemical analysis of possibly incriminating dust from Repentigny's caves and of any other forensic evidence.

The second grower who got through the filtering process -- Valentin Lemorge -- was a more subdued candidate for guilt. He was obviously cleverer than Lonniaux, but no less bitter and motivated to kill the victim. Caron called him into her office for his filmed interrogation.

"Monsieur Lemorge, thank you for coming in."

"I am at your disposal, Madame."

"You maintain wine-fields near Bouzy, I believe, and you have in the past supplied grapes to the *Maison Repentigny.*"

"That is true."

"Why do you think we called you in today?"

"Not for anything you know I did. But perhaps because you are questioning anybody at all that you think might have a grievance against Monsieur Repentigny."

"It's no secret that we have several suspects. But we brought you in because we have especially strong evidence tying you to the crime."

"You must be referring to that stupid letter I wrote to Repentigny three years ago, threatening revenge after he cheated me on his underpayment for some grapes."

"Yes indeed, we do have that letter. You accused him of delaying the pressing process for your grapes – with the result that roughly forty percent of them went bad. This, you alleged, was his fault, and a mere pretext to pay you only sixty percent of what the grapes were really worth – had his people pressed them on time."

"That's exactly how he cheated me."

"Be that as it may be, you also threatened in the letter – and on later occasions – to kill him. Quoting from your letter, I see you said, and I cite your words: 'I will bash in your brains, cut off your head, then stuff your balls down your throat.' Quite a program."

"Well, you know how men talk."

"I know a few who don't talk like that. But also, unfortunately, I know a few that do --- especially characters met in this line of work."

"Commissaire, I was beyond myself with rage. Repentigny destroyed my entire profit for that year. I'm still struggling. My loss then lowered my family's standard of living – no more vacations, and I can't support my son at university."

"That's awfully distressing, monsieur Lemorge. But we're not questioning you today over your intemperate language or even your fury at your family's suffering. We have other evidence suggesting that you might have committed the crime."

"What can that be? I had absolutely nothing to do with it."

"Really? Then why were you seen the morning of the crime lurking around the police lines? It's common for criminals to return to the scene of their crime to discreetly watch the police at work. Sadly for you, you were not discreet enough: one of the Repentigny staff recognized you from a wine fair, and in passing mentioned your presence to a policewoman blocking access to the caves. The witness also said you suddenly ran away, looking frightened."

"Two things, Commissaire. First, showing curiosity at a crime scene is a perfectly natural reaction of passersby. Everybody does that. Second, I had my own business in Reims that morning, and was on my way to it. I was to see my bank manager for a bridge loan on a new property. After waiting too long gawking at the police lines, I suddenly realized I was late, and ran back to my car."

"Can you prove that?"

"Easily. Just call up my bank manager at the Crédit Lyonnais.

She is manager of the branch at 25 rue Carnot. Her name is Adélaïde Ducoisy."

"One more small thing before I let you go, monsieur Lemorge. What size are your shoes. Size 46, I believe."

"Would you mind taking them off for a few minutes? This is only a routine procedure, but I would like our technical and scientific police to check their imprint, and maybe to give them a good brushing."

"You don't have to brush them for me, Commissaire."

"That will be our pleasure, monsieur Lemorge. Thank you so much for your answers."

Caron sent the shoes down to Dominique Flochard. It was unlikely that useful chemical traces would remain in the dust several days after the crime, she thought, but you never know. Even now, back at Lemorge's place in Bouzy, Flochard's assistants were dusting all his other shoes for incriminating evidence.

Would cave-dust betray either Lonniaux or Lemorge? Caron was beginning to think that this was her last chance to find a culprit among the growers. She told Duroselle not to count on finding the attacker there. She believed that with no new factual evidence, or a betrayal by one of the two wives, no court would convict either of her two grower-suspects.

Next category: the three mid-sized houses. Then, finally, the two *grandes marques*. Might they have worked independently? Or in tandem, to divide up the Repentigny spoils?

CHAPTER SEVEN

Suspects Galore

Le Château Fort, Sedan...

Philippe Rigaud and his DCRI Economic Protection team barely had time to bug the ancient, imposing castle-hotel before the Chinese arrived. The hotel nestled in a huge medieval fortress in the middle of quiet provincial Sedan – a strategic town the Germans had captured in both 1870 and 1940. The delegation of thirty-five Chinese Trade Mission staff rented all forty-five of the hotel's rooms. But they occupied only thirty-eight.

Rigaud had installed his recording equipment in a basement suite, marked DÉFENSE D'ENTRER - HAUTE TENSION -- DANGER DE MORT. To lessen the risk of discovery, they bugged no bedrooms. This paid off, even at the risk of losing some key conversations. Within four hours of the Chinese group's arrival, its technicians reported that their electronic sweep showed all the bedrooms were clean. So were the meeting-rooms. The Chinese relaxed, strolling to the courtyard for an early evening smoke.

The Chinese Trade Mission liaison officer, an agent of Beijing's Ministry of State Security, warned hotel staff not to visit any of the elegantly decorated bedrooms. He said commercial secrets were in luggage, and they couldn't risk losing them. Hotel staff, he said, should only serve meals in the dining-room, and drinks and snacks in the main meeting rooms.

While serving, however, two admirably trained DCRI agents disguised as servers discreetly slipped four almost invisible microphones into places guaranteeing full-room eavesdropping. DCRI equipment was not off-the-shelf kit for amateurs. No online-bought Lavalier mikes or pin-hole cameras here. Only ultra-performing stuff, FSB-CIA-class, the world's best wizardry.

Cleaning up after dinner, the 'servers' unobtrusively removed the bugs -- in case Trade Commission security agents found them on a surprise night-time sweep. At the next morning's meetings, the DCRI servers slipped the tiny mikes into place again. Rigaud's recording crew, accompanied by native Mandarin-speaking agents, could now make a complete transcript of the two-day meetings.

Of course, DCRI made a complete photo album of attendees. Among the group, it spotted Ma

Chuntao. Beautiful and vivacious, and dressed in a deep-blue, thigh-split *cheongsam*, she was hard to miss. Her carousing with the President, then Repentigny, had made her a star at DCRI. And at the Chinese Trade Mission, she starred in currency swaps.

The Chinese Trade Commission team met formerly the next morning.

Guang Xiaoli the Mission chairman, opened the meeting.

"Comrades and esteemed colleagues, we are here close to the world's most famous champagne caves. Champagne, we know, is a product intimately identified with France. Now entrepreneurs from our country are starting to produce champagne in both France and our homeland. For now, our Trade Ministry has no fully-defined policy on how China should develop its interest in champagne. Or indeed how far we should go in taking a predominant role in this prestige market. It is our task to recommend how China should proceed in the worldwide champagne market. In the first instance, plainly, that means deciding what to do in France."

"To begin this morning, our research chief Quan Ye will offer an overview of the background and opportunities. Then I will invite our market strategist Ma Chuntao – who has nurtured some personal relationships in this area – to summarize approaches we might take if we wished to move aggressively."

Quan Ye spoke first. Around fifty, bald and with thick glasses, he shuffled through his papers.

"Dear colleagues, allow me to summarize the history and current figures for France's champagne industry. Production of wine in this region goes back to at least the fifth century A.D. Having a moderate northern climate, producers in this region could not compete with the rich, fuller-bodied red wines of Burgundy just to the south of here. Up until the late 17th-century, vintners tried to rid local wines of bubbles – then a cause of exploding bottles."

"Benedictine monks, by tradition Dom Pérignon, decided then to capture the bubbles. And over the past two hundred years, complex procedures have developed the immensely popular, sparkling wine we know today. For memory, the taste of today's champagne emerged from the interplay of French and British consumers. The British pressed for sweeter, bubblier champagne. But the French, as usual more subtle, insisted on drier wine with smaller bubbles."

"The whole world now knows champagne as an élite product, identified as one of the highest expressions of French good taste, elegance and celebration. Those few countries – America, Australia, Spain, Italy and Germany – that have tried to compete offer only cheaper, less subtle versions of sparkling wine. But although these have sold well in some markets, none has reached the level of quality and prestige of real French champagne."

"How large is the world champagne market? After surviving the loss of Russian and U.S. markets during the 1917 Revolution and Prohibition, as well as two world wars, champagne today sells some two hundred million bottles a year. Expanding markets are putting pressure on France's certification authorities (INOQ) to expand the definition of "champagne" soil. This will likely continue. But we predict that as countries such as China, Russia, Brazil and even India get richer, their emerging prosperous classes will demand more champagne."

"We see no logical limit to the world market for champagne. Why? Because buying champagne is not logical. It's emotional, symbolic, linked to pleasure, consolation, and even conspicuous consumption. So from China's perspective, this is a market worth entering. If we could get a serious foothold in it, we could change the image of *all* China's exports – moving, as we want, to higher-added-value prestige goods. Instead of being only the 'world's factory,' China could gradually become the home of high luxury and craftsmanship."

"How we do this is a delicate question. For to the French, champagne is a mythical product, deeply linked to France's self-image. A brutal, even too-direct, approach to this market might risk dangerous diplomatic tensions. Not only would the French government be upset. The French press and public would probably unleash a virulent attack on China's perceived arrogance and attempted domination of a key French industry."

"This in turn could lead to costly retribution against China's exports to France, and even to Europe as a whole. You can't discuss champagne as though it is like socks or refrigerators. We're dealing here in the realm of magic, self-respect and identity. The analogy is a little rough, but it would be like France claiming ownership of Peking Duck or acupuncture."

"Well put, Quan Ye. You have given us an excellent feel not only for the considerable monetary value of this market. You have educated us to some crucial diplomatic, political and commercial dimensions of the champagne challenge."

"Thank you, Mr. Chairman. This is indeed a very special and even tricky market for us."

"Now," said Guang Xiaoli, I ask Ma Chuntao to outline some possible schemes that her team has under discussion. Ma Chuntao, you should know, is not only our main expert on central-bank currency swaps. In her spare time, if I may put it that way, she has developed some intriguing, if rather unorthodox, ideas for a bolder Chinese entry into the champagne market.

"Ma, having heard Quan Ye's cautions about the political and diplomatic delicacy of France's champagne market, what options have your people discussed? And what course do you urge?"

"Mr. Chairman. If you will forgive me, I will first outline three conceivable options to weaken France's champagne market against Chinese competition. Then I'll give you my best judgment as to the wisest course."

"Excellent, Ma Chuntao. Please go on."

"As our chairman knows, I have been able to cultivate some quite influential people in the Reims-Épernay champagne corridor. Two in particular.

But for security reasons you will understand, only the chairman and I – as well as my supervisor in Beijing – can know their names. One of the contacts has now retired, but the one remaining still plays a key role. He has enviable contacts throughout the world, and he is a respected figure for his accomplishments in raising the quality of recent vintages."

"I believe he is the one," interjected the chairman, "who worked out with you the three possible strategies for destabilizing the champagne market."

"Indeed he is. His three hypothetical strategies all sound plausible in theory. Personally, I think they are rather naïve. I caution you: all carry very serious risks. Risks for our investors, and, if our government were to back them, risks for China-France diplomatic relations. Quan Ye has already outlined why champagne is a uniquely sensitive product. The French cherish it as a spectacular aspect of their national identity, as a perfect symbol of French elegance and *joie-de-vivre*. Do we even," smiled Ma, "*have* such a word as *joie- de-vivre* in Chinese?"

"As we get richer," chuckled the chairman, "I'm sure we'll find one. But let's get on with those three subversive options."

"My source calls his first strategy the 'Killer' option. In this scenario, a huge industrial group – for example, one of our gigantic government-backed holding firms – would buy up a major French champagne house. It would pour into this French house enormous sums to let it steamroller smaller French houses in the market. This forced-march approach could include several elements: tying up supplies of raw materials (mainly grapes); massive discounts in the U.S. and UK markets; even more generous loans to hotels, restaurants and bars to expand space or services – such loans being a traditional marketing tool. Finally, the Chinese holding company could launch a gigantic publicity campaign to induce the middle classes to drink more champagne. The holding company could hide its losses in its many other activities."

"The result of all this? A lot of medium-sized French champagne houses, crowded out of their markets at home and abroad, would face bankruptcy. The Chinese-owned holding company, through its initial purchase of a prestige French house, then could scoop up the weakened houses for a song. It could do this while parading as just a patriotic French house buying other French houses. In a couple of years, continuing to buy up small houses, China could begin to exercise a commanding indirect presence in the champagne world though its increasingly powerful subsidiary."

"Needless to say, we could then let prices creep back up to where they were before the 'steamroller' attack. And happily, lower prices would have created a huge new class of consumers, people increasingly accustomed to buying champagne to celebrate. In China alone, that would constitute a major cultural accomplishment. And with hundreds of millions of new drinkers, an economic bonanza."

"As you warned," said the chairman, "such an approach, once analyzed by the vigilant French competition and economic-protection authorities, as well as the economic press, could look pretty brutal. A kind of classic loss-leader strategy. To work, it would have to be spread over several years. It would have to be stealthy and gradual."

"Absolutely right, Mr. Chairman. I am only sketching out the underlying strategy. I am certainly not arguing for us to carry it out in a thoughtless, heavy-handed way. As the French say, we would 'make haste slowly.'"

Rigaud's Mandarin-speaking translators, listening in a room down the hall behind the HIGH-TENSION warning door, gave him a thumbs-up. The meeting was giving them exactly what they hoped.

"Now the second option?"

"We could call this the 'Mirror' option."

"And how would that work?"

"It's a tricky one. Once again, a large foreign holding company – that could be one of ours – buys a major Reims or Épernay house. It orders the house to saturate the markets of the BRIC countries: Brazil, Russia, India and China. Why the BRICs? Because although some of their élites know a little about champagne, their mass-market clients are pretty unsophisticated. The French house, now controlled by the foreign holding company, could use its French name, and its new owners' cash hoard, to promote a fraudulent 'French champagne'. A champagne denatured with lower-quality grapes and 'still wine' bought locally or from low-cost Argentine producers."

"And then?"

"And then the foreign-owned French house would sell this inferior product under its own respected label – but at low prices that cut honest French champagne exporters out of these markets. The risks of this approach are easy to see. First, you would have to produce grapes from hard-to-trace vineyards. Second, you would have to hide these foreign profits from the French tax authorities. And finally, the low quality of this ersatz 'champagne' under a famous French label would catch the attention of serious connoisseurs in a flash."

"That sounds like a very complicated and dangerous option," said one attendee, a woman versed in trademark and quality issues.

Several heads nodded assent, as did the chairman.

"Well, that second option will probably not fly," he said. "For one thing, it would tend to drag down the image of champagne. And if we are seriously thinking of entering this market, we have every interest in following France's example of protecting, not undermining, quality."

"The third option," concurred Ma, may be more plausible, if highly cynical. We might call this the Divide-to-Rule option."

"God forbid that we should be cynical," smirked a bank elder, provoking general laughter. "But even our great historical strategist Sun Tzu would bless divide-to-rule."

"Fine. Now consider this," went on Ma. "As we all know, Europe's economy faces severe difficulties. The euro has been almost on life-support. Brutal deficit-cutting has impoverished and unemployed millions. People have less to celebrate, and they have to tighten their belts. So they're not buying as much champagne as before."

"This softening market hurts both growers and merchants. The growers have also faced a long dry spell; this drastically reduced their high-quality crops. To maintain their income, they demand higher prices for their grapes. Unfortunately, the blending and marketing houses are facing weakened markets, and want to pay *less*, not more, for grapes. Result: an impasse. Several houses will go under unless the growers soon accept lower grape prices."

"At this point – and this is where the cynicism comes in – that mythical foreign industrial group decides to secretly back the most radical growers. With this clandestine funding and encouragement, the growers' high-price radicals block any softening of grape prices. Several mid-ranking champagne houses, unable to borrow in these tight-credit times, are driven under. The foreign holding company, probably again using a local 'stalking horse' or complicit French company, buys up some attractive houses at ridiculously low prices."

"Clever, Ma," said a senior officer. "Devilishly sneaky, though a little crude. But this is really capitalism at work, isn't it?" His eyes lowered in a gesture of mock contentment.

"Thank you Ma," Chairman Guang Xiaoli concluded, "for this menu of options. You and your industry source have thought hard about how to ease China's large-scale entry into the champagne world."

"The risk with option three, however, which you haven't mentioned, is that the large champagne firms, and even less radical growers, might find out that foreigners were *funding* discord. Playing one side against the other, in fact, to create a paralyzing impasse. To create helpless takeover targets. Were such a plan to be unmasked, that would prove disastrous for us. It could sow anti-Chinese fury for years. And banish us for decades from the champagne world."

"My job was not to decide, Mr. Chairman. Only to show what might be conceivable."

"You have done so clearly, Ma Chuntao, and I thank you. However, dear colleagues, I would ask you all now to adjourn overnight and to ponder these three options. Should we favor one or another, and try to follow through on it? If so, within what time-frame and with what means? Or are all these options simply too risky?"

"A fourth, unspoken, option is that we borrow elements from each option," urged Ma.

"And a fifth one," replied the chairman, "is that, because of the dangers, we do nothing. There is much to be said for prudence. For taking a very long-term view. That could consist of investing in champagne as opportunities arise. But with no strategy for destabilizing the French. Or for trying to take over an industry which they claim as part of their national heritage. Meeting adjourned."

Rigaud's transcriber-translators worked all night. He would have his transcripts in French the next morning. He would be able to peer inside China's entire champagne thinking. This would make interesting reading for several ministers – commerce and foreign affairs at a minimum. Possibly even for the prime minister and president, the latter known to be close to Hubert Repentigny.

At the continued meeting next morning, chairman Guang Xiaoli realized that he had no consensus. He listened to a vigorous, even sometimes bitter debate – broadly speaking with young activists accusing their elders of lacking imagination and boldness. Coming to a common position would take a few days longer. Guang Xiaoli ended the seminar, proposing that members meet two weeks later in a bug-proof room of the Chinese Trade Commission building.

Delegates left in several cars. Ma decided to spend the weekend in a charming old bed-and-breakfast called *Le Prieuré*, half an hour from Reims. Her champagne-industry accomplice, leaving wife and worries, would meet her there in a lovely loft where sunlight and starlight would play on their wide, eiderdown-covered bed. It was, for everybody's record, just a business consultation.

CHAPTER EIGHT
Impasse

Hôtel de Police, Reims...
Caron had spent the night before with Stéphane, her lover, her "warrior's rest," and... was he becoming more? He had shown a tenderness she had missed before. Or which was only now developing. Something was happening between them, and she wasn't sure it was good for her police work. Stéphane, the man in her life, was beginning to feel like the man of her life.

At a near-impasse in the Repentigny investigation, Caron needed to play the tough, clear-headed, logically focused cop. The case had invaded her mind, leaving little room for anything else.

Now something totally unfocusing was invading her heart. There were times when she was just plain scared. Terrified of messing up the investigation. Of losing the confidence of her colleagues, both above and below her. The cursed imposter complex was back. Late at night, alone, she sometimes didn't care about becoming a police superstar. She would settle for putting her head on the strong shoulder of a good man, who would hug back her confidence.

The official and human Caron were at war. What could she do?

Talk with Stéphane, for one thing. Then talk with her father, her idol, and her mother, her womanly refuge. All three told her to do her job, but not to confuse it with her life. In her job, she could find the moral and professional satisfaction of helping other people. In her life, she could put herself and her own people first. Family, someday the right man and, she hoped, some lovely children, would warm her thriving, and later twilight, years. And if ever an irresolvable conflict arose between job and love, she should go with her heart – and never look back.

This classic advice was a soothing theory, she scoffed. But she knew it was true, and her only path to peace. The trick was to put theory into practice.

Her intimates' counsel fitted perfectly the advice of her bedside philosophers, both ancient Romans. At one difficult stage of her professional life, the ugliness and violence of a street-cop's life had briefly led her to feelings of martyrdom. Hairshirt-wearing Marcus Aurelius suited that phase to perfection. She became a tight-lipped stoic, and survived. As she grew out of this phase, she discovered Seneca, the *bon-vivant* stoic, the wise old uncle who always spoke sense in adversity.

Ever since she won her promotion as a Commissaire supervising a team of thirty, she would dip into Seneca for ten minutes every morning. He gave her a carapace of good-humored fatalism. A toughness and flexibility to face nasty surprises. A confidence that she could do this job of her life, and do it damned well.

Plus an instinct to handle the new stirrings in her heart? Control, Denise, control.

New evidence from the police scientifique...
Dominique Flochard had not been inactive. Over the weeks since the attack, she and her lab sleuths had been digging deeper. They had analyzed the cave dust to try to track it into suspects' homes. But in passing, she discovered that the *racodium cellare* mold (popularly called wine-cellar mold) had other effects than dissipating odors and causing respiratory problems. Like the alcohol it feeds off, she had learned, *racodium cellare* speeds up the effect of other drugs, such as psychedelics. Combined with LSD, it can lead to advanced hysteria."

Caron arrived at Flochard's lair with her usual healthy skepticism.

"Would that presume a predisposition to hysteria? Or latent hysteria?" asked Caron.

"I would think that a person already vulnerable to hysteria, or who was on any kind of mood-altering medication, would be in extreme danger of losing all sense of reality. Oh, by the way, the

Communists used a drug called psilocybin. If you mixed that with the cellar lichen, you would risk a whole pharmacopeia of effects: euphoria and a feeling of power, hallucinations, spiritual experiences, and panic attacks. Not something to put in your grandmother's night-time chamomile tea."

By this time, Caron was rolling her eyes. Flochard, in love with her arcane data, was again telling her far more than she wanted to know about cave dust. Caron thought of an impatient James Bond as his tech-wizard "Q" explained in grinding detail his latest exploding belt or cigarette camera.

"All of that is fascinating," said Caron. "But I still don't see any immediate application of that information. Let's let it all marinate. If it doesn't fit this case, maybe it will another. Dominique, you're always teaching me intriguing things."

"I try, Denise, although some of my speculations may stretch belief."

"Keep stretching, mon amie. Our problem is not too much imagination, but lack of it. By the way, I've been thinking of revisiting the scene of the attack, and spending some time there trying to imagine whether there are facts we've missed. Can you come with me tomorrow morning? Around 10?"

"Of course. I'll come to pick you up at your office."

Next morning, Caron and Flochard, accompanied by two other investigators, went down again to the attack site. It still felt like a murder scene: Repentigny remained in a deep coma, and doctors saw only a tiny hope he might regain consciousness.

For a long time, they stared at the spot of the attack, still blocked off by yellow police tape. Together, they re-enacted the attack: the victim on one knee examining something on the hard dusty ground, the attacker standing above him to one side in the shadows. The attacker had plainly tricked Repentigny into kneeling to look closely at something on the ground. How? By luring him to exactly this spot.

"Let's go back again to the victim's e-mail and text-message accounts. We must have missed something in our searches at the outset – such as a message urging the victim to come here that night. Or maybe there is suspicious timing in a phone call to or from him. Or even to or from his wife or secretary."

"I'll get on all that," said one of her young techies.

"Now, as I look around," said Caron, "I'd like to try a couple of far-out ideas of my own. See that huge alcove of bottles behind the attack scene? There must be thousands of bottles in there. But thinking as a criminal under high pressure after committing the attack, I wonder if there are places here where I might throw incriminating evidence with some assurance it wouldn't be found for years."

"Now where could that be?" Flochard and her investigators asked almost in unison.

"The only immediate place I see is right over the top of this mountain of bottles. I see they're marked as very recent, and may not be touched for a long time. I could imagine throwing something all the way to the back of the pile, and if possible behind it."

"What would you want to throw away?"

"I don't know yet. But it would have to be small, tied to the crime, no longer useful, and in little danger of turning up soon enough to relate it to the crime."

"So what can we do?"

"We'll ask the Repentigny *chef de cave* to have his workmen remove all the bottles so we can look."

"That's Painteaux. He won't like that. It's a lot of trouble for the slim possibility of a useful result."

"He may like the idea better if I ask him," said Caron, sure of herself and stern-faced.

Caron also wanted to take her small team to look a little more closely at the alleged link between the Repentigny caves and those of Saint-Remi. She knew this was an extremely unlikely discovery. It was essentially superstition. But the publicity surrounding the amateur archeological expedition had piqued her curiosity. If there really were an ancient treasure in here somewhere, all the stories led to the caves of Saint Remi, leading in turn to the Abby of Saint-Nicaise. A walled-up stairway heightened modern curiosity. But the supposed treasure of Saint-Remi, including gold hidden by persecuted Christians, seemed lost in the medieval mists.

True, a 1750 search found 800 gold pieces in an unearthed leather sack. And more had turned up after a 1918 bombing.

In 1980, archeologist Daniel Réju had tried to interest authorities. They paid no attention.

The small police group, guided by cave staff, walked the maze-like corridor for a couple of hours. Clearly, nobody would find the mythical treasure short of having a road-map, compass and GPS.

The road-map for true believers, of course, was Remi's Great Testament – the apocryphal 'long' one revered by many pilgrims. Including Sophie-Charlotte Repentigny. She, like most of these fervid faithful, knew it by heart and believed in its prophecies, blessings and curses. In it, Saint-Remi named the Church as sole beneficiary of all hidden treasures. To protect the treasure and the Church with divine power, Remi's curse stood terrifyingly clear: Any thief or desecrator, after seven warnings, would become a "traitor, for whom no indulgence..."

Caron was too sensible a person to believe a word of this superstition. Its only interest to her was academic. It reminded her of her medieval studies. These she pursued at a youthful time she still cherished every time she managed to decipher a Latin inscription. Or to ponder a really satisfying, mind-filling curse.

Caron ended the day with a more prosaic request to Flochard. "Dominique, we've done a fine job on the immediate crime site. Any more ideas?"

"Thanks, Denise, but I'm still uncertain about a few things. If you reach beyond the immediate place of assault, the caves are a huge crime scene. For example, we don't yet know enough about the attacker's shoes and where they went."

"We did check the exits. But maybe we need to look further beyond them. Are there any places, even outside the exits, where he might have left clues?"

"That's like looking for a needle in a haystack. But I'll check even the loading-docks and the flower-beds around them. We might get lucky. We might even find some traces of blood from the attacker's clothes or some of that rare cave-dust from the attack room."

"Good thinking, Dominique. You'll need to mobilize some guys with strong backs for digging."

"Yes, guys – they're perfect for that." Both women laughed at the many talents of their male colleagues.

Guilt and reasonable innocence among the barons...

To deal with her most powerful suspects, Caron assembled a many-faceted team. It comprised first of all her financial and political experts. All were very familiar with the champagne world – and as close to understanding *les grandes familles* as any outsider might become. She also had three officers nosing about the media and certain restaurants like Reims's everyday power trough, the warm, elegant old mansion near the railway station called the Brasserie Flo.

A favorite of the Reims establishment, Flo is where 'good families' could hold a classic medium-budget wedding dinner – outside in the shady courtyard in summer, inside under the chandeliers at colder or rainier times. It's there that prosecutors and magistrates could lunch and gossip, amiably shaking hands with passing senior police and politicians. It's here that the champagne barons, when not dining in conclave, could display their prominence to wide-eyed people from outside their charmed circle.

The Police judiciaire hesitated to haul in members of this champagne aristocracy unless it had grave reason to question them. It couldn't go fishing with their time, or browbeat them the way it sometimes could with dubious, tainted or socially marginal characters. Like humble growers.

After meeting Sophie-Charlotte Repentigny, Caron had decided to clear up the angry mistress hypothesis. Nearly all Hubert's identifiable exes seemed to have forgiven him. His tragedy also brought out apparently genuine affection.

That left Anne Varendal. Anne was the only baron's wife who, after Hubert dumped her, Sophie-Charlotte thought might still despise him enough to kill him. Madame Varendal entered Caron's office at the appointed time.

The lady was angry, for sure. She had long yearned to spend more time with Hubert

"I just wanted to be the most important person in his life, not own him," she said. For a normally twitchy male, and Hubert was twitchier than most, that could sound perilously close to ownership.

Like most women of her class, of course, Anne had no wish to disrupt her own marriage, if at all possible. Too much money, security, status and face were at risk. These were indissolubly associated with a 'good' marriage – meaning, all things considered, a sensible one. An income-boosting one.

And in some women's lives, there comes a time when wags might argue that social position trumps the missionary position.

Hubert was game to make Anne his semi-official mistress, in some soft penumbra. But he insisted on two terms. First, any such arrangement should not limit his wandering eye to Anne; and second, it must meet Sophie-Charlotte's unspoken acceptance.

Anne rejected the first condition, as younger women in love are wont to do. Sophie-Charlotte's uninquisitive silence gave Hubert licence enough. Hubert, caught between formal and informal attachments, decided to cut the weaker link: Anne. She was not amused. However, as Caron soon ascertained, over two or three years her anger had grown more philosophical. As time passed and wrinkles deepened, she had the wisdom to forgive Hubert more than he had thought possible.

But for him, it was too late to reheat the romantic stew. He had too often borne Anne's reproaches and occasional harangues. Now his heart was cauterized – well, except perhaps for some other lovely woman who might come into his purview.

Hubert, like many men wanting perfection in this world, once again passed up his own version of a healthy balance in love. He was starting to feel older. Aches, stiffness and recurring recitals of Andrew Marvell eroded his optimism: "The grave's a fine and private place, but none methinks do there embrace."

When the attack took place, Hubert's mind was nowhere near the grave. He still found time to reserve himself a comfortable space in life. But really just enough space to contain his ineradicable failure to understand women.

Now, Caron's angry-mistress card pretty well discarded, she turned to her financial sleuths. First, her forensic accountants. Did they find some trickery, a shell-game, an awful scandal, a betrayal that might drive a competitor to violence? The bean-counters had spent several weeks going through Repentigny's books. These, plus his files, correspondence, e-mails and text- messages fascinated Caron and her superiors, Baraquant and Duroselle. This was the big stuff they had to know. The stuff that might finger the culprit or – who knows? – maybe blow Champagne-land wide open.

What did the diggers find after three weeks? Much, and not much. There were, as expected, secret offshore accounts – Hong Kong, Cayman Islands, Luxembourg and Liechtenstein. Maître Alexandre Gueillot, his cobwebby old family notary, held only the basic family documents: Wills, titles to personal property. Félix Corzelius, the family BNP bank manager, reserved no surprises either. Two single accounts (for Hubert and Sophie-Charlotte) and one joint account for family expenses. Pension-like assurance-vie accounts for Hubert totaled seven million euros; for his wife, two million.

One thing the financial sleuths missed dwarfed all of this. For even over the months Ma Chuntao had been hatching potentially aggressive Chinese plans for champagne, Hubert had discreetly prepared his own spectacular coup.

For reasons he kept to himself, Hubert had long held his business accounts at the HSBC bank at 17 Cours Jean-Baptiste Langlet. One reason he liked going there was to see his charming branch manager Brigitte Bartolo, a cute fiftyish blonde he had long admired. Another reason was HSBC's strong worldwide connections. That was especially true for the gigantic, almost virgin market he had had his eye on for a decade: China. The original name of HSBC was, after all, the Hongkong and Shanghai Banking Corporation.

Repentigny had long confided in Brigitte that he wanted his *maison* to break into the Chinese market in a big way.

"I have a two-stage plan," he confided to her over lunch at the cozy, 1930s-décor Café du Palais downtown. "Over a year or so, I'll echo the Champagne Bureau's efforts to educate Chinese tastes to appreciate chilled, not-too-sweet sparkling wine. In a huge and witty publicity campaign, we will try to accustom the fast-rising middle classes to drinking champagne as their primary drink of celebration."

"I've heard that is the industry's major challenge."

"Yes, a big one. In this first phase, I want to borrow from you 30 million euros to help change Chinese celebratory-drink habits – but also to start making our brand famous in key markets such as Shanghai, Hong Kong and Beijing."

"That's a lot of money, but with your holdings and reputation, I think we can swing it. But I will have to consult HSBC on the Champs-Élysées."

"In the second phase, I foresee a much larger investment -- to implant our brand nationally. To position our products as a prestige family of champagnes. Pricey, yet affordable."

"How much do you need for that?"

Repentigny paused. Lowering his voice, he leaned forward and fixed her eyes:

"I foresee a new, market-development line of credit of 160 million euros more."

Brigitte's eyes widened.

"That's quite a jump. For what exact purpose/"

"To launch and run a three-year market-saturation campaign. To build our Chinese brand into a universally known name to seduce the gigantic, aspiring middle classes."

"Pretty ambitious. But conceptually classic: key city markets first, then the whole nation."

"Precisely."

"Positioning, of course, is critical. How advanced is your thinking on that, apart from the idea of affordable prestige?"

"Brigitte, only my *chef de cave* and I share the details. I trust you personally, of course. But our community is so porous that I have to fear leaks and pre-emptive actions."

"A sensible precaution."

"Thank you for meeting me for lunch, Brigitte. I'm always delighted by your company."

"And I by yours, monsieur. I shall get back to you soon with headquarters reactions to both your proposals. Goodbye, and thank you for lunch."

Repentigny had already thought through in some detail how he would conduct his two campaigns – initial branding, then market saturation. His positioning would promote the various types and vintages of *Les Champagnes Repentigny* as the most chic of French champagnes. The tag-line: – *"The champagne of presidents and princes."*

To Chinese ears, he thought, that would echo two titles of political, economic and social influence: the 'presidents' of prestigious national bodies (including the President of the People's Republic of China); and the envied 'princelings' – descendants of high-ranking Communist Party officials."

"Of course, many Chinese despised the princelings' party-bestowed career and financial privileges. But *to live* like princelings could suggest an appealing association for the millions who aspired to wealth and power.

Repentigny's idea: to dominate the Chinese champagne market in a blitzkrieg of seduction and snobbery. To make *Les Champagnes Repentigny* synonymous with success in China. Before the other barons could wake up, he would seize the top-tier market, then leave them to pick over the crumbs.

The only other person privy to Hubert's plans was Painteaux, his loyal, prize-winning, sworn-to-secrecy *chef de cave*. Hubert told Brigitte that he and Painteaux had made a trip to Beijing and Shanghai, where they had met and convinced all the requisite officials and potential partners – who, in China, are often the same people.

For Repentigny's move to work, it had to look like just a legitimate try at carving out a prestigious place in the Chinese market, along with other brands. By its daring and financial muscle, the strategy aimed of course at seizing market power from all the other barons.

In spite of Repentigny's great discretion, two of his rival barons, Martineau and Lemberg somehow caught wind of his plan. Through bankers' gossip? Or through an improbable leak?

In any event, they decided to combine with a few other barons to defeat Repentigny. They would plot to head him off – even to take over his business – by a blitzkrieg of their own. In the gentlemanly *milieu champenois,* a shocking idea!

The key to the schemers' game? Repentigny's rivals would conclude a secret deal with the Chinese Trade Ministry to divide the world champagne market. Eventually, this would dilute French control of it, and give China predominance. The deal: French expertise for massive amounts of Chinese capital.

Repentigny would have to spend his HSBC cash against even better-funded and better-informed rivals. He would slowly bleed to death until he too had to sell out -- to Martineau, Lemberg and Company, discreetly funded by China.

This came very close to Ma's first hypothetical scheme for China to destabilize, then dominate, the champagne market using French 'partners.'

Happily for the Chinese, Ma's secret source was perfectly placed to help counter Repentigny's game. Beijing had already recruited Painteaux to betray his boss.

In sum: goal: *Les Champagnes Repentigny* would not take over the *Chinese* market. A Chinese government-backed offensive – with top French insider advice -- would take over a decisive chunk of the *French* champagne market. Not only would this entail buying several more French houses. With bitter irony, it would even lead some barons to expand... by investing in Chinese vineyards.

By doing this, these proud barons would illustrate Lenin's prediction that "the capitalists will sell us the rope with which we shall hang them."

The whole effort would in time cost the Chinese-funded barons over 1.5-billion euros, a staggering sum. Within a decade, it would give China a dominant role in worldwide champagne sales. It would leave the French only a few prestigious brands. Owned, of course, by China's subordinate French 'partners' – the cabal of anti-Repentigny barons.

A breathtaking, unthinkable ploy. It could only work through the handful of well-funded, French insiders. The term 'collaborators' might readily apply.

The HSBC, with its unparalleled contacts, caught whispers of the two barons' plot. But it couldn't believe such a massive betrayal of a fellow champagne baron – and, much worse, of France itself. It queried fellow French banks to check suspicious loan applications.

This quickly turned up a request for a whopping 250-million euro loan the two barons were negotiating with the BNP and the Crédit Lyonnais. By a consortium of a French shell companies and various Chinese banks. The Chinese Trade Mission kept its distance, to avoid scandal. But it followed the schemers' every move. It stand by toe mobilize from Chinese banks the far larger sums the plot needed to seize world-market domination of champagne.

The accountants' report contained only a few lines hinting at talk of a large new Chinese investment program in Champagne-Ardenne. The report landed on Caron's desk on a Friday afternoon, just as the banks were closing. She immediately alerted Baraquant and Duroselle that there would be no weekend for anybody.

Baraquant, following the rules, alerted the Interior Ministry that P.J. Reims now needed to swap all relevant information with DCRI Reims, with as few prohibitions as possible. Protocol observed, he called the P.J.'s local counter-espionage cousins, and asked ahead for three more coffees. In five minutes.

Until now, a Chinese connection to the Repentigny attack had been only a fleeting shadow on the wall. Now Caron and her colleagues saw the shadow casting itself over everything. Or so they thought.

DCRI and P.J. Reims – kissin' cousins...
"It's a pleasure to meet you guys in your inner sanctum," said Baraquant to the DCRI's local director, Pierre Renouvin, as he, Duroselle and Caron

walked into the DCRI's unpublicized offices. Caron rarely had a chance to talk with these secretive cousins, and felt a small thrill at the meeting.

"Denise would really rather be a spy," chaffed Baranquant. "She's beginning to find our work a bit too tame."

"A pretty girl is always welcome in the spook business," bantered Renouvin, a middle-aged man of military bearing. Caron winced at the pretty-girl tag. So tiresome on the job. So often welcome elsewhere.

"We've been eager to see your photo collection," retorted Caron, cutting to the chase. "And to see if you all still have those stereotypical brushcuts."

"Not me," smiled a young long-haired DCRI agent. "But I do have some pretty pictures to show you."

"Let's see them"

He pulled out a thick album apparently featuring a beautiful young Chinese woman, identified as Ma Chuntao. The first thirty pictures showed her outside the Chinese Trade Mission, then in a dozen Paris street scenes where she seemed to be window-shopping. A few others showed her in international meetings, recognizably Europe-China meetings on trade or the sagging euro.

The next page startled the P.J. trio. "What in God's name is she doing entering the side door of the Élysée Palace?" said Baraquant.

The photo specialist commented; "First, she sometimes visits number 14 rue de l'Élysée, where many of the President's personal advisers work.

This could be normal for her currency interests. But then – and this is getting fishier – she's walking along avenue Gabriel beside the Élysée gardens. She turns a corner... then disappears."

"Where?"

"We learned later from one of our agents within the Palace that a year or so ago she often visited the private quarters of the President. This at a time when he often met an old friend of yours: Hubert Repentigny."

"Incredible! How do you interpret this?"

"About the time we took these photos, the president and his friend Hubert were, dare I say, sharing the favors of this lady. As soon as we alerted the President that under her cover-job with the Chinese Trade Mission she was working for Chinese Intelligence, he banned her from the Palace."

"And Repentigny?"

"He was much freer to see her. He too was warned about her darker role, but decided he could see her as long as he breathed not a word about the President. The liaison went on for several months. Then she dropped him to transfer her interest to another man."

"Anybody we know?" asked Caron.

"We don't know the name of her new boyfriend, but we're collecting photos."

"How promising are they?"

"Not much so far. Here, for example, is Ms. Ma exiting a breakfast meeting at the Café de la Paix in Paris. Her interlocutor, whom we followed, turned out to be an insignificant mid-ranking official of the Banque de France. When interviewed, he seemed astonished that he or his breakfast companion was of the slightest interest to us. Other enquiries about him confirmed that he was just picking her brain on currency-swaps."

"He must have had other ideas. She's a stunner."

"We learn to our dismay that many Banque de France officials are not interested in women. Only money."

"That's reassuring, I suppose."

"We have lots more photos of Ma, showing her all over Paris. Sometimes with a man who just might be a lover."

"When you find out who he is, let us know. At this point, we're eager to see whatever you have, in case it turns up something we can use in our murder investigation. Anything Chinese is starting to get our attention."

Baranquant spoke up again.

"Indeed. We're hearing stories from Denise's Repentigny investigations that the Chinese seem inordinately interested in our champagne industry. But apart from suspicions about Repentigny himself at one point, we now have a rather spectacular lead. Denise, would you please run our DCRI colleagues through that financial intrigue?"

Caron spelled out the findings of her forensic accountants, Riquet and Bardy. She explained Repentigny's plan to break into and dominate the Chinese market. She went over his request for a stand-by loan to do so. Then she detailed the gigantic loan application of two of his main rivals, who just might be in cahoots with the Chinese.

"In relation to China, there is major action afoot in the champagne world," she summed up. It's going both ways, to and from China."

The DCRI officers expressed surprise – but not much. "We've been watching for and expecting something like this," said Renouvin. "Now you're fleshing out some information that may help us see more clearly."

"With luck," said Caron, "we may have more for you soon. A few days ago, I asked France's Champagne Bureau in Beijing to send us anything at all on Chinese plans to invest in champagne. I also asked for any relevant photos, including of the trip Repentigny and his *chef de* cave took there two years ago."

"Will you share those with us?"

"Of course. With 1.3-billion Chinese, it's unlikely we'll luck onto any face we know. But at this point in our investigation, we live in hope."

The DCRI cousins ended the meeting. Caron summarized the status of the Repentigny case to Baraquant and Duroselle. Then she briefed the whole P.J. team.

"So far, *mes amis*," she told the officers, "we've done a lot of solid work. We've followed up on many suspects. But plainly, we're at an impasse. The only recurring theme seems to be the Chinese. But we have no idea at all if and how they might be linked to the Repentigny case. Any suggestions?"

"If we're at an impasse," piped up a grizzled old warrior from the back of the room, "we need to do three things: a) admit frankly, for our own credibility, that our leads have run dry; b) review all our earlier interviews and clues to look for anything we missed; and c) brainstorm this whole thing anew to imagine some weird truth that's staring us in the face."

"A brilliant summary, Jean-Jacques. Anything else?"

No other proposals bubbling up, Caron continued.

"Here's an old idea I've flown past Georges and Philippe. It's just a classic tactic against public distractions. The media, especially *L'Union*, are alleging we're incompetent and rudderless. We could push back with a barrage of information setting the Repentigny case into a broader perspective of our activities. This won't directly solve our murder case. But it might snag us a little breathing space – time to work on Repentigny more serenely."

"How, exactly?"

"Well, we could publicize successful investigations we've been running. We could play up our gains in fighting teenage crime, maybe highlighting rare hopeful cases of Arab or black kids in the Croix-Rouge district high-rises. We could outline our collaboration with Dutch and Belgian police in attacking their heroin gangs' pipeline into Reims and Troyes. We could publicize the reduction in large-scale break-ins and bank robberies. We could update, with payoff statistics, stories on our new high-tech equipment for recovering stolen cars. This is less flashy stuff than murder. But it touches people's lives, and reminds them of the complexity and value of police work."

"Excellent, Denise," offered Duroselle, "as long as it's short-term and doesn't make us flacks instead of cops. Making good news eclipse the bad is sound basic PR. Even if it's hard for teenagers and cars to make some people forget the attempted murder of a celebrity."

"I agree," said Caron. "I would only see such news management as temporary. As a quick way to shade the one-dimensional Repentigny narrative of key media."

Outside the Hôtel de Police, busy delinquent minds did their best to 'shade' the Repentigny case with a kaleidoscope of crime. That same week, the cops had to deal with a series of other crimes: a couple of hold-ups, murder of an 82-year-old woman, a lovers' crime of passion, a Muslim "honor" crime slitting a beaten wife's throat, a shoplifting wave, a racist, homophobic crime, teenage gangs invading the town's center.

Caron and her P.J. colleagues were always juggling horrors. But – combining money, champagne and sex - the "murder in the caves" story was irresistible. It would bring *L'Union* thousands of new readers. Caron's diversionary tactic would run head-on into commercial reality and public voyeurism.

A new voice spoke up: "Alhough it's just a rumor, I think we ought to blitz that shadowy Chinese angle, if only to distract the public. Already people are alarmed at so-called Chinese commercial 'invasions.' Champagne, both drink and region, could be portrayed as just another example of that."

The team joker suffered a final idea. "I agree with all the others. But if nothing works, we can always hide under our desks and cry."

"I'll leave the crying to the men," smiled Caron. "If any women choose to hide, it would likely be just to touch up their lipstick."

The mood lightened, and a hint of activist consensus emerged. Caron could breathe slightly easier. But none of the defensive stuff could change the situation: the case was at a dead end. And Caron's job was looking just a little more fragile than a month ago.

Empty caves, empty hopes...

The next day, Caron got the report from the investigators watching Painteaux's workmen clean out the large alcove behind the attack scene. Before his forklifts went in, he could barely hide his contempt for Caron's inspiration.

"A piece of evidence might be in *there*? This woman has no idea how hard it would be to throw anything back there and land it behind the bottles. She's grasping at straws."

Now he smirked as his men moved out. The *police scientifique* moved in with lights, antiseptic suits, dusting brushes and small plastic evidence bags. After three hours, they concluded there was nothing there. No incriminating glove or mask, for example. Nothing.

Painteaux would make sure the media learned that their little female Maigret was getting nowhere. That she was wasting police and other resources on wild goose chases.

Next day, *L'Union* ran another page-one story. Its headline: "Police lose their way in the caves: Commissaire Caron wasting time and money?"

For the first time in the investigation, Caron retreated to her office, locked her door, and wished she could afford to weep. In ordering the shifting of bottles against Painteaux's advice, she had acted too cockily. She should have reflected more on his practical objections. She pulled herself together. She thought a moment of her dad, and how the headlines would hurt him.

Her phone rang. *"Bonjour princesse,"* began Gilles Caron in his rasping, cheery voice. "I see the bloodhounds are short of news today. Don't let them spoil your coffee." Her father could change her spirits in a split second. "Just keep doing what you're doing, *ma petite,* and they'll end up looking like idiots."

"Thank you, papa. This has not been a fun day so far. But you've just made the sun shine. Thanks for thinking of me. I send you a big hug. Bye-bye."

Caron needed some kind of victory to impress her bosses, her own troops, and maybe even the "clowns" in the media. A breakthrough? New evidence? A new idea? Maybe even that crazy Chinese fantasy? Her mind reeled, beset by too many unproven theories.

CHAPTER NINE
Despair and Wild Thoughts

A gentle rain ended the week from hell. Caron slumped into the stuffed easy-chair before Saturday lunch at her parents' place. To be closer to Denise, and to enjoy easy mobility for her father, they had moved into a downtown apartment.

Today, Stéphane was along. Her parents thought he was a decent, kind young man, even though a bit young for Denise. But they would not be upset if the relationship went further. Over an affordable small-grower's bubbles, they all chatted warmly, though with an undercurrent of worry for Denise.

At a lunch of squash soup, *poulet chasseur* and a cool bottle of *Bouzy rouge*, they warmed up and talked of happier times, past and future. Stéphane was easy and unpretentious, and his good humor lifted spirits.

After a rest following dessert, Caron and Stéphane took a long walk trough the downtown streets. As usual in recent years, Reims looked like a huge Meccano set, with cranes and scaffolding everywhere. Families, kids and lovers filled the streets, and ultra-modern trams skimmed at ground-level down the broad avenues. This was a good place to live. A people place.

As they walked into the imposing square in front of Notre-Dame Cathedral (the coronation place of twenty-nine kings), they looked up at the richly-carved, just-cleaned façade. They ignored the tourist shops selling swords, coats of mail, and of course acres of champagne bottles. They did a brief, familiar tour inside the great church, then crossed the esplanade to the modern glass Médiathèque. Here, on the fourth floor, you could sit on a sofa before the floor-to-ceiling windows, and marvel at the Cathedral's stunning panorama. It was like seeing the Church up close on a very wide, high-definition TV screen.

"Looking at this spectacle, and thinking of the scores of kings and bishops, and millions of people, who have prayed there, I gain a bit more perspective on my own tiny problems," sighed Caron.

"Your problems aren't small," soothed Stéphane. "But you'll solve them. Tell me whatever you can. As you explain things, perhaps some new ideas will come."

"Stéphane, you know very well that I can't tell you anything. I would love to unburden myself sometimes, but it would be a gross violation of police rules even to hint at details of our investigation."

She paused, and smiled at him.

"But there's no rule, I think, against briefly leaning my head on your shoulder here in the Médiathèque -- at least when nobody's around."

"I understand perfectly. I didn't mean to try to worm secrets out of you, just to relieve your stress a little."

Caron stared at the grand scene at their feet, and remained silent for a long moment.

Then she said:

"Stéphane, you have better ways of relieving my stress. But for now, let me just sit here quietly for a while. Maybe the peace of this great church and library can help me imagine new ideas."

"Yes, let's just sit here for a while. And while you're thinking, I can slip over to the racks there and pick up a magazine."

"Thank you, Stéphane, for understanding."

Caron paused again, furrowing her brow. She remembered her university days of specializing in medieval studies. She had studied Latin and the history of this region during the Middle Ages. History in those days was largely about the church.

"Maybe the pressure is driving me crazy," she thought, "but my guts are telling me that there might be some religious angle here. Living among the ruins of these great cathedrals, basilicas, monasteries and convents, we often forget that religion is what made Reims. We're drenched in religion, and we don't even realize it."

Visualizing the crime scene, Caron recalled that those hundreds of kilometers of champagne caves, dug by slaves, were often used by early Christians to hide from persecution. In fact, that archeological expedition she had read about a couple of years before alleged that there was still a hidden treasure of Saint-Remi, our patron saint.

"So now I just have to untangle the Chinese, Repentigny, buried treasure, and Christian martyrs," she groaned.

Her thoughts stayed with religion. "Religious belief is an awesome psychological weapon. It can cause wars; unite and oppose peoples and individuals. Why couldn't it somehow be used to make things happen in a society like Champagne-Ardenne? There are plenty of people here who go to church. And a whole cult around Saint-Remi. Maybe – just maybe – there's an answer here."

After further long reflection, she walked over to Stéphane and whispered: "I see you brought along your knapsack with your latest toy."

"Don't joke about my iPad while you brood on crumbling cathedrals and weird saints, I prefer state-of-the-art religion!"

"Let's combine your high-tech religion and one of those 'weird saints' -- Saint-Remi, for example. The old guy still has fans, maybe even more than your iPad will have in 1,500 years. Every October 1, there is at the Basilica a huge celebration in honor of Saint-Remi. It features a long Procession under a chandelier with ninety-six candles. The faithful walk slowly behind Saint-Remi's relics in a state of intense emotion."

"Bullshit."

"That's what Repentigny used to say. And at the very least, I guess it didn't motivate Saint-Remi to intercede for him. Now haul out that iPad."

"OK, anything to help the Reims Police judiciaire meet the modern world."

"I could kill you, but then I would have to investigate myself."

"Fine, it's on now, What next?"

"Get online, then pull up your music video apps, *YouTube* or *DailyMotion*.

"Now how did you hear about them?"

"I don't spend all my time reading medieval manuscripts. Or writing with a quill-pen."

"I'm sure you cops do use quill-pens."

"OK, pull up *YouTube* and type in "Translation Saint-Remi Reims.""

"What are they translating? Latin?"

"No, the relics of Saint-Remi. Translation can also mean moving something from one place to another. This procession is supposed to recall the bringing of Saint-Remi's bones to the Basilica."

"Wow, I see the blazing chandelier and the guy with the funny hat."

"That's a bishop, sir. But look behind him in the procession. See the pilgrims folding hands and looking solemn. They advance slowly, reverently, moving toward... Oh my God, look! There's Madame Repentigny! No husband in sight – he hated this stuff. And look at the tears running down her face!

I already knew she was devout. But this shows her faith in technicolor."

"Too bad about that noisy music."

"You mean Bach's Great Fugue in G Minor? You mean those clear, sharp, celestial notes played on the new Bertrand Cattiaux Franco-Flemish organ?"

"Oh give me a break! You're such a snob. What do you know about Foo Fighters, Coldplay or Seether?"

"You've just told me more than I ever wanted to know about Foo Farters, or whatever they're called. Sorry. Rock music doesn't rock my boat."

"I can rock your boat. Either we should have a duel, or go back to my place."

"Have you washed the sheets yet? Maybe my place instead? You'll be under police protection."

"Arrest me, and I'll go."

Digging for new facts....

Over the weekend, Flochard had directed four technicians to scour the loading areas and adjacent cave exits. This hadn't seemed necessary at first, but now Caron and the P.J. were desperate to solve the case. Flochard also set three gardeners to digging up the enormous flower-beds. This would annoy the owners. But after studying possible escape routes from the caves, she had spotted barely-visible, suspicious mud-tracks on three of the pathway's flag-stones. So she decided, with Caron's blessing but little hope, to kill a few flowers.

Caron knew the loading areas were probably a cold trail by now, almost a month after the crime.

But maybe the P.J. had missed something in those frantic early days. Maybe the attacker was also frantic after committing the crime, and got sloppy as he rushed away.

Staring at old facts...

The next day, a sunny Sunday, Caron couldn't stay home. After a lazy morning with Stéphane, and croissants with two double espressos, she went into her office around 1 p.m. She wanted to think afresh, even far-out thoughts. To get started, she pulled out the unfinished album of reports and photos assembled so far.

The reports demonstrated the investigation's fast, professional beginnings. The P.J. team had identified, then filtered out, key categories of suspects. Its checklist: strongest suspects vigorously questioned; visits and revisits of the caves; inconclusive rumors of Chinese nosing around the champagne world. About the Chinese: Why? To what avail? Was there even a distant or indirect link between them and the Repentigny crime?

The media, especially *L'Union*, would be on Caron's back from now on. Relentlessly. Once they think they have an angle – here the cops' alleged "incompetence" (especially hers) -- they rarely back down.

Turning to the photos, Caron shuddered at the bloody color photos of Repentigny's head. No way will he survive this. And the look of shock and surprise on his face, mouth wide open as in a final scream. He had fallen flat on his face, apparently from a kneeling position: his face was not too smashed up in the fall forward, just badly bruised, with those obscene shards in his eyes.

Slowly, she leafed through the other photos. The bottle-weapon on the ground carried blood stains on its heavy end. The cave dust around the victim looked seriously disturbed. Two clearly visible shoe-prints indicated where the aggressor had waited. Those huge size 46 monsters.

No more secrets here.

The final photo showed the splash of blood on the wall at the level of a kneeling victim. The middle of it was roughly star-shaped, with splatters of blood-drops high and wide. Conceivably the splash had left traces on the attacker's clothes, shoes or body? Unfortunately, Caron had none of these to examine. Only the victim's clothes, tested and stored at the start.

At wits' end, Caron's eyes returned to the wall splash she had seen so many times. She stared at the furious top-to-bottom line the attacker had drawn through the letter "R." With his glove? A stick? With what?

As she stared, her mind wandered from objects to meaning. Deliberately, she let her eyes unfocus, then refocus as she stared at the killer's message of apparent triumph. Her mind drifted back to the caves. Her imagination strained to delve into the attacker's psyche. Into context. Into motive. Into history.

Suddenly, the blood-image seemed to recompose itself before her eyes. She let herself go, gasped, and turned white.

Swapping photos with the spooks...

The DHL courier package came in from Beijing at 11:15 a.m. the next day, Monday morning. Caron opened it quickly but carefully.

The Champagne Bureau's written report on the earlier Repentigny-Paintaux visit to Beijing rang no big alarm-bells. But it did confirm that the two visitors, while splitting up for some weekend tourism, had apparently established some close new relationships. Clearly, their *maison* hoped to make some kind of breakthrough in the Chinese market.

Representing the entire champagne industry, the Bureau couldn't play favorites, or pry too much, for fear of betraying commercial discretion. All it saw, and reported, was a normal, market-exploring visit from a major house from Reims. The story was neutral enough to appear in *La Champagne viticole*, the growers' publication, and in a Council report of the UMC, the merchants' Union des Maisons de Champagne.

How close the new relationships might prove came out in two photos near the end of the pile. In one, Painteaux was engaged in animated conversation with a beautiful Chinese girl. Interesting, but routine. In the second, a shot of Repentigny making his farewell speech, Painteaux beamed from the end of the group's line. Beside him, and almost touching shoulders, was the Chinese girl again. Caron took out her magnifying glass. The Chinese girl had clearly bound her little finger around Painteaux's.

Still perhaps just a business-trip flirtation. But from both shots, the lady looked noticeably like the

woman in the first photos DCRI showed the P.J. –
the ones of Ma Chuntao at the Café de la Paix and
the Élysée. What did *that* mean?

Caron, like many Westerners, had trouble distin-
guishing unfamiliar East Asian faces. But she decided that a superficial coincidence of faces might turn
out to be a useful lead. Besides, she and Painteaux
had never hit it off. She distrusted him, finding his
mix of cockiness and hard eyes annoying.

She asked Baraquant to arrange a new visit to
the DCRI cousins to compare all the mystery lady's
photo-files -- both still-shots and videos. To assess
subjects' intentions, they would note the date of
each item – before and after the cave attack.

Renouvin warmly greeted the P.J. team of Caron
and two officers. Sensing a break in the case, she had
also invited Duroselle. Renouvin apologized for his in-
sipid home-base java. He knew P.J. coffee was far tasti-
er (Caron's premium-espresso influence, he learned).

The DCRI photo-librarian brought out Ma
Chuntao's whole file. There were almost two hundred photos and ninety minutes of video, mostly
from before the crime. They showed her all over
Paris – mainly in the well-off Sixth, Seventh and
Eighth *arrondissements*. Her interlocutors there –
though not all yet identified – looked like routine
business acquaintances. People like the tedious
Banque de France banker. People emerging from,
or re-entering, buildings where talk was of investments, official visits, and especially currency.

Then some less official-looking photos started turning up. They showed Ma in more artsy or

bohemian *arrondissements* – the Third, Fourth and Fifth. They showed her shopping for art under the arcades of the Place des Vosges, and strolling past, at no. 13, the apartment of the infamous "DSK" of New York hotel-maid fame. They showed her wandering into nearby *Carette,* her favorite pastry and tea house.

Inside, a DCRI briefcase movie-camera caught the subject seated at a small table next to the table of a handsome, fair-haired man about fifty. Ma savored a Saint-Honoré, closing eyes as she reveled in its oozing *crème Chantilly.* The man made short work of a moka éclair. The pair barely exchanged glances. Suddenly, Ma signed her credit-card slip – then wrote something on the back of it. She left promptly, barely casting another glance at the macaroons in the opulent display-case. Opening her umbrella, she disappeared into the rain.

Soon after, the man put on his raincoat. Sliding through the narrow space between the two tables, he took care not to let his coat sweep a glass onto the floor. He steadied himself briefly on Ma's abandoned table and, in a furtive gesture, scooped up her credit-card copy.

The man was Painteaux, noted Caron. And Ma had left him a message.

"Can we look at your photos and videos of just these two people?" asked Caron. "They may," she suggested, "even be the link between the Chinese and the Repentigny attack we've been speculating about."

The librarian pulled together a new series. It showed not only a clear complicity between the two subjects. It revealed something even more startling: an apparently well-advanced love affair. The interlaced fingers in Beijing were a flirtation. Now you saw the intimacy of a full-blown relationship.

"We did see her in this liaison," said Renouvin a little defensively. "But we hadn't focused seriously on identifying the gentleman. We hadn't yet put a tail on him. We had his phony name from hotel bills paid in cash. Most of the time, when they met in isolated places, he just seemed a lover. We thought that if he was only keeping her busy in the sack, that was fine. She would have less time for spying. That credit-card trick was the first sign we had that they might be discussing more sinister things. "

Caron asked: "How busy was she, as you gallantly put it, in the sack?"

"Busy enough. We have five or six examples of hotels over the last three months. Plus two or three out-of-the-way hugging and kissing episodes: a tiny park on rue Payenne in the Marais; and another on a remote bench of the Jardin du Luxembourg over by the rue Guynmer."

"We need evidence of more than romance, lovely as that may be," said Caron. "We're trying to see if they were – and still are – colluding in some kind of Chinese plot against our champagne industry. And whether this ties into the Repentigny attack. Here's our file on Chinese champagne activity. For now, it's pretty fragmentary and indirect, being mainly in press clippings. But these do show China starting to move significantly into the champagne business, both here and at home."

Renouvin, with a sly smile, pulled out a new file of both photos and transcripts.

"Maybe we can help you with some new evidence just in," he purred. These photos show a large group from the Chinese Trade Mission meeting last week at a secluded hotel in Sedan. We presume they chose Sedan because it was close enough for visiting champagne country, but far enough away not to raise a frightening profile in Reims or Épernay."

"Let's see it." said Caron.

"To speed things up, we've photocopied the transcripts. Maybe we could all get a quick idea of what they're up to by reading them right now, if you wish. During the Sedan meetings, these pages were translated overnight from Mandarin, thanks to the fast work of our DCRI Economic Protection colleagues in Paris."

"An impressive coup," whistled Duroselle. "But what does all this prove?"

"Read on and see. You'll 'overhear' this high-powered Chinese group discussing a series of extremely aggressive strategies for crippling, then taking over, our champagne industry. They're only reviewing hypotheses. And their chairman, sounding cautious, insists on a delay to ponder these options against less manipulative means. Nevertheless, reading this stuff will give you a scary idea of how some of their radicals are thinking."

A half-hour later, the P.J. and DCRI reconvened.

"This is devastating stuff," marveled Caron. "It proves that Ma Chuntao is at the very heart of the Chinese radicals' scheming. And to think that we now know she's consorting intimately with the *chef de cave* of one of Reims's major champagne houses – the house of our victim. The link is shocking. This will be the most explosive scandal the champagne world has known in decades."

"The question now," she said, "is how we should move on this information. And how we can work with you, our DCRI friends, to better understand and stop this plot."

"I agree," said Renouvin. "Being both under the Interior Ministry, we have complementary mandates and skills. We need to concert our efforts. I suggest we immediately inform our Ministry masters that that's our plan."

"Absolutely," echoed Duroselle. "We'll alert our DCPJ bosses while you contact your superiors."

"May I suggest," asked Caron, that you people -- DCRI Reims -- intensify your tracking of Ma Chuntao? And that you see if you can acquire even more conclusive eavesdropping proof of Chinese intentions? Then we, P.J. Reims, can close in on Painteaux at our end."

"That makes sense," said Renouvin.

"We already copied Painteaux's hard drives at the start," said Caron. We'll copy them now to you. Maybe, with your advanced tech skills, you can dig out even the deleted e-mails in his Yahoo e-mail bin."

"Thanks, very useful," said Renouvin.

"Short of enough technical staff, we've had to pursue a lot of other tracks. Now we have an urgent reason to get back to Painteaux's hard drive – to see if his e-mails reveal more about the Chinese affairs or the attempted murder. We're already reading his text-messages and accessible e-mails. It's the deleted ones that escape us."

"Glad to help," assured Renouvin. "Summing this up, it looks like DCRI should handle Paris tailing and deep electronic investigation, while the P.J. handles movements and interviews of suspects in Reims."

"Inevitably," cautioned Duroselle, "there will be overlaps. But this sounds to me like a logical dividing of the pie."

"Let's get going immediately," said Renouvin, "and meet every day to coordinate. We can swap urgent news by secure text-messages, OK?"

"Perfect. Let's move," said Duroselle.

Caron, her Beijing hunch confirmed by DCRI's transcripts, smiled a collegial smile. On her way back to her private office, she began humming "Voi che sapete" from Mozart's *Mariage of Figaro*: "You who know what love is..."

Paris, le Quartier Mouffetard...
DCRI's eavesdropping on Ma Chuntao's phones had so far produced careful nothings – only normal banking and trade business, and a bit of personal trivia about hair appointments and shopping hours. It decided to put several of its top geeky counter-spies on both Ma Chuntao and her recently identified lover, Sébastien Painteaux.

The day after the Reims P.J.-DCRI summit, Renouvin's boss, Rigaud in Paris, had six agents tailing Ma Chuntao, loaded with their sexiest toys. Tiny cameras and videocams, miniature, easy-to-plant microphones, even a small shotgun mike and parabolic mike. These could capture conversations a hundred meters away.

DCRI could also monitor e-mail and text-messages from smart phones, but counter-measures made this unreliable. Old-fashioned shoe-leather and plenty of bodies would make the difference. And yesterday's meetings of the Reims P.J and DCRI Reims had suddenly moved this file up to the required high-priority status for releasing more bodies and toys.

With his boss out of action, Painteaux could now absent himself from the labs and caves more readily. On her credit-card slip, Ma had scribbled three rendezvous points, number 1, 2 and 3. Henceforth, she could meet Painteaux with no exceptional electronic communication, just by leaving a message in a disguised voice from a public phone saying "RDV 1 b16" – meaning rendezvous at point one tomorrow (b) at 4 p.m., but really at 4 p.m. minus two hours. Codes for days were "a" for today, "b" for tomorrow, and "c" for two days from now. A crude but effective code.

However, Ma had not counted on being under much heavier surveillance, both human and electronic. When she arrived to meet Painteaux, she would unknowingly bring along a team of DCRI recording engineers, tailing her since morning.

Both Ma and Painteaux knew that their complicity in love alone, or in love with commercial plotting, put them at extreme risk. On the love front, Painteaux had already warned Ma that his wife was intensely jealous – and many times, she had found cause to be jealous. She was a bit of a loose cannon, he said, who could go berserk when cuckolded.

This had a less-than-joyful effect on Ma. Would her lover be thinking of betraying his mistress with his wife? An old story. And a cocktail for new drama.

As for the champagne plot, Painteaux and Ma knew they would wreck their careers if the plot blew up. Ma was beginning to curse herself for getting romantically involved with a player from the other side. Not cool for one of Tsaï's star agents. In fact, utterly stupid.

Painteaux, as a scared (though hardly guilt-obsessed) husband, cringed when he imagined his spouse's wrath. He might survive her storming, as he had before, by refusing to identify his paramour. But he couldn't survive if his wife implicated a woman who turned out to be a foreign spy.

These doubts on both sides were the first worms to wiggle in the apple of the lover-schemers' Garden of Eden. The slimy little invertebrates would grow. In exact synchronicity with the sinners' fears of getting caught.

Sinners indeed. For Ma's first coded post-*Carette* phone message brought Painteaux to the venerable little 14th-to18-century Église Saint-Médard in Paris's Fifth arrondissement. This historic church had welcomed wars of religion, famous philosophers (Blaise Pascal) and sexual shenanigans disguised as religious trances. Louis XV allegedly forbade "miracles" here that clergymen performed with gullible young girls. On several counts, an imaginative choice of venue.

The church sits in a charming little movie-set of a square at the intersection of rue Mouffetard and rue Censier. Rue Mouffetard, originally a Stone Age path, became the Roman road that probably brought Julius Caesar into Paris. For sure, it brought his legions.

In the Saint-Médard Square sit a lovely fountain, two bistros facing each other, two bookstores, and a lively vegetable-and-fruit market. Not a customary place for either currency-swappers or champagne-blenders. But a fine place for lost-in-a-crowd spies, and certainly for lovers.

As soon as Ma entered the church, three DCRI friends slipped in, one by one: two mature women, one young man. Heads bowed, or wandering about to study the alcoves and parish bulletins, they waited. Twenty minutes later, Painteaux drifted in. He had been watching for Ma from the tiny children's playground beside the church.

Ma, after walking about as a tourist, sat down half-way to the altar, off to one side, leaving three chairs between hers and the aisle. Painteaux, unrushed, slipped in two chairs away.

DCRI's parabolic mike, hidden on a chair twenty seats away, could have picked up their voices easily, recording as it listened. But neither Ma nor Painteaux, staying silent, obliged the eavesdroppers.

Ma wanted to shake any tails right there. She left a note on an empty chair between her and Painteaux. The note said: "We have company. Get lost in Métro, then meet me at the Mosque tea garden in one hour.

Ma got up abruptly, gathered her purse and dignity. Erect and steady on her high black heels, she walked out with a toss of her long black hair through one of the side doors. She stopped there to place a euro in a waiting gypsy-child's hand.

Painteaux waited ten minutes, pretending to pray. As he had good reason to. When he left, he glanced up at the famous allegorical painted façade of 134 rue Mouffetard, across from the church's high wooden front door. The façade fresco's twin wild boars, diving pheasants, prancing deer and weird curlicues seemed a perfect image of his life.

He took the Métro Line 7 to Pyramides, near the Opéra, and wandered into Brentano's bookshop. He browsed there for 15 minutes, then window-shopped at men's clothing stores before buying *Le Figaro* for the Métro ride back.

Ma walked in the other direction, up the avenue des Gobelins, getting on the Line 7 Métro at Gobelins station. She rode up one stop to Place d'Italie. There she idly shopped for shoes, got lost in the crowd, then turned and rode back down toward the Censier-Daubenton stop, a short walk to the Mosque.

They met as agreed at the vine-covered, outdoor tea terrace of Paris's Great Mosque.

"Come and have a nice hot Arab tea," said Ma, still on guard against counter-spies. "And especially one or two of their honey-drenched pastries."

In case DCRI bug-artists had followed them there, Ma continued talking about lovers' hopes and quarrels.

At the same time, she recognized one of the middle-aged female parishioners from the church. She got here pretty fast, thought Ma.

The church-lady had both a high-gain bracelet mike and another in her purse videocam, now pointing obliquely at them as she fussed over her menu.

"We should stop meeting like this," started Ma.

"Why? Said an anxious Painteaux.

"There's too much at stake, including your marriage, and I'm not sure your nerves are steady enough to follow through."

"Oh, and yours are?"

"Of course," said Ma, cautiously making their plot talk sound like lovers' banter. "I'm a woman. I'm used to romantic scheming. The other lady doesn't faze me. She's an idiot, and is completely at sea. She has no idea how to handle you."

They nibbled their sugary pastries in silence, daintily holding the hot glasses of tea with their fingers. They ordered a second tea, then Painteaux settled the bill.

"Wait. Where can we meet next to clarify all this?"

"I thought I was very clear. Stick by your phone. By the way, calm down, darling."

Happily, Caron's own 24/7 tail on Painteaux had also seen everything. Now she was eager to listen to the DCRI recordings – if they had any – to hear what the lovebirds (and accomplices?) had said.

Reims, Hôtel de Police – the Chinese angle strengthens...

DCRI's Paris recordings went immediately to both the Ministry and to the P.J.-DCRI group in Reims.

"A pretty rough recording," regretted Baraquant. "Scraps of it point to some kind of complicity – or trade-off – between Ma and Painteaux. To discover exactly what that is, we would need to fill in a lot of blanks."

"Yes," said Caron. This gives us intriguing hints, but we still have no clear idea of how the love affair fits into the plot suggested in Painteaux's e-mails and text-messages. He has an iPhone 4S, and he uses it rather incautiously.

"Yes," said Baraquant. "Now may I point out that in addition to cracking a hypothetical Chinese plot, we're also looking for an attempted murderer? For the P.J., that's our priority."

"Yes, said Duroselle, thanks for bringing that up."

"So far," said Caron, "Painteaux fits the criteria of means and opportunity for murder. But what exactly could his *motive* be?"

"I can imagine several, but with little hard evidence," said Baraquant.

"I have serious suspicions about Painteaux's movie alibi," said Caron. He claims he was at an early movie the evening the crime occurred, then went to bed with his wife. She of course confirms this, as wives do."

"So, I understand, do his work colleagues," added Baraquant.

"I'm not satisfied that their corroborations are precise enough," said Caron. "What was the *actual* time he left his lab the evening before the attack? No witness so far could nail that closer than within half an hour."

"An eternity," said Baraquant. "Lots of killers have lost their freedom for a difference of ten minutes."

"Right." said Caron. "That's why we're widening our enquiries about Painteaux's movements just before the attack. Already we're getting some intriguing observations from a bystander."

"Who's that?"

"A guy who knows Painteaux, and who happened to see him around the movie theater that evening. Our guys are just cross-checking his facts against the timing of phone records. I should know within hours if this stands up."

CHAPTER TEN
Saints and Sinners

Basilique Saint-Remi...

In the days following the crime, Madame Repentigny had continued her walks in the Déambulatoire and the Crypt. She still attended Mass every day. And she shared her sins and fears with her reliably consoling Father Vladimir Farfelan.

"Father," she would repeat. "I feel so safe here with you. And with the presence of Saint-Remi, ever here. I am also enjoying the unfailing support of my husband's *chef de cave*, Sébastien Painteaux. You may have seen him here a few times keeping a distant eye on me. He fears for my welfare, and especially my health. To sustain me, he often even drives me here. He consoles me by listening, and by supporting my faith as no other layman ever did. He too is clearly a believer."

"He seems like a saintly man, Madame, or at least a very good man."

"Yes, I think he understands me better than my husband, poor man."

"Have you confided to him your thoughts about Saint-Remi?"

"Not nearly as much as I have to you, Father. He would be shocked."

"I admit that I am still a little shocked myself. But as your spiritual guide, it is my duty to accompany you wherever your needs may take you. As a priest, I understand the nature of spiritual ecstasy. And how it can shape one's outlook."

"Thank you, Father. You are my anchor."

Hôtel de Police...

The first batch of Repentigny's e-mails and text-messages came to Caron at noon. She sent out for a Panini and Diet Coke to read them at her desk.

Surprises, small and big. Not on Chinese plots. But on Repentigny's tom-catting.

The first surprise was Frédérique Pommier, chief of the cave tourist-guides. In spite of what everybody thought, she was not over her infatuation with Hubert. Secretly (except to him), her flame was still burning high. Her fall-back husband in Épernay had turned out to be a life-sucking bore. While Frédérique remained full of ideas and joie-de-vivre, he had no inclinations beyond vegetating in the countryside and drinking.

For the past three years, showed the e-mails, she and Hubert had started up again – she for what she rationalized as love, he just for fun. They met at the intersection of mind and body, in theory for a light-hearted, no-strings liaison. Hubert – again – hoped it would stay that way. Their after-hours romps in the caves gave him a handy and amusing release. Hide-and-seek among the millions of bottles, zig-zagging in the tunnels' scores of twists and turns' was endlessly entertaining. Frédérique never knew exactly when and where he would catch her. Only that she would elude, then *help* him catch her.

The revived affair thrived on special new private e-mail accounts. The lovers' early messages read like teenage text-messages:

"RDV [rendezvous] at 17:00 today on corner leading to Argentinian racks," went a typical Hubert summons. "Hungry for you." Or just: "Come to Gallery C now."

Pommier was always available. Within winking distance of forty, she was an accomplished *allumeuse*. She could turn on a saint, which Hubert certainly wasn't.

"Take me now," she would urge. "No, sooner than now. NOW. Hurry. When and where?"

As time went on, their exchanges grew more graphic. Trusting their secure e-mails, each would tease the other with an X-rated reminder. Or promise. As long-familiar lovers, they had their tastes, their codes, soon their habits.

One was for Pommier to hide a sexy note for Hubert under a rack at a specific spot in the caves. Her text-message summons would identify in code the first location. There a handwritten note would tell him where the second was. Then the third. And maybe a fourth, until he was mad to mate.

An enchanting, playful, secret erotic world.

Their meetings grew as frequent as before. The reasons were self-evident: they both had distracted spouses; and playing at love in the caves – just below their offices – was convenient, discreet and thrilling. They didn't seek extravagant comforts in the caves. The very roughness and sudden unpredictability of the place made their encounters deliciously primitive, even savage.

So did the history and mystery of their strange, shadowy labyrinth.

As Caron scanned more recent e-mails, however, she tracked a slow, sad descent into the ancient misunderstanding: between love-struck woman and love-wary man. As in many such relationships, one came to crave more, the other less. The disconnection of their earlier affair returned. E-mails and text-messages started echoing frustration, then sometimes irritation. Hubert felt harassed and trapped; Pommier felt ignored, even rejected.

"You're turning into a totally selfish bastard," finally exploded one of her recent missives. "You treat me like your toy, a convenience you can use, abuse, and forget at will."

"But didn't you volunteer to be my toy? I've played with you as you begged. But now, frankly, I'm finding this whole thing rather tedious." replied Hubert.

"You will regret saying that," warned Pommier, "I could kill you. I could really kill you."

"You and a cast of thousands."

"You're despicable. And an arrogant, insensitive idiot."

"I've been called worse things by worse people."

"I've warned you. You had better be careful."

"Thank you. I shall. Especially when hunting in my own chicken-coop."

"You're a pig. All those girls in your guides' harem think you're just a gross, ridiculous old fool."

"I don't care what they think of me, as long as they enjoy touring the caves with me."

"One day, you monster, you will die in these caves – no doubt by a heart attack while *in flagrante delicto*. Or, better still, drowning in champagne..."

Pommier had just put herself back on Caron's serious suspects' list.

The Repentigny blending room...

After informing the prosecutor, Caron sent Jenneret and Marcambault to question Painteaux's colleagues again about the latter's movie alibi.

"We understand," said Jenneret to the blending staff, "that monsieur Painteaux left early the evening before the attack to attend a movie. You gave us approximate times, but we need to narrow down that time."

"Of course," agreed the senior man of the five colleagues, assembled in their white lab coats. "But I'm not sure we can really be more precise."

"But having talked now among yourselves, could you not offer a consensus about the time he left?"

The staff conferred for another two or three minutes.

"About 6:45 p.m., we think."

Jenneret persisted:

"The film he said he went to – *J. Edgar* – was at the Gaumont-Pathé on the Place Drouet-d'Erlon, and the showings were at 4:00 p.m., 6:50 p.m. and 8:50 p.m. The first showing was too early for the time Painteaux told you he was leaving; the second would have been too tight a timetable for him to get there. That leaves the 8:50 p.m. showing – so late that he would not have had to leave work early. Are you absolutely sure he left around 6:45 p.m? Even taking into account a 20-minute commercial segment before the 6:50 movie, that would be tight."

"I leave such calculations to the police."

Smiling, Jenneret said "All right. We're not bad at math. We'll work with that."

Police scientifique, Reims...

Dominique Flochard called Caron down to her crime lab, two floors below. Amidst the fingerprint screens, microscopes, test tubes and horrific color murder photos, Flochard had set out a table of what looked like junk and dirt. The scattered mess –already studied and reported to Caron -- included some whitish dust, a scrap of black head-scarf, two wigs (black and blonde), and two large dirty rubber boots with curious inside indentations, and one workman's glove with blood stains.

The cloth and dust were detritus culled from a badly swept corner of the loading docks. Flochard's team had dug up the boots from the adjoining flower-beds.

Flochard had already told Caron that these artifacts would clearly tie back to Repentigny's attacker as he bolted out of a rarely-used cave exit at the back of the dock.

"I have your preliminary reports on these items, Dominique. Now have you got final, detailed readings on them?" asked Caron.

Flochard straightened her big thick glasses.

"The one piece of positive evidence is the glove. The blood-stain matches the victim's blood type. Not conclusive, but highly suggestive."

"Good. That's' encouraging. Maybe it's the glove that drew the crossed-out "R" on the wall."

"Yes, quite plausibly. The dust contains the usual cave lichen called *racodium cellare* – the well-known wine-cellar mold. But it also carries minute traces of something astonishing: mescaline."

"Isn't that the hallucinatory drug you told me about when explaining so-called 'psychic driving,' that Korean War-era brainwashing drug?"

"Precisely – so I see you *were* listening to my boring little discourse."

"It was a bit of a detour for me at the time, for I was obsessed with finding answers I could use immediately."

"Well, I think – and this was a long-shot, as I said – that maybe we can use some of this info now."

"Wasn't that psychic driving sometimes linked to endless loops of suggestive tapes?"

"Yes, that was the MKULTRA approach at Montreal's McGill University."

"OK, now what about the head-scarf?"

"It doesn't tell us much yet, but it might. It appears to be just some sort of loose black cloth that a woman might throw over her head to enter a church."

"Under our most powerful microscope, we can see traces of dandruff, spittle from the wearer's mouth, and one blonde hair."

"Please get us a DNA check on all that, Dominique, and let me know ASAP. I am starting to ask myself where we might look for a match."

"Can we check the DNA of everyone close to Repentigny, or even in contact with him?"

"Of course, we'll work up a priority list for tomorrow, and get at this."

"Oh, and the boots?"

"They're size 46, as expected from the crime site. Then two particularities. Inside each boot is a curious indentation, like a large insole, no longer there. On the outside of one boot, we've identified faint traces of blood. We've already matched these with the victim's blood."

"At last, a real break. This is our first hard evidence. Now comes the tricky part – finding who *wore* the boots. And of course the glove."

"I have no leads on that. I will have to leave that to you."

"Thanks, you always leave me the easy part!"

"Denise, as for acquiring DNA and other specimens, should we leave Madame Repentigny out of that?"

"No. But go at her tactfully to avoid scandal. She's a beloved figure in this town. And she enjoys enormous public sympathy now because of this tragedy. At some stage, we might quietly slip an agent into her private quarters to take even more samples. If we don't do this, someone will blame us for lack of thoroughness."

"Got it. We'll proceed with infinite care and delicacy."

Parc Mendès France, Reims...

It's one of the most charming of Reims's eighty-two public green spaces. Le Parc Mendes France, named after the most respected French prime minister since 1945, is quiet, bucolic, and full of trees, lakes and creeks.

Rarely frequented by champagne barons, it was an idyllic place for the still-shattered Sophie-Charlotte to take restful strolls with her friend Ludovine Pfaffenzeller or Marie-Laure, her daughter.

Soon Sophie-Charlotte resumed her habit of driving herself to daily Mass. She lingered at the Basilique for her walks through the peace-giving Déambulatoire. She loved every corner of the church – its high galleries, its alleys, its vaulted ceilings, its four dark, carved Confessionals, its Crypt.

On her strolls at Mendès France, she would talk with Ludovine or Marie-Laure about Hubert, the children, and the *maison*'s future. But also of faith and Saint-Remi.

Her religious mood thrived too on visits to the Musée des Beaux-Arts de Reims. Harboring one of the richest multi-century collections of any French region, it sits in the disaffected Abbaye de Saint-Denis. Sophie-Charlotte wondered there at the 16th-century Christian paintings and the portraits by Lucas Cronach, Elder and Younger.

She also sought refuge in the Musée Le Vergeur in the long Place du Forum. The museum building, started in the 13th century, was a unique repository of the Reims heritage – with religion never far.

Such tourism was a break for Sophie-Charlotte from her loyal and depressing visits to Hubert's bedside. Lost and dreamy, gripped by broodings on the afterlife, she would sit with him for an hour or two, and hold his hand. Then she would see the brain-activity monitor flicker and droop ever more weakly.

The doctor's faces and low, slow voices told her Hubert would soon leave her forever.

CHAPTER ELEVEN
Catching Up On (Other People's) Mail

Caron's office...words from Hubert's coma...

With help from DCRI hackers, the P.J had managed to break into Painteaux's secret Yahoo account. He had a Repentigny business account he used for only two types of messages. Delicate personal matters. And confidential messages to and from his boss, Hubert Repentigny, of whom he was the most trusted associate.

Caron's team plowed through several thousand of Painteaux's e-mails. Now they could ransack his mind at will. To do so, they went back a year.

Before Ma Chuntao warned of such an electronic break-in, she and Painteaux exchanged "love" notes coded to set rendezvous. But they also indicated obliquely where the plot was going. It wouldn't take long for the two police allies to get the drift of both activities.

Thanks to DCRI and P.J. tracking, the police already had a good handle on the love affair – its early budding, its flowering, and now its fading. But DCRI's Economic Protection specialists naturally had a predominant interest in the Chinese plot.

The P.J. focused on the attempted-murder investigation. Painteaux remained a leading suspect. But there was not yet   conclusive evidence.

Painteaux's recent pre-attack e-mails with Repentigny raised intense suspicions. Between a *chef de maison* and his *chef de cave*, there is something like a marriage. Together they made good or great champagne, their *maison*'s distinctive brand.

Now, suddenly, the police found a text-message exchange preceding the attack by only three days. Repentigny opened the Pandora's Box, leading to this exchange on their company account: "Sébastien,as soon as you return from your current vineyard tour – Thursday? Friday? – I need to spend an afternoon with you. I need to discuss something of terrifying import to our house, and even to the whole French champagne universe."

"*Mon Dieu,* what could that be? You have all my attention."

Painteaux, alarmed, wrote: "Tell me the essence of this."

"Earlier this week," said his boss, "I met with five other *chefs de maison* in *La Rotonde* bar at *Les Crayères*. Only top houses. Then we adjourned upstairs to lunch in a private Impératrice suite at *le Château*. Going back down, we left through *La Rotonde* one by one not to attract attention."

"You really think you could visit incognito the fanciest hotel and restaurant in Reims?"

"Not entirely. But the prices alone give some assurance that the wrong people won't see you."

"The wrong people being the media? The tax people? The Competition Authority?"

"All of the above. But some other people you might never expect."

"Who, for heaven's sake?"

"The Chinese, Sébastien, the Chinese."

"What? You're joking."

"No."

"I'm stunned. What on earth are you talking about?

"Calm down, and register this. Several leading *chefs de maison* have heard rumors that Chinese investors, in league with their government, are discussing how...basically – to take over France's champagne industry."

"Shall I laugh or cry?"

"Laugh a little, then get ready to cry a lot."

"I'm laughing right now. This is nonsense. The Chinese could never in a thousand years dominate the world champagne market. And even less could they imitate the quality of our bubbles – our *terroir*, our grapes, our savoir-faire."

"We can't argue this by text-messages, Sébastien. Just come in to see me as soon as you return."

"Will do."

"Ah, and wrap your mind around this shocker. The rumors are suggesting that the whole take-over effort, spread over several years, will be teleguided by a French insider, a senior person in our industry. A mole."

"You mean a traitor?"

"Yes, that's the perfect word. A Quisling who knows all our secrets – blending techniques, current blending reports, methods, technologies, expected profits, and current and future worldwide marketing plans."

"That's a breathtaking hypothesis. I have difficulty believing any of it. This is either a prank or paranoia."

"Neither applies to me, Sébastien, as you well know. Come in and listen to me. Ask all the questions you want. But take this seriously. Then we'll review all the facts and possibilities. We'll try to imagine how to stop this monstrous plan -- if it's true. And initial evidence here and in China tends to favor that."

"Any idea who the traitor might be?"

"Nothing firm yet, but I'm making a short list."

"I hope I'm not on it."

"Of course not, *mon cher Sébastien*. Remember: You're the guy who came with me to China a couple of years ago to build a Chinese market for *us* – not to hand our market to the Chinese."

"Yes, it was an instructive trip."

"It's sickening to imagine a Frenchman betraying us," said Repentigny. "One thing is sure, if we ever catch the rumored culprit, and find he's one of ours, we'll hang him from a meat-hook."

"Ah, the colorful phrase Nicolas Sarkozy used about the guy he hoped to unmask in the Clearstream affair, where another politician mounted an elaborate scheme to smear him."

"Sarko did have a way with words, in a vulgar sort of way. I would suggest we slowly drown the bastard in a vat of lousy so-called Chinese champagne."

"Sarko?"

"Now you *are* laughing at this. Just look in the mirror to make sure the bad guy really isn't you after all!"

"Spoken like a true baron. See you very soon."

From Ma Chuntao to Tsaï Yong-kang

From the beginning, months ago, Ma had instructed Painteaux to use the code-word "river" to signify disaster. That would mean that the plot had leaked to influential French milieux, either government or industry. In that event, Tsaï had given a standing order: stop all activity, disconnect from all sources, deny everything, and lie low.

To trigger the shut-down, it would not be necessary for the French to have detailed, iron-clad proof of the plot. It would suffice that China's principal agent in this, Ma, notice a critical mass of suspicion directed at China.

On getting Repentigny's tip-off about the plot, Painteaux sent Ma an ostensible love-note on his private text-messaging account:

"Sweet spring peach, I cannot forget you. Today, as I walked along the river in the park here, I thought of you tenderly. Too busy to see you, alas, I need to help my boss all week.

Love, Sébastien."

The second part of the agreed disaster code was this: mentioning any other person in the message would indicate from where the danger came. Repentigny (as 'boss') was thus in Tsaï's sights. Ma would ask Beijing's instructions. And Caron, reading the 'river" note, took note of this apparent confirmation of her suspicions.

But, whatever his links to the Chinese, was Painteaux really the most likely murder suspect?

Chinese Trade Mission, Paris...

On getting the "river" and "boss" disaster message from Paintaux, Ma raced to her handsome cryptographer friend, Lin Yi.

"What can I do for you today, peach flower," he said.

"You can encode and immediately send this message to Tsaï in Beijing," she said. Make it HIGHEST PRIORITY. Her message:

"Our key source advises that half a dozen top champagne houses, including Repentigny's, are aware of our broad strategy. They are planning to counter it. That will certainly include trying to identify our primary source and ally himself. Note:

This may or may not mean that the DCRI Economic Protection unit is on this. Even if not, the local Reims Police judiciaire soon will be. As per orders, am shutting down all activity. Request further instructions."

Fifteen minutes later, Lin confirmed he had sent the message.

At the caves: the guides' office...

Frédérique had written her last threatening message to Repentigny in anger. For the second time with him, she had felt scorned, abandoned and – in her mind – humiliated. Hubert's get-over-it nonchalance only made her more furious.

But today, she would have to explain herself. And explain actions far more than humiliating.

Caron went with two investigators to Pommier's office. It sat just behind the guides' desk where tourists stop to buy tour tickets for the caves.

Caught off guard, and watched by her amazed multilingual tour guides, Pommier blanched on seeing Caron and her colleagues. She stood up, and said: "What can I do for you, Commissaire?" She looked more than a little alarmed.

"We would like to ask you a few questions in the privacy of your office. Then make a brief visit with you to the caves."

"Of course, Commissaire." She shut the door.

"In our investigation of the attack on Monsieur Repentigny, we have gained access to a confidential e-mail account used by the victim. Inevitably, we discovered that you and he had maintained a very close relationship."

"Of course, we worked closely together."

"I am referring to your love affair, not work."

"It wasn't really a love affair, Commissaire."

"That's usually what men say about these things. Reading your text-message exchanges over the past few months certainly reveals a love affair – a very joyful and lusty love affair."

Pommier blushed.

"If you've been reading everything I remember you must have read, I guess I can't deny something like that."

"No, not really. But what concerns us today is not that you and he had some happy times. We're interested in what happened when your relationship recently turned sour."

"I would rather say disappointing."

"Just disappointing? In one of your last text-messages before the attack on Monsieur Repentigny, you made a specific threat against him."

"Specific? I don't recall anything specific. I never said I would shoot or stab him – and certainly not hit him over the head with a champagne bottle."

"Let me read you part of your final exchange with him:

[The victim] "But now, frankly, I'm finding this whole thing rather tedious."

[Pommier] "You will regret saying that, you bastard. I could kill you. I could really kill you."

"You and a cast of thousands."

"And later, you said:"

"One day, you monster, you will die in these caves – no doubt by a heart attack while

274

in flagrante delicto. Or, better still, drowning in champagne..."

"You call that a specific threat? I was just annoyed, not really eager to kill him."

"Given that someone attacked your employer only a day or two later, I would call this a credible threat – or at very least a highly suspicious threat."

"I note that each time you change adjectives, Commissaire, your accusation grows a little weaker."

"In the end, Madame, if you are guilty of this crime, it won't matter what my adjectives are."

"All right then, how are you going to prove that I was the criminal?"

"At this moment, our *police scientifique* are inspecting your apartment to search for evidence. They will scour your place for any scrap of proof, whether that's a document, blood, DNA or even dust from the immediate crime scene."

"That's outrageous! How dare you invade my apartment illegally for no serious reason!"

"It's up to us to decide what is a serious reason, Madame, and following the law, we obtained prior authorization from the *procureur.*"

"This is disgusting. Hubert and I may have had a lovers' spat. Most couples do. But maybe lovers are not something you've ever been personally familiar with."

"My, my. And you think insulting a cop is going to improve your case? Now we'll go down to the caves with you. The elevator being small, we'll take the stairway. Maybe that will give you a little more time to think of a good story."

"I'll save my stories for the judge."

"He will enjoy them."

Once reaching bottom, the group walked straight ahead to get out of the brightly-lit reception room. Then they turned left toward the galleries.

Caron asked Pommier to go over some of the hide-and-seek games the now-alienated lovers had played. Humiliated at this intrusion in her intimate life, Pommier snapped at Caron again:

"What is this, Commissaire, an exercise in voyeurism? Are you really that sexually frustrated that you have to pry into every detail of another woman's love-making?"

"We are not the slightest bit interested in your *Cirque du Soleil* prowess, Madame. We just need to ascertain if anything you did here with Monsieur Repentigny could conceivably have led to his death."

"Meaning that you *really* think I tried to kill him?"

"We don't think anything yet. We're only speculating on why and how you might have attacked him with the rage of a twice-abandoned mistress."

"You really enjoy wallowing in that so-called 'twice-abandoned' description, don't you? Nobody would abandon you twice, because they wouldn't want you in the first place."

"Are you really naïve enough to think that ridiculing the police will distract us from your highly suspicious situation? I've tolerated your childishness so far, but let me sober you up with this: article 433-5 of the Penal Code stipulates that attacking the dignity of any public officer, including police, is punishable by a fine of 7,500 euros *and* six months in jail. Try your little insult game once more and we'll charge you. Then, in jail, you'll have time to ponder even more clever stories for the judge."

"That's an outrage!"

"You seem to see outrages everywhere."

"Is that law the work of that rotten little Guérin?"

"An even bigger mistake, Madame. Not only is Monsieur Guérin protected against insults as a normal public servant. As President of the Republic, he is also protected by four articles under the 1881 Law of Freedom of the Press."

"What the hell is going on in France? Whatever happened to the free speech and democracy we claim to have invented in 1789?"

Caron laughed.

"I'm sure every loyal French man and woman asks that every day. We love to complain. But when you're under a strong suspicion of attempted murder, it's not very smart to test the limits."

"All right. What do you want? Why did you bring me here?"

"Three reasons. First, tell us again where and when you were on the evening and night of the attack?"

"I told your two cops – forgive me, policemen – that I worked late until about 8:30 p.m., cleaning up some overdue work."

"What was that?"

"Oh, just routine paperwork."

"What kind of paperwork?"

"I don't remember. Why do you need to know exactly what it was?"

"Because if you can't remember a simple thing like that, maybe your memory of that whole evening and night is unreliable."

"OK, let's say I was checking our annual visitor statistics."

"In early October? Isn't that something for the end of the year?"

"Well, we do monthly stats too, then compile the monthlies for the annual."

"When you were working late on the fateful night, did you see anyone else?"

"No, not that I remember."

"Are you sure?"

"I can't swear it, but I am pretty sure."

"Where did you go after work?"

"I drove home to Épernay."

"To your husband?"

"Well, I am married to him."

"I gather by your ongoing affair with Monsieur Repentigny that your marriage was not entirely... fulfilling."

"How many marriages are?"

"The fact that your affair with your boss revived a year or more after your marriage suggests that it was something you needed, something that filled a gap in your married life."

"It certainly made the marriage more tolerable. My husband – lacked – lacks -- everything that Hubert radiated."

"Radiated. Which was?"

"Energy, confidence, panache. Hubert was quite a compelling package."

"So it seems. Now please tell us how the caves figured in your adventure."

"I don't like the word 'adventure.' It sounds like a one-night stand."

"Let's call it your 'relationship' with him."

"Thank you."

"We met here as often as we could. We played here, we loved here."

"Yes, this is quite a romantic place if you're engaged in a secret rendezvous and are not put off by the rather eerie atmosphere."

"I never was."

"Did you have an elevator key?"

"Of course, I am the chief of the tourist-guides."

"Did you sometimes wander through the tunnels?"

"Yes, of course. That was part of the excitement. We could leave notes and hints, and make the other seek out his or her partner. I could easily slip down from the office and plant some notes, only telling him by text-message where the first note was."

"Did you use any disguises?"

"Sometimes, just to heighten the fun. Hubert had hidden a few masks, and usually black robes. I used to wear one to make it hard for him to see me."

"So you could hide pretty well anywhere in your black robe?"

"That was the idea."

"Like behind the rack where you clubbed Hubert over the head in a fit of rage?"

Frédérique's face contorted. She shrieked: "No, no, no! How can you suddenly accuse me of trying to kill him? You have no proof."

"No proof? You mean you did it, but you think you made your crime hard to prove?"

"You're twisting my words."

"Maybe I'm just catching a nuance. In any event, I'm afraid you just now completed the three tests usually applied to evaluate suspects: motive, means and opportunity. In messages we have read, you declared your hate and repeated wish to kill him. You had at hand millions of bottle-clubs and convenient racks for hiding. And you had the elevator key, plus a job just upstairs that allowed you to creep down at will to plan the attack."

"Fascinating, Commissaire. But after blasting him to hell in my message, how do you explain that I was able to lure him back down to the caves for a so-called last fling?"

"You might have phoned him *in extremis* to beg for a final meeting in the caves. Under strain, lovers do often flip-flop. Or you might have somehow tricked Hubert into believing that one of his latest conquests among the guides wanted to meet him there."

"Those are just wild speculations."

"Really? I notice that they're alarming you."

"It's this whole charade that's alarming me. Stop this! I am innocent!"

"Madame Pommier, I think we've heard enough to justify putting you in temporary detention."

Pommier collapsed, and broke down, sobbing pitiably.

"I didn't kill him, I swear! But I did love him. I *do* love him. I love him so much. This is so unjust. He rejected me. Again. He was cruel and cold. So cruel, so cruel. But I still love him. I love him, and regret nothing."

Caron notified Baraquant and Duroselle, who advised the prosecutor. Then Caron, Flochard and the two officers brought Pommier to the surface. They drove her to the Hôtel de Police, and placed her in a cell until she calmed down.

There she alternated between screaming and babbling. She was a broken woman. Nothing she said made any sense. To drown her grief, she would blame everyone in sight – for insensitivity, stupidity and scheming.

"You're all plotting against me!" shouted Pommier.

"Plotting what?" asked Caron.

"Plotting to have me replaced as his mistress! Do you think I was the *only* one? He trained at least one other to walk and hide at night in the caves. It was his twisted ritual. One night, I even saw another black-robed wanderer, but couldn't catch her. If she became as crazy as I did under his direction, she probably still goes there some nights."

"How did you feel when you felt crazy?"

"Love-sick, of course. But once I also felt I was floating like a powerful princess, almost flying to my destiny."

"Did you see visions apart from the other black-robed person?"

"Yes, visions of strange or famous people. But also explosions of color, like a kaleidoscope. Then when my lover came and took me in his arms, all the visions melted away, and I disappeared within him."

"You must remember Gustav Klimt's famous painting 'The Kiss,' where the man bends the woman's neck to kiss her, and their bodies seem to melt together? Remember her long robe of gold and dreamy colors?"

"That was exactly the feeling and the vision I drowned in. It was almost like being on some kind of drug."

"Before you met Hubert, did you ever take a drug?"

"No. I don't believe in that. My only vice is *langues de chat* dessert biscuits. As a prelude to love, we used to eat them in the caves with a glass of bubbles – at least I did; Hubert preferred to just drink his champagne, with no pastry or *amuse-gueules*."

At end of day, Caron asked her two bosses to release Pommier. She had finally calmed down, and made more sense. But Caron imposed on Pommier the obligation to report to the P.J. every day until the case closed. This was risky. Pommier might still be suicidal. But Caron wanted to run an unusual test to clearly prove or disprove her guilt. Reluctantly, Baraquant and Duroselle let her run her test.

First, she needed to confirm some key suspicions. With her bosses' approval, Caron made highly unorthodox preparations to identify the mysterious late-night cave-prowler. It was likely somebody with restricted cave keys or knowledge of door codes: for example, Pommier, Painteaux, Henri Lonniaux the furious fired employer and grower from Aÿ-Champagne. Perhaps an over-looked cave worker. Maybe even a weird long shot Caron kept to herself

Madame Repentigny's quarters...
Dominique Flochard and her *police scientifique* eagerly followed Caron's instructions – pre-approved, again as law required, by the state pros-ecutor. From a distance, and in an unmarked car, they watched the victim's wife drive to her habitual Mass and promenade. As soon as she drove away, Flochard's team again searched her entire large liv-ing area. Earlier, with her agreement and offered key, they had already done an initial search to catch likely clues.

This time concentrated on Sophie-Charlotte's bedroom and Hubert's, a few meters apart. Applying the same collection methods and tests they used for other suspects, they again went through cup-boards and drawers, but with an eye to more prob-ing chemical analysis. They checked bedding and clothing, and dusted key places for fingerprints and Flochard's exotic substances. They scoured Madame's bedside table in case anything new had appeared. Would this second search tell them more?

After two hours, they brought back to the labs an impressive new haul for further chemical tests. Among items noted: a Spanish-style *mantilla* or head-shawl, a few blonde hairs, photos and samples of rug stains, and a black penitent's robe (presumably for the annual Saint-Remi Translation ceremony).

The team also reported a considerable collection of books about Saint-Remi. Beside Madame's bed were his most famous sermons and admonitions, and his two Testaments, the great and the small. And a black family Bible embossed with the omnipresent Repentigny "R."

On every item, Flochard tested for unusual chemical traces, the results coming in quickly.

Flochard laid all this out on her briefing-room table for Caron and her colleagues, then gave a new oral report:

"I'll leave it to Denise and her team to interpret what all these items might mean. I'll just offer a brief and tentative report about the scientific findings.

In three places we found an unusual mixture of traces. Basically, these places were the head covering, the black robe, and the rug stains. Again we found tiny traces of *racodium cellare*, but also mescaline and a rarer hallucinogenic drug called psilocybin. We also found minute traces of the particular dust seen in the cave's art-galleries. Madame Repentigny earlier confessed, we know, to walking in the galleries to meditate, so in principle this would fit what we knew already."

"Yes, said Caron, she said she occasionally strolled there, as in the Basilica's Déambulatoire, to meditate and find inspiration."

"Two other discoveries raise questions. First: Why two or three earth stains on the bedroom broadloom? Does this tie into our recent digging effort to identify an escaping attacker? Probably not: for such stains would have been on the large size 46 boots, not on Madame's rather small feet."

"Would that rule out her as being involved in the attack?"

"Too soon to say, but that's probably right. Yet it's the second discovery that really leaves us mystified. On Madame's dressing-gown we found tiny traces of mescaline, the hallucinogenic drug. This drug is known in some countries like the U.S. and Mexico as a recreational drug. As a liquid, it can be mixed into a drink. It can cause strange visions, a severely altered state of consciousness and euphoria. But also revulsion and anxiety."

"Ah, Dominique," said Caron, "could this also act as an aid to brainwashing?"

"Of course. But for anyone to manipulate Madame Repentigny's brain, he would need to establish an extremely close relationship with her. And a means for programming her mind. I see no other evidence to suggest that technique of so-called psychic driving."

Said Caron: "Just as a long-shot. Did you find an audio playback device anywhere?"

"You mean a dictation and recording device like the ones we sometimes use?"

"Possibly."

"In fact, beside the lady's bed was a white iPod in a speaker dock."

"Did you listen to it?"

"No. We presumed it was for listening to music. That's what we found in the first twenty minute of listening."

"Caron snorted. "What? Only twenty minutes? You mean you didn't check the entire recording? I'm not impressed."

"For now, we'll ponder what you found. But meanwhile, go back to check all the recordings are on the bedside iPod. You can copy them onto your iPhone or a USB drive so we can study it all at our leisure."

"OK, Denise."

"Back to the recreational-drug idea: That hardly sounds like Madame Repentigny."

"You never know. Mescaline also has fans among the bored or dare-devil wealthy."

"Bored might fit Madame, but hardly dare-devil."

"As you often say, Commissaire, in our trade, the predictable, more often than not, is the unpredictable. If religion is her consolation, maybe drugs are her secret sin."

"OK, Dominique, let's just take note of the mescaline and see if and how it might tie in with anything else."

"Right."

"Meanwhile, I'm going to dig a little into those books about Saint-Remi on Madame's night-table. Your notes and photos identify them perfectly. I'll get copies from local libraries and bookstores. This should be fun for me. It's a bit of a hobby of mine.

And oh, Dominique, when you lift the sound-file off the bedside MP3 player, please send it to me right away."

Hôtel de Police -- daily briefing...
From the outset of the investigation, Caron and the P.J. had struggled to imagine Sophie-Charlotte as the actual assailant. But they kept their professional skepticism about murdered men's wives – whether as killers or accomplices.

At their evening briefing, officers debated her case.

"Her convincingly proclaimed loyalty to her husband," Caron told her assembled colleagues, "hardly guarantees her innocence. The same goes for her ostentatious Christian devotion.

"We shouldn't look at her only as a possible assailant," said Baraquant. "She could have hired the assailant."

"I doubt that very much," said Caron. "Where would a woman of her social status find a hit-man?"

"I agree," said Duroselle. "Again, no hint of motive, means or opportunity. Madame Repentigny associated with the cream of Reims society, both civil and religious. Not with gangsters and hit-men."

"As for some weird mystical motive," said Caron, "she is clearly a religious cultist. But does that make her a killer or accomplice to murder? At most, Dominique Flochard's mescaline traces suggest she might be relaxing with a recreational drug. Trapped in an unhappy marriage, and forbidden by her faith to take a lover, drugs might well be an escape for her."

Baraquant whistled. "Let's be damned careful that we don't let any such speculations leak to the media. That's potentially libelous, and in our community downright explosive – not to mention wildly unfair."

"Now," said Caron, "to sum up: conceivably, Pommier might remain a plausible lead. But a far stronger one is Painteaux – terrified that his complicity in the Chinese plot is about to come to light. That is his motive. And his opportunity lurks in the discrepancy – or at least confusion -- in the time he says he went to the movies the night before the crime."

"Yes," concurred Duroselle. "And you could argue that Painteaux had ready access to the caves, and was husky enough to wield a heavy bottle as a weapon: after motive and opportunity, the means.

Baraquant warned: "DCRI's Paris bosses are about to bring in Ma Chuntao to blow the whistle on her little games. Let's now also bring in her boyfriend Painteaux."

"Right," said Caron.

"As for Ma Chuntao," said Duroselle, "To crack her, I presume that it will be enough to show her photos and movies of her movements, including the Sedan hotel meeting."

"Yes, that's quite likely," picked up Baraquant. "We can just let the Chinese worry that DCRI monitored them. Then, if they deny they were plotting,

some Sedan sound files or transcripts might myste-
riously turn up to shake them."

"I'm not sure it will shake them all that much,"
said Caron, Remember DCRI's pants-down mishap
on November 30, 2010? Chinese officials stumbled
on three French agents with recording equipment
in the Toulouse hotel-room of Liu Shaoyong, president of China Eastern Airlines. Authorities hushed
up the incident. But this confirms how common
international industrial spying and counter-spying
really are."

"Don't mention that to our DCRI friends,"
smiled Baranquant. "And for God's sake, don't
joke about Inspector Clouseau being at work in
Toulouse."

"*Patron*," said Caron to Baraquant, I'm being attacked by a small armada of flu bugs just now. And
I have a ton of evidence and documents to go over.
Do you mind if I lock myself in my apartment for a
day or two to work on them? I'll stay in touch and
be available at all times."

"Of course, Denise. With luck, you'll find the
culprit from afar – if you can see through the smoke
of those smelly cigarrillos."

"No guarantee, but I'll try. I've got a fabulous
view of the city from my living-room window.
Maybe I can spot him from up there."

CHAPTER TWELVE
Intuitions

Caron's apartment -- new homework...

A heavy morning rain made it seem even more sensible to stay home. Caron's snug modern lair was her refuge and inspiration. Her place for fresh thoughts and perspectives.

She was in no mood for 'carpentry' lessons just now. Stéphane, delightful as he was, would just clutter her mind. Her head was aching, and she felt drugged from her flu-fighting pharmaceutical cocktails. To decompress, she played Chopin's heart-breakingly sad, slow Prelude No. 4 on her electronic keyboard. At times, she would switch it to church organ or harpsichord to fit her mood or the original music.

Then she slipped into her cozy, all-forgiving police sweat-suit. She curled up in her chaise longue with her black-and-white "tuxedo" cat, Mendès. Convinced he was really a dog, Mendès constantly followed her around, even when not hungry. He offered his affection and playfulness with an astonishing prodigality.

Caron was eager to nail down the murder case. The jackals at *L'Union* were still on her back, and she sensed even loyal colleagues were beginning to look at her skeptically.

To set a mellow mood, she lit a *Panter* cigarrillo. Soon, to put her soul at peace, she set it down and turned on her booming stereo to hear two of her favorite *Magic Flute* arias. Both were sung by the Finnish bass, Martti Talvela. First, his deep, virile version of *O Isis und Osiris;* then, like the voice of God, his *In diesen Heil'gen Hallen.*

Caron breathed a few long, relaxing breaths, then opened her research materials.

First, the books. Caron had done her *licence* at the University of Reims in History, Heritage, Musicology and Civilizations. She loved to nose her way around the specialized libraries, those touching on medieval history and culture. Now, having visited the University library, she held most of the books found on Madame Repentigny's night-table.

In the Latin Caron could still follow, she found a *Vita Remigii* (Life of Remi) written by archbishop Hincmar before 882. She also found translations of the four extant letters of Remi; then a survey of medieval history and archeology by Professor Bruno Dumézil of the University of Paris-Nanterre. Finally, a remarkable 2010 biography-hagiography of Remi by a University Jean-Moulin (Lyon) scholar called Marie-Céline Isaïa: *Remi de Reims. Mémoire d'un saint, histoire d'une Église.*

Settling in this morning, she searched for phrases, ideas or myths that might help explain Sophie-Charlotte's fascination with Remi. Caron read Remi's two famous letters (481 A.D. and 507 A.D.) to King Clovis. The 507 letter set out for Clovis -- baptized by Remi -- a generous and amazingly modern program of government. It urged tolerance toward all, fair justice, wise councilors, kindness to slaves, avoidance of unnecessary wars, care for widows and orphans, freeing of prisoners of war. This letter -- *Epistola sancti Remigii ad Clodoveum ante bellum Gothicum* – was a model of balance, wisdom and style.

But the two famous Testaments, the long and short, mattered most now. Both repeated the curse, seven times spoken, against anyone who would "usurp, ravage or destroy God's churches, and declare himself His enemy..." Punishment, they urged, should be swift and pitiless. It should "shorten his life."

Dramatic, prophetic, menacing. Even now? Caron decided that it was all just overblown medieval style. In today's terms, mere superstition.

Inspired by dipping into her old academic field, Caron pulled out a lined police report-book. She listed all the investigation's loose ends. After each, she noted its status, possible solution, or at least a path of enquiry.

But not before cooking up half a dozen buckwheat *gaufrettes*, to be kissed by some bitter-orange marmalade. A little energy break.

In point-form, she listed the hanging threads:

* <u>Painteaux</u>: Overtly loyal to Hubert R. Also to bereaved Sophie-Charlotte. Badly-explained relationship with Ma: lover, but also accomplice in Chinese plot. Likely motive to kill Hubert emerging: panic at unmasking. Fuzziness about movie time. Did he return to caves? Exactly when?

* <u>Mistresses</u>: only one left standing (so to speak!). She is chief guide, Frédérique Pommier. We continue grilling her to see if she confirms her still plausible guilt – see her death threats.

* <u>Chinese link</u>? Core question: spell out more the link between the Chinese and Hubert attack. Decision: Haul in Painteaux for further questioning on both Chinese plot (include DCRI) and movie times. Strong suspicion: Hubert killed just after summoning Painteaux re Chinese plot.

* <u>Dust, mescaline and mud chez Sophie-Charlotte</u> – from Hubert or someone else? Did Hubert take mistress Pommier to wife's bedroom?

* <u>Size 46 boots</u> – indicating a large man? Or could a smaller foot fit inside with other footwear, thick socks or insoles? Flochard had quickly studied pressure points on footprints to reveal how heel, instep and ball of foot registered; but she needed further study. Could sniffer dogs help identify cave prowlers?

Hôtel de Police... seeing and hearing the culprit?
Feeling better the next day, and pleased with her new research, Caron went in to her office. She was beginning to form a new hypothesis, but needed

to check some electronic evidence. And to recheck some older photographic evidence.

The first new evidence came from the remote video monitoring in the caves. Caron had junior officers run through the last two weeks of tapes from elevator, stairs and crime scene. For hours, nothing happened beyond tourist and staff visits. Then, on two occasions, an officer spotted an unidentifiable figure in a black headscarf and robe staring at the blood-splash on the wall beside the attack. This barely lasted three seconds. Then the figure scurried off to the right, never to be seen again.

Who was this? How did he or she get into the caves? The intruder couldn't have been anyone with an elevator key, for the elevator shots showed no unauthorized personnel.

Caron called in her tape observers.

"Did you see any strange-acting people in the tourist groups? Man or woman?

"Not that I could say," both said.

"Then go back and study the tourist groups on the two days in question, starting with the 10 a.m. tour and ending with the 6 p.m. tour. Look very carefully at the tourists' faces. Can you identify the same person visiting on two separate days? Watch for possible easy disguises such as glasses, wigs, scarves and hats. If it's a woman, she may also be carrying a large hand-bag."

"Will do," Commissaire."

"If you can identify such a person, I would like blowups of their face. Better get moving on this. We may be getting somewhere."

"Exciting, it's about time."

"Oh, by the way, I also want you to scan the tapes from the motion-activated night-time cameras. We left these running just in case. Can you identify any people there besides obvious employees? In fact, look again at the staff photo album. You need to be able to recognize these people, and to report any unusual activity by them. Remember: At this stage, everybody is still a suspect – including all employees. Remember too that we also have an unsupported allegation from Frédérique Pommier that one of her rivals may occasionally prowl the caves. That is most unlikely though, with her lover Repentigny out of play."

The second piece of electronic evidence was the sound track on Madame's bedside iPod. Flochard had copied it during a visit to Madame's quarters. Easy: She plugged the iPod into iTunes on her PC, and found all the sound listed as an iTunes 'song.'

The third piece of evidence was in a color photo that Caron had studied many times. It was the blood-splash on the wall beside Repentigny's body. It still made her shiver. For its goriness? Or for some mysterious meaning? Given all the contexts, what might it truly mean?

At day's end, Caron called a general briefing. With all hands present, including Baraquant and Duroselle.

"*Chers collègues*, I believe we may finally be reaching a conclusion to our investigation. Or rather conclusions. First, we're developing a compelling new theory about the attempted killer. And second, in cooperation with our DCRI friends, we may have solved the suspected international economic plot. A plot to dominate the principal industry of our region: champagne. At the intersection of these two files we find a familiar name: Sébastien Painteaux, the victim's *chef de cave.*"

Baraquant spoke up to support this assessment. "Yes, from what I've seen, this is beginning to look like a case of killing two birds with one stone."

"I'll refrain," smiled Duroselle, "from adding a metaphor about killing two evils with one bottle of champagne."

Everyone groaned at this dubious humor.

"We still have to collate final proof of Painteaux's implication in either dossier," said Caron. "But this, I believe, is imminent. We also hope – to our surprise – to be able to tie both murder and Chinese plot together as one major case."

"How will you do that?" asked three voices at once.

"Give me two or three more days, and I hope we'll be able to tell you all the details."

"Sounds good," said Baraquant. "And by the way, let's avoid the media until we have a solid final story. We don't want details to seep out to create false news or expectations.

The briefing ended. The tension held. But with a cautious touch of excitement.

Caron's office, two days later...
Caron's two officers reviewing the daytime TV surveillance tapes came in by 11 a.m. with startling

news. First, they had observed among the tourist groups a nearly-identical – perhaps even familiar – face in two separate groups. In one, the rather plump woman had black hair; in the other, blonde hair. She wore glasses lowered over her nose, and carried a large, stylish bag. A different bag in each shot.

Caron kept a poker face. But her heart began to race.

The next piece of electronic evidence was the sound-file recorded off Sophie-Charlotte's bedside iPod. Caron opened it. After the few initial minutes of music, she heard a deep, distorted male voice.

She told Baraquant and Duroselle what she had seen and heard. She said she had formulated a rather complex plan to sort out the night-visitor suspects. She asked her bosses' permission to test it in a wildly unorthodox manner.

She made sure her TV surveillance cameras were ready and rolling in front of all entrances to the caves. Their vigilance included daytime tourist groups and the night-time elevator and stairs. To save staff time, police would activate night-time surveillance by turning on the cameras via motion detectors.

Her instructions: to alert her night or day, at office or home, as soon as they had spotted the mystery person.

With the prosecutor's eyebrow-lifted approval, Caron also had her tech people install a remote-operated playback device. This controlled two powerful, well-separated speakers bordering the crime scene. When triggered, they would immediately play back the iPod voice recording. It would start sending the solemn cavernous voice throughout the area – on command, minutes after the motion-activated night cameras clicked on.

Police technicians tested the speaker volume. They could adjust it from whispering to thundering. Caron wanted first a whispered voice. To haunt the visitor, perhaps even cause a revealing panic. Then police would crank up the volume to an almost deafening, and disorienting level.

If and when the mystery figure appeared, Caron and two colleagues would race to the cave, and confront the person. Thinking of her most likely caveprowlers, Caron assessed the probable impact of the recording on each. In every case: terror, though for very different reasons.

"I know you find all this more than eccentric," Caron told Baraquant and Duroselle. "I only ask you to trust my hunch that we may be in for a shocking, definitive ending to the murder case. I want to lay a trap to provoke a confession."

"This is as weird as anything I've ever heard," said Baraquant. "Your reasoning is either brilliant, or utterly crazy. It's certainly not textbook police procedure. The result is doubtful, and could make or break our careers. If it flops, I may have to apply for reposting to a South Pacific backwater – Wallis-and-Futuna no doubt."

"I agree," said Duroselle, with a fatalistic grin. "And I would end up in Mayotte, off South Africa.

By the way, Denise, if you have by any chance not-ed *L'Union*'s headlines hammering you as the "am-ateur girl-sleuth," prepare for the worst."

"Or the best, if they care to be fair," smiled Caron.

CHAPTER THIRTEEN

Closing In, Closing Down

The caves come alive...

The next day, Caron's TV surveillance team reported no clear candidate for the mystery figure among the tourists. One of the latter, a plump lady with an unfortunate blonde bouffant, seemed to have disappeared into the crowd. Maybe, maybe not. Nobody was counting the group at the exit.

That evening, Caron went to bed early at 10.30 p.m., secure in the knowledge that no plausible suspects had appeared – just slovenly tourists in white sneakers, some obvious provincial retirees, four East Asians, and that overweight lady with the Alpine bouffant. Night-time surveillance was through motion-activated cameras in the caves.

Two police officers posted upstairs at the caves would rush to watch when an intruder turned one on. Caron went to sleep, emptying her brain into a charming mind-movie of her last carpentry lesson.

Just before 1 a.m., her bedside alarm sounded. Had someone entered the caves? How? She called the monitoring team and asked what they saw.

"About ten minutes ago, a motion-activated cave camera started sending us images, now taped. We saw a slim, black-veiled figure suddenly appear at the crime scene, linger a moment then move on. This might be Pommier, or her night-walker."

"Perhaps."

"It could have been man or woman, but on balance the figure moved more like a woman, though with awkward steps. A woman who knew where she was going."

"Which way did the person head?"

"If you're facing the crime scene, to the right."

"Thanks. Keep watching. I'm on my way with two colleagues and will start searching from the crime scene."

Caron, Jenneret and Marcambault squeezed into the cave elevator. The two cops noted that Caron was carrying a pair of light-enhancing night-vision goggles. These would give her a bright, green-tinted picture in almost complete darkness.

If the figure turned out to be a love-crazed, and perhaps drug-crazed Pommier, Caron would have her likely murderer. But what about Painteaux? And what about Caron's mysterious long- shot trap?

Caron and her two colleagues bee-lined for the crime scene. Nothing seemed changed there. But they did see partial imprints of large shoes -- size 46 again.

The remote speakers had turned on automatically via a motion-activation system similar to the camera system. This guaranteed that as soon as the intruder triggered the cameras, a slow, solemn man's voice would challenge them.

The first phrases came in a stately whisper. Then, turning louder and prophetic, the deep male voice intoned these heavy, echoing words – the ones taken off Madame Repentigny's bedside iPod:

I am Remigius, buried with Christopher. I speak this solemnly through the ages to the sinners of Reims, my bishopric:

Bend your neck, proud Sicambre, humbly lower it. Adore what you have burned, and burn what you have adored.

Caron had remembered that the early name of the Basilica was the Église Saint-Christophe. The words following were, she also recalled, the famous injunction of Saint-Remi in 496 A.D. to Clovis I when Remi, as bishop, baptized the warrior-king, a member of the Germanic Sicambre tribe.

Could what was "burned" refer to the two growers crippled by Repentigny? There was no proof he had really meant to hurt them. But in the Champagne rumor-mill, and in the minds of the two growers, such speculation quickly turned into agreed certainties.

To the paranoid or deeply credulous mind, the Remi-Sicambre allegory might even carry over into the "adoration" of what was "burnt." Stretching the point, it just might refer to Hubert's casting aside his wicked ways in church: he had generously supported his wife's construction committee for the Basilica's great new Bertrand Cattiaux Franco-Flemish organ.

Wild fantasies, of course. But not necessarily to a mind eager to believe.

Three times, and at increasing volume, Remi's recorded words to Clovis echoed through the caves' corridors. They were a compelling admonition to sinners to repent. Exactly what Repentigny was reputed to need.

After a long pause, the deep voice spoke again. Ricocheting off the high walls of the crime scene, the words of Remi's famous curse thundered. Caron recognized them from his Long Testament, the one preferred by Sophie-Charlotte Repentigny:

I Remigius, fifteenth bishop of Reims, now warn of punishment for all who render evil for good, and who display hostility to the Church.

After seven warnings, the rebel will be separated from the Church's body and treated as Judas the Traitor. This, because he forgot mercy toward the weak and poor.

May his days be shortened, as with all in authority who neglect his punishment.

Again, the message sounded three times. Enough to make sure a listener could decode it.

To a normal listener, Remi's threat would seem a dusty medieval formula. But to the literal-minded or emotionally fragile believer, it could seem imperative. In the case of Hubert Repentigny, known for his brutal business methods toward smaller or distressed firms, it might even seem a fitting and actual command. A threat to "shorten the days" of a bad man.

All these interpretations raced through Caron's mind. She knew the medieval spiritual and cultural mindset. And from both training and experience, she knew how egregious could be the wanderings of the criminal or psychotic mind.

How would the mystery cave-visitor react? Who *was* the visitor? Soon Caron would know.

At most times, the caves' temperature is a steady eleven degrees Celsius – ideal for storing champagne. But unless dressed warmly, visitors soon begin to feel a chill. The dank and gloomy caves are no place to linger. The millions of bottles seem like judgmental eyes watching each guest. They also look like an infinity of sinister hiding-places.

About twenty minutes after the last echoes of Remi's curse, Caron was walking toward the distant caves that legend claimed opened into Remi's own treasure caves. Jenneret, also with goggles, followed Caron fifty meters behind in case of mishap. It was a long and winding itinerary, with false endings, alcoves and sudden twists. One could easily get lost for days here.

Armed with her night-vision goggles, Caron saw a surprisingly bright horizon. But for minutes at a time, when long stretches of the caves were in total darkness, she couldn't catch even a flicker of wall-light silhouettring the mystery visitor. Then she could barely catch a fleeting view of her prey.

Fearing to reveal herself, Caron often held back and stood still. Wall-lights might betray her too.

After a long half-hour, the tracking began to resemble a cat-and-mouse game. Instinctively, Caron sensed that the mystery person, approaching some goal, suspected pursuit. Again, Caron held back, sometimes disappearing for three or four minutes. But she tried to keep a broad sense of direction to a goal she suspected.

The person ahead was clearly intelligent, and alert to the subtle twists and turns and hiding-places of the caves. The figure often stopped, as if looking behind to catch a glimpse of a pursuer.

At this stage, Caron knew that the deep, broadcast voice of "Remigius" would have instilled panic in the night-visitor. It would also have made clear to the figure that, somehow, he or she had been identified. The dénouement would depend on which of Caron's suspects she found at the end of the tunnel.

Caron felt a cold sweat around her neck. She had rushed from home so quickly that she had only thrown on a tee-shirt, jeans and her heavy police jacket. She wanted the pursuit to end, but didn't dare rush it for fear of losing her prey again.

Suddenly, on turning a corner, her goggles showed in the distance a yellowish, bright aura. She took off her night-vision goggles and placed them gently on the ground. The yellowish light was enough.

Caron turned and waved to Jenneret to keep following. Then she crept forward softly on rubber-soled shoes.

One hundred meters. Seventy-five. Fifty. Then she lowered herself onto hands and knees to advance silently without shadow.

In the eerie twilight, she saw a black figure lying face-down before a kind of altar lit by two large candles. Head and body covered in black. Strangely oversized rubber boots.

The altar carried the huge black letter "R" of the Repentigny house. Again, the killer's trademark downward slash appeared -- this time in bright red.

But now, the flat top line of the "R" had also been traced in red. Caron shivered, her eyes wide. Together, the two red lines gave her dramatic confirmation of her hunch. For superimposed on the so-called family "R" was... the Cross of Remi.

Caron stood up, and cautiously walked the final few steps toward the prostrate figure. She crouched down, put a reassuring hand on the person's shoulder, and whispered:

"Madame, I understand you. Please come with me and you will be safe."

The figure's head turned sideways to look up at Caron. Then Sophie-Charlotte, her anguished face bathed in tears, peered into Caron's tender eyes and murmured:

"I have fulfilled Remi's curse. I have been waiting for you, Commissaire."

Jenneret, his eyes staring in shock, and with concern for Caron, advanced to help. Caron gently raised Madame Repentigny to her feet, put her arm around her shoulder, and walked her slowly back toward the elevator. For safety, Jenneret followed a few meters behind.

During the long walk back to the exit, Sophie-Charlotte could not stop talking, even as she sobbed.

"He told me the devil now inhabited the body of a man who mocked Remi. This devil-man would soon kneel at the first rack to the left of the room exiting the main gallery. My friend told me Remi had decided the moment had come to carry out his curse. To end the days of the infidel."

"Madame, you don't have to tell me this at present. You have the right to call your family, a doctor and a lawyer who will be present at your first questioning."

"Thank you, Commissaire, but I need to tell you now. I trust you, and need to explain myself."

"I have cautioned you, Madame. Only go on if you insist, but you are not obliged."

"I acted that night because I heard a voice I also trusted."

"A voice?"

"Yes, that of Sébastien."

"Your *chef de cave.*"

"Sébastien is much more than that. He has become my nightly guide in my devotion to Remi."

"Nightly?"

"A few months ago, in Hubert's absence, Sébastien borrowed my iPod. To support my spiritual life, he kindly recorded on it several sacred texts, especially Remi's Testament that he knew I revered."

"I see."

"Oh, and Commissaire, I have to tell you something else.

"Again, Madame, you don't have to tell me anything more."

"But I need to."

"If you insist, Madame."

"Father Farfelan at the Basilica is the only person on earth who knows this. But my devotion to Remi has many dimensions."

"Of course."

"Spiritual, cultural, intellectual and even, in my imagination... physical."

"My goodness, Madame, are you really sure you want to share this with me?"

"Yes, I must unburden myself. I simply must."

"Whatever it is, I'm sure no court needs to hear this."

"Maybe not, but here it is. For many years, my marriage having turned cold, my imagination took over. I began having uncomfortable... very intimate... fantasies about Saint-Remi. About Saint-Remi, the only man I could love without betraying my marriage vows. I am shocked and ashamed at this, but I cannot help myself."

"Perhaps there is some human aspect to this? A real man? A lover?"

"Again, only Sébastien. We were never lovers, but... well something very vivid and tangible occurred between us a couple of years ago."

"Really?"

"We were walking in these caves in all innocence, just looking at my artworks, and when we accidentally touched... it was electrifying."

"Ah."

"Then I slipped on a crooked stone stairway and landed full-on against his body. His hands flew up and held me for a split second... at a place no man had touched me for years, and which completely shook me. With shame. With delight. And much more."

"Could it be that somehow this moment in the caves heading to Saint-Remi's caves led you subconsciously to confuse the saint and the man?"

"Amazing, Commissaire. Maybe that *is* what happened. And what allowed Sébastien to move from *chef de cave* to sexual fantasy to spiritual guide."

"And finally to a voice that could counsel murder. The human mind plays many tricks, especially when there are underlying tensions. Or passions."

"Murder? When Sébastien phoned me two hours before the attack on Hubert, he said such an act would only be the carrying-out of Remi's curse. And the victim would only be the devil in disguise."

Caron noted this confession. If repeated, it would convict Painteaux. She would confirm it during her formal investigation.

She handed the suspect over to Jenneret. Her cell phone not working in the deep caves, she went to an emergency wall-phone. She quickly got transferred to Baraquant.

"It's over, *patron*. The assailant was Sophie-Charlotte. But the *real* guilty party is Painteaux. We have convincing evidence that he was drugging her and manipulating her religious faith. Now we have enough to break his alibis."

"This certainly sounds like it. Good for you, Denise. This is outstanding police work."

"Obviously, you can brief DCRI on tonight's murder arrest."

"DCRI have already nabbed Ma in the light of their counter-espionage investigation. And as of this evening, we have Painteaux under bars."

"Excellent."

"Now Denise, you had better go home and get some rest."

"That can wait. Tonight's drama is going to keep me awake anyway. And in any event, first I want to get Madame medical care under our supervision."

"I'll go with your judgment, Denise. Thanks for wrapping this up. You really did a brilliant job – and now I won't have to take a job in a cop-shop in the South Pacific."

"Obviously, arresting both Painteaux and Ma should close both cases. And our parallel actions will tie the P.J. -- via Painteaux -- to both cases."

Baraquant laughed.

"I appreciate your suavely linking the P.J. to solving the Chinese scandal as well as the Repentigny attack."

"Well, DCRI helped us indirectly with the attempted-murder case," replied Caron. "Given the degree of collaboration between our two services these past weeks, I think we want to emphasize how each service helped the other."

"Impeccable diplomacy, Denise. The Ministry will love us for that. Let's hope our DCRI neighbors show the same generosity."

"After the hospital for Madame, then I'm back in play."

"Goodnight, Denise. Or rather, good morning. If possible, come in to see me and Philippe around 10:30 a.m."

"Count on me."

Caron called her father at 9 a.m. that morning to tell him of her success. They shared their relief and joy. The media attacks on her had taken a toll.

Shortly after, she woke up her carpenter. Claiming her warrior's rest at last, she would see him later that evening. Suddenly, she needed him to build some new bookshelves.

Hôtel de Police... the story told

The day after the cave pursuit and discreet arrest of Madame Repentigny, rumors about many supposed culprits flashed through Reims and the Champagne region. The Hôtel de Police suddenly went silent on the case. Its spokeswoman would only say that later that week the P.J. would hold an important press conference.

Meanwhile, Caron and her team grilled a stunned and terrified Painteaux. They let the damning evidence fry his nerves. Sophie-Charlotte's confession left him no exit.

The only leaks were dilatory rumors: Sophie-Charlotte had supposedly fallen ill at home; and Painteaux was being briefly held on a "domestic" matter. But the faces of several members of the Police judiciaire telegraphed bigger news. News more breathtaking than anyone might guess.

Two days later, with local and national media alerted, Baraquant, Duroselle and Caron stood beside the beaming *Procureur de la République,* Alexandre Simon, at a packed and televised press conference. The *Procureur* opened with these words:

"Mesdames et Messieurs,

I am immensely pleased to confirm that our Police judiciaire seem to have solved the heinous crime committed against Monsieur Hubert Repentigny, still in a coma at the Centre Hospitalier Universitaire de Reims. Through a remarkable team effort led by Commissaire Denise Caron, they have identified a presumed attacker. I regret to say that she is Madame Sophie-Charlotte Repentigny"

The crowd gasped. Everyone talked at once: "Impossible! I don't believe it! They must be joking!"

"However," picked up Baraquant, "I hasten to say that there is possibly an attenuating aspect -- of a medical nature. Doctors have conducted psychiatric and blood tests that may cast the crime in a still more surprising and complex dimension. These tests suggest that the crime occurred while the attacker was not in a normal frame of mind."

Listeners shook their heads in disbelief.

"We have made a second arrest," he went on, "that of a likely accessory to the crime. The suspect's name is Sébastien Painteaux, well-known *chef de cave* of the Repentigny house."

Again, the crowd went wild. What could the link between Painteaux and Madame Repentigny? A classic murder-and-love affair?

Baraquant, sober but pleased, added:

"Painteaux has also appeared in a related case: an alleged foreign plot to destabilize much of our champagne industry. Our sister-service, the *Direction centrale du renseignement intérieur*, carried out most of that investigation through its Economic Protection unit."

"A plot?" shouted a reporter. "From which country?"

"China. The Chinese, you probably know, have already been actively interested in our Bordeaux wines."

"How did you and DCRI get along?" The crowd, aware of service rivalries, tittered.

"Much better than some cynics might suggest. The DCRI worked in close cooperation with the Police judiciaire, and we with them. In the end, the two cases became so inextricably linked that you could say this has all been an exemplary joint effort."

"But who was really in charge?" insisted a reporter from *L'Union*.

"As I said, we have worked jointly on aspects of both cases. But if I had to assign special credit, I would say that DCRI did the main work on the Chinese plot. And the P.J. did the essential work on the Repentigny case."

"How did you do that?"

"At this point, I would like to turn over the press conference to the lead person on our side, Commissaire Denise Caron, Chef des Divisions Opérationelles. I understand that you at *L'Union* have long admired her work."

The room exploded with laughter. "Admired" was not exactly the attitude anybody could remember. "Undermined" was more like it.

Caron stepped forward.

"Yes, I have enjoyed very much the interest and support of *L'Union* in my humble efforts... even though I don't always have time to read this important newspaper."

More laughter, and applause for Caron's cool repartee.

"But let me put credit where it belongs – with a lot of key players. First, my two bosses, Regional Director *Commissaire divisionnaire* Georges Baraquant and Assistant Regional Director *Commissaire principal* Philippe Duroselle. Throughout a complex and demanding investigation, my two superiors have sustained me and our entire investigative team with unqualified support. I can even say that on several occasions – particularly in the final stage of our effort – they took measured but serious risks with some of our proposals. For that, I thank them heartily."

"I also thank my brilliant and hard-working colleagues directly or indirectly engaged in this investigation: the thirty members of our team, our scientific and technical police, the *Identité judiciaire* staff and all the others who helped. Everyone was essential. All our officers worked hard and intelligently. But I must say the scientific knowledge and intuitions of *Commandant de police* Dominique Flochard broke the impasse."

Flochard blushed and looked down as Caron pointed to her.

"Our *Identité judiciaire* chief, Commandant de police Louis Trumaut, and his hard-digging staff also deserve special mention. They sifted through our many suspects, and dug out nuggets of information that told important stories. They form the police's collective memory. They may know more about all of us that we know ourselves."

The crowd chuckled nervously.

"On the procedural front, finally, I would support Commissaire divisionnaire Georges Baraquant's words about the Direction centrale du renseignement intérieur. DCRI's expertise and professionalism substantially helped us. Just after this conference, you should know, DCRI's regional director Pierre Renouvin will speak."

Caron paused, and looked down to a familiar face off to one side of the front row.

"There is one other man who helped me personally more than anyone," she said, with a slight tremble in her voice. "Just by being who he is." Stretching out a hand toward the man in the wheelchair, she simply said: "My father, Captain Gilles Caron, who is well known within these walls."

The audience, even a few hardened journalists, stood up to salute an old soldier of the Reims Service régional de police judiciaire (SRPJ).

"Now some basic information, then I will take questions."

"Earlier this week, in a carefully arranged setting within the Repentigny caves, we obtained a spontaneous confession to the crime from Madame Sophie-Charlotte Repentigny. The details of this setting will emerge in court. So too will vital reports from doctors, psychiatrists and even some religious witnesses. This is a remarkably original case. The motive, means and opportunity all present unique characteristics."

"What are they?" shouted a journalist for France 3 TV-Reims.

"Madame Repentigny," as you know, is widely respected for her devotion to Saint-Remi. We believe she was drugged and brainwashed into believing that she was killing a sworn enemy of Saint-Remi. Perhaps even an incarnation of the devil."

Journalists sucked in their breath. A few smirked.

"You're joking," yelled a journalist from *L'Union*.

"I assure you I am not," said Caron.

"How then?"

"By a combination of mescaline – a type of psy-chedelic drug -- and a technique of recorded sug-gestiveness well-documented by brainwashing experts. Preceded by shock-induced domination, this two-pronged method is a variation on what is sometimes called 'psychic driving.' We believe Painteaux used this, and was indirectly but in fact behind the crime."

"Absurd! Nobody will believe that."

"We think they will when they hear the full evi-dence. These are complex, but interlocking. First, Madame Repentigny's bedrock belief in the sacred, commanding nature of Saint-Remi's message: after his blessings, she heard on her iPod what she took as an ancient incitement to destroy his enemies. Second, she heard documented, historic allusions to Remi's supposed wishes. Third, she heard a dev-astating, recorded message purportedly from Saint-Remi. A voiceprint analysis identified the speaker as Sébastien Painteaux."

"What is this? Disneyland?" snarled the *L'Union* reporter.

"I promise you that the P.J. does not pursue Mickey Mouse. Just the truth wherever it leads. And in this case, it leads to a highly improbable -- yet we think credible -- conclusion that Monsieur and Madame Repentigny were both victims of the same man."

"Painteaux?" shouted several reporters.

"Exactly. Sébastien Painteaux, the *chef de cave* of the *maison* Repentigny. We arrested him earlier this week, and he has confessed that he orchestrated the attempted murder. He also admitted backing the Chinese plot against France's champagne industry."

The room exploded with astonishment. TV reporters from France 24, TF1 and France 3 moved to the back of the room to send live stand-ups with Caron speaking in the background. Painteaux was a well-known personality among the élite *chefs de cave*

"What was Painteaux up to?" asked an agitated local reporter. "And what the devil is this talk of a so-called Chinese plot?"

"DCRI Regional Director Pierre Renouvin will spell out the Chinese matter in short order. But I can already tie Painteaux to both the Repentigny crime and his hope to profit from the Chinese operation. Not to jump the gun, Painteaux seems to be a greedy, unpatriotic man."

"Unpatriotic?"

"How else could you describe a Frenchman willing to sell out one of his country's major industries? That's indeed how we believe Monsieur Repentigny may have seen him two or three days before being attacked. As soon as the eventual victim learned of the Chinese plot, he began rallying other *maisons* and the State against it."

"Then, when Painteaux sensed that his cover was blown, he decided – perhaps with Chinese complicity – to strike. He had already poisoned Madame Repentigny's mind for her active role."

"Are you claiming that Monsieur Repentigny was a hero in this play?"

"In a literal sense, yes. While Painteaux was undermining France's economy, Monsieur Repentigny was trying to defend it. And, according to Painteaux's confession, it appears to have cost him his life."

"Returning to the brainwashing issue: Are you implying that Painteaux manipulated a fragile Madame Repentigny to kill her husband?"

"Yes, exactly that. And he did so first by stalking her at the Basilica. Then by flattering her growing fantasies of Saint-Remi. Then by drugging her. Then, by making her listen to a recording he made of the alleged murder command by Saint-Remi. Then, finally, by urging her in her delusional state to hide in the caves to assassinate Saint-Remi's enemy – who, in the cave's darkness, turned out to be her husband. By the way, we also found fragments of Painteaux's fingerprints on several key items – including her iPod."

"It sounds like your entire case rests on proving that Madame Repentigny is crazy."

"I did not use that word. And I never would. I have only said that we have her confession that she made the attack, convinced that she was obeying an order by Saint-Remi. And now, we have Painteaux's confession that he tricked her into carrying out the attack. I think – subject to proof in court – that those two confessions close the circle."

"What exactly did Painteaux admit to?"

"You'll hear it all in court. But I can tell you that when we confronted him with a considerable amount of circumstantial evidence – including the arrest of the Chinese agent – he broke down and told all."

"Examples of such evidence?"

"For example, we compared incoming phone calls to both Monsieur and Madame Repentigny. To our surprise, we found calls on the night of the murder originating from a sidewalk phone booth on the Place Drouet-d'Erlon. Painteaux had already told us he had gone to an early showing of the film *J.Edgar*. The showing started at 6:50 p.m. at the Gaumont-Pathé cinema at no. 72, Place Drouet-d'Erlon. Half an hour earlier, someone had made a brief call to Monsieur Repentigny from a phone-booth near the cinema. Then a longer call to Madame Repentigny."

"How did you know that was Painteaux?"

"We didn't, at the start. But we got lucky. 'Lucky,'" Caron smiled, "is what we call good, basic police work. Soon after the crime, we checked for clues at Painteaux's favorite restaurant, *l'Apostrophe*. That's just across the street from the cinema at no. 59. The *maître d'hôtel* there knows Painteaux as a regular client. Standing near the door to greet customers, he told us he twice saw Painteaux leave his drink to go out to use one of the two phone-booths on the sidewalk opposite.

The first call took place at roughly at 5:40 p.m., the second one at around 6 p.m. That's just before Painteaux's announced movie. The *maître d'* found Painteaux's behavior surprising. He had always seen Painteaux with his ear glued to a cell phone. Using the outside phone, not normally bugged, was strange -- unless Painteaux's cell phone was broken or left elsewhere.

It wasn't: his phone (that we quickly inspected) showed he made two short cell calls to his office three minutes after his second phone-booth call, the one to Madame Repentigny."

"Now, are you telling us that the *maître d'* guessed that those two phone-booth calls went to the Repentignys?"

"Of course not. As soon as he told our officer assigned to watch Painteaux about the strange phone-booth activity, we obtained the booth number's records from the phone company, Orange. Obviously, this took us from curiosity to even stronger suspicion of Painteaux. We had been watching him closely for a long time."

"But all you had was phone numbers from the booth to the Repentignys. What's so sinister about that?"

"First, the timing, just before the attempted murder. What did Painteaux have to tell each of the couple so urgently just then? Second, Painteaux's bizarre action in phoning from a sidewalk booth when we have records proving that his cell phone was working perfectly three minutes later. And third... when we confronted Painteaux with these final facts, and linked them to our other evidence, he was clearly shaken."

"Did he confess then?"

"No, but he did when we caught him out on the very movie he claimed as his alibi: the movie, *J. Edgar*, that he said he had seen with his wife. We asked him: whatever became of J. Edgar Hoover's secret files? This was a memorable scene at the film's end. It shows Hoover's secretary slowly shredding his notorious blackmail documents. No filmgoer could ever forget that pivotal scene. But Painteaux blushed, stuttered, and said he couldn't remember. Then, exhausted, he finally admitted that he had walked out of the movie over an hour early. This gave him just enough time to push a brainwashed Madame Repentigny to act --- including time to guide her to the crime scene himself. For the record, Painteaux's wife confirmed he had left the movie early, claiming his cell-phone vibrator had summoned him to an urgent meeting."

Some journalists began to smile. Admiringly?

"How exactly," said one, "did Painteaux provoke the assault?"

"He told Madame Repentigny to hide in the shadows behind rack Y-435 by 8:20 p.m. and wait with a full bottle of champagne to attack a mysterious figure, no doubt a devil in disguise. Then he phoned her husband to say he had just received explosive new information spelling out the Chinese plot. Telling Repentigny he thought he was being followed, he suggested a meeting where nobody could possibly spot them – in the caves. Near the wall beside rack Y-435."

Having personally placed Madame in ambush, Painteaux then decamped quickly to watch from fifty meters away -- to make sure Sophie-Charlotte followed through. She did, said Painteaux, screaming *Dixit Remi!* – loosely, Remi ordered this!"

A few listeners winced in shock. "You must be inventing this," snorted a *L'Union* reporter.

A TF1 reporter jumped in. "Was there something in the calls to the Repentignys that prefigured the crime?"

"I just told you. The trap was Madame de Repentigny. The bait – in the call to Monsieur Repentigny -- was the secret Chinese plan. This bait, which never existed, purported to offer Repentigny the proof of the plot needed to rally the industry against it."

"And the call to Madame?"

"As I said, just before Painteaux called Monsieur Repentigny, he rang Madame to tell her that she had to act right away. To fulfill Remi's command – his curse.

"Madness! That's just too unlikely and complicated to pull off."

"Maybe, but not to a tired, credulous, indeed drugged mind. Remember: our chemical and iPod evidence proved that for weeks Painteaux had already fed Madame mescaline, and had brainwashed her about her alleged lethal duty to Saint-Remi. By the way, we also found trace amounts of psilocybin -- a drug that, when mixed with cave lichen, can cause hysteria, panic attacks, delusions and wild fantasies. Such chemical assaults arguably made Madame Repentigny a victim of manipulation. She was a fragile, even abused, woman. Abused by Painteaux."

"Why did Painteaux crack, in the end? Merely because of some dubious phone numbers?"

"The phone number surprise was, for Painteaux, just the straw that broke the camel's back. The combined pressure of the Chinese plot, and his emotional relationship with a Chinese agent called Ma Chuntao, had ground him down. So had his unconscionable manipulation of Madame Repentigny. That, and his late-blooming guilt at betraying his boss."

"How did he betray his boss?"

"Having long feigned loyalty to Hubert Repentigny, Painteaux finally confessed to us that his real plan was to sell out France's champagne industry in league with the Chinese. In any way he could. Of course, a leading *chef de cave* has a multitude of contacts. Then, went the supposed deal, when Repentigny died the Chinese would step aside so Painteaux could scheme to marry the victim's widow."

"Not very likely!" interjected the *L'Union* reporter. "A widow revered as a pillar of Reims society far above Painteaux's social status?"

"Remember this: In Painteaux's insanely ambitious mind, she would be a widow deeply confused by drugs and sophisticated brainwashing. A widow grateful for Painteaux's flamboyant religious consolations and timely practical advice."

"You're dabbling in pop psychology. And probably wishful thinking," said another reporter.

"Thank you," said Caron.

"Now Commissaire, how realistic was Painteaux's plan?"

"Good question. But speculating on Chinese investment plans is hardly the business of a humble regional police woman. All I can say is that it's no secret that the Chinese sit on a lot of investment cash. Working perhaps through a French shell company, conceivably they might have made an offer that neither the Repentigny board nor family could refuse. But all that is pure conjecture."

"As for the family, I leave you to imagine their reaction to a hypothetical marriage to Painteaux – especially after Painteaux was tried for murdering their father."

"Tell us more about the mescaline," pressed another reporter, eager for facts, not theories.

"We found it scattered as a powder in several places in Madame Repentigny's bedroom. Sometimes it showed traces of racodium cellare or cellar-rot, a possible accelerator of the mescaline's hallucinogenic effect. Both were present on her personal effects."

"This is incredible. It's totally, totally nuts," said a reporter from *Le Monde,* who came by TGV from Paris for the occasion.

"I have to agree," said Caron. "But the evidence and confessions support it all."

"Evidence? Does Madame Repentigny wear size 46 shoes? That was the aggressor's rumored shoe-size."

"No, but DNA heel scrapings showed that her smaller shoes fitted tightly into the larger boots meant to mislead us."

"When did you first begin to suspect that Madame Repentigny was the aggressor?"

"Consciously, only in the past month. That's when Commandant de police Dominique Flochard of the *police scientifique* brought in the fully analyzed mescaline evidence, plus her further research into Korean War-era brainwashing techniques. Then we found Painteaux's voice inciting violence on the iPod recording."

"Anything else?"

"Well, *un*consciously – when I think back – I believe it might have been Madame Repentigny's frequent touching of her gold "R" pendant. Given her emotional detachment from her husband, this touching raised the question of whether the "R" signified something more than Repentigny. Something like, as we later confirmed, "Remi.""

"Still other hints?"

"Yes, for several weeks I kept returning to the crossed-out splash of blood on the crime-scene wall. It troubled me from the outset. As I stared repeatedly at the color photos of the splash, I began to imagine... well, you might call it an optical illusion. Originally, we thought the downward slash was the assailant's cry of triumph. But if you combine this slash with the horizontal top line of the R, you can almost imagine a cross."

"The R might then mean not Repentigny," she went on, "but Remi. This highlighted Cross is exactly what we found at the cave altar. The vertical and horizontal lines, thickened in bright red, stood out clearly as a Christian Cross. The Cross, believed Madame Repentigny, of Saint-Remi."

"Are you superstitious, Commissaire?" teased a journalist.

"Worse – I have a *licence* in medieval studies in the Champagne-Ardenne region. A region drenched in religious history. Thus," she said smiling, "I suppose Saint-Remi was never far from my mind."

"Where exactly was this cave-altar?"

"At the blocked-off passage rumored, believe it or not, to lead to the adjoining caves of Saint-Remi. Some archeologists think there may even be a treasure there – treasure accumulated by early Christians. I'm afraid I'm too prosaic to believe that. But to a sensitive mind deeply attuned to Saint-Remi, maybe the symbolism of that place made it a logical venue for the make-shift altar we found there."

"A legal question: When you intercepted e-mails and text-messages, weren't you breaking the law?"

"Absolutely not. We followed the rules to the letter. Before intercepting anything, we secured permission from the state prosecutor. And, for the Chinese plot, we also got that of the Commission nationale de contrôle des interceptions de sécurité, the CNCIS. Since the Chinese plot was linked to an attempted-murder suspect, Painteaux, this met the condition of being connected to organized crime."

"Didn't you also need pre-clearance from the Judge of Liberties and Detention?"

"Indeed. We obtained that too before acting. It was easy to get from Orange, the phone company, Painteaux's critical pre-attack telephone records. But the various formal authorizations we obtained let us monitor *all* relevant electronic communications. We were 'legal' from beginning to end."

"Allow me another point," pressed the *L'Union* reporter. "A full standard 75 cl. bottle of champagne weighs almost 1.6 kilos. How could a slight woman like Madame Repentigny possibly swing that as a weapon?"

"Madame may be slight, but she's far from frail – as her partners at the Club de Tennis de Reims can readily testify. They say she wields a devastating backhand, and an impressive serve."

"Speaking of slight," pursued the reporter, "we've heard a rumor that the suspicious lady in the tourist line was plump. But now you're saying she was actually Madame Repentigny, a far thinner woman."

"It was indeed Madame. She stuffed her black robe under her coat for wandering the caves, as she sometimes did in her grief and delusions. This was a disguise to fool the surveillance cameras."

Several people laughed, and began to clap. Journalists shook their heads incredulously. The cops had played a smart game right to the end.

Baraquant and Duroselle beamed. Caron, calm and controlled, looked down at her proud father Gilles with a tender smile.

Baraquant spoke up to end the P.J. part of the session.

"Thank you, Commissaire. And thanks to all of you who have come here today. And now my colleague and friend Pierre Renouvin of the DCRI Reims will outline the Chinese matter and its conclusion."

Renouvin, happy to share the spotlight (an unaccustomed role for "secret police") praised the collaboration with the Reims P.J.

"This was an exceptionally complex case – actually two intertwined cases – and this demanded exceptional cooperation. We believe we brought useful insights and skills to the Repentigny investigation – run with brio by our P.J. colleagues."

Then, with telegraphic concision, he summarized the Chinese plot. Under orders from his boss Dominique Morel in Paris, he kept methods and personnel confidential. Renouvin could only say that DCRI's Economic Protection unit had discovered a foreign plot. It might have allowed elements of the Chinese government and business community (essentially a single entity) to destabilize, then dominate, France's champagne industry.

He announced that DCRI had arrested a key Chinese plotter, long under observation. She was a woman associated with banking and trade. Her fate: deportation or criminal prosecution, depending on further evidence and her willingness to speak. So far, she wouldn't talk.

"*Mesdames, Messieurs*, this being an extremely sensitive matter, that is all I can tell you today."

The press room erupted in frantic conversation. The TV reporters rushed to update their stand-ups. Print reporters started typing their leads.

CHAPTER FOURTEEN
Plus Ça Change...

The Quai d'Orsay, brilliant at futile gestures, had already lodged a discreet protest in Beijing. It told prying media that there would be no more information available in the near future. Inconvenient scandals in France have a habit of fading conveniently. Experienced observers expected the plot would get a first-class funeral. Franco-Chinese trade and diplomatic interests required a twin-shovel excavation for the grave. So did the endless euro crisis. A crisis in which China might prove Europe's banker of last resort.

Front page, L'Union -- next day...
The region's newspaper of reference outdid itself to play fair with Caron and the oft-maligned P.J. Its page-one main headline trumpeted:

REPENTIGNY CASE SOLVED
Baron's drugged wife, chef de cave, confess
Commissaire Denise Caron
leads astonishing P.J. investigation

Introducing a package of twelve sidebars, profiles and secondary stories, the lead story began:

*After six weeks, police interviews with 324 witnesses,
and complications from a parallel industrial-espionage
plot, Procureur de la République Alexandre Simon announced yesterday that he had charged Madame Sophie-
Charlotte Repentigny with the attempted murder of her
husband, Hubert Repentigny. He had also charged chef
de cave Sébastien Painteaux as her accomplice.*

*In an astonishing tale of drug-fed religious delusion
which may border on insanity, Madame Repentigny is
under police guard and suicide watch at the Hôpital de
Jour Psychiatrique. Painteaux sits in a cell at the Hôtel
de Police. His interrogation continues to cast light on
both the attempted-murder and industrial-espionage
cases.*

*The Repentigny investigation alone engaged thirty
full-time detectives and technical experts. It was a remarkably broad team effort. But many police colleagues
gave Commissaire Denise Caron – head of Operational
Divisions of the regional Police Judiciaire -- effusive
credit for her imagination, intuition and discipline in
leading the collective effort. Even her medieval studies
at the University of Reims, some said, brought unusual
insight to bear.*

*"Said one twenty-year police veteran: 'We had our
doubts about Denise when she came in over the heads of*

many older, more experienced investigators. We doubt no more. She is really one of us. Possibly even the best of us.

The paper's updated profile on Caron echoed this. And taking Caron's collegial lead, the other stories highlighted other members of the team. Caron steered special mention to Commandant Dominique Flochard of the *Police technique et scientifique*. "We could never have cracked this case," said Caron, without Dominique's erudite intuitions and the incredibly careful, imaginative work of the team under her direction."

Flochard beamed through her signature designer glasses. Her rosy plump Norman cheeks glowed like twenty-year old Calvados.

Caron drove home through light rain, stopping briefly only to hug her father and mother and to share a little glass of bubbles. Once in her glassed-in lair, she turned up her hi-fi and put on her best Koss earphones. She called up Cecilia Bartoli singing the aria *Non piu mesta* ("No more sadness") from Rossini's *La Cenerentola*. She sang along with Cecilia. Caron's admiring neighbors marveled at her apparently sturdy (if a bit overstretched) *a capella* performance.

No more sadness indeed. At least until the horror of the next crime. The next tangle with suspicious media. The next mad tracking of a fiendishly improbable culprit.

Having sung out her heart and her stress, Caron punched Stéphane's number into her cell phone. They had a quiet dinner at *L'Antr'Act*, their *cantine* on the rue Salin. Next, a chat about a holiday escape to unwind from Caron's latest drama. Finally, a charming tussle about where to spend the night. Caron's cleaner sheets would win again: Stéphane's washing-machine, he said, was still broken.

CHAPTER FIFTEEN
All's Well

To mark their success, Baraquant, Duroselle and Caron shared a celebratory lunch at the 1920s Brasserie du Boulingrin – fated to end an epoch as its lease expired. The head-waiter, like every Rémois, had learned of their exploit in *L'Union* and on radio and TV. He brought them three glasses of complimentary bubbles

"To the P.J!" toasted Baraquant. "To us!" added Duroselle. Clinked Caron with a grin: "To the first three honorary members of the Ordre des Coteaux de Champagne!"

Denise Caron's apartment, next day...
Baraquant had awarded Caron an extra week of time off, which she tacked onto a week of her regular holidays. She announced that she was first

going to supervise some renovations of her apartment. Then she would take off ten days to visit family in Grenoble related to her carpenter-cousin.

To fuel the renovations, Caron and her 'cousin' stopped at her favorite gourmet épicerie, Le Bon Manger at 7 rue Courmeaux – a "confidential" address she normally kept to herself, not to invite envy. They picked up three days' worth of *foie gras*, roast duck, pâté de chevreuil, fine cheeses, caviar and other delicacies, a bottle of blonde Lillet apéritif, two bottles of Riesling, four velvety Burgundies (Pommard, Côtes de Beaune) and two Bordeaux (Pomerol, Saint-Émilion). Plus, need one add, memorable champagnes, and an excellent "confidential" Daviault-Quinet from Chouilly – all to be accompanied by exquisite pink *biscuits de Reims*. At the *tabac*: two packages of Panter Mignon Deluxe cigarrillos.

Then they pulled down the curtains, and got on with the renovations.

Four days later, the Air France pilot flying the pair to Grenoble via Paris made a small navigation error. To their astonishment, he landed them on Ibiza, playground of Europe's young and irresponsible party-animals.

Certainly no place for a Commissaire and her carpenter.

Élysée Palace...
President Roland Guérin, Hubert's close friend, and warm acquaintance of Hubert's wife Sophie-Charlotte, had reacted with horror to the news of her

implication in her husband's attempted murder. He took note of the parallel arrest of Ma Chuntao, the sometime Guérin mistress shared with Repentigny. Having cast her aside on DCRI advice, he faced no serious embarrassment from her few brief visits to his office. But he had the Quai d'Orsay tell the Chinese Trade Commission to hustle her out of France with no fuss.

As the twin-faceted case wound up, Guérin called a newfound friend. He was the just-installed new President of China, Xi Jinping. Chuckling into his phone, the French president drowned the "absurd" story of a beautiful Chinese spy in effusive congratulations... and the promise of a case of *Cristal Roederer*. With the case came a handwritten note subtly suggesting *Realpolitik*, solicitation, and hoped-for better times. It read: "Champagne is the wine of civilization and the oil of government."

Xi, a big man in every way, took it all in good spirit, even recalling his family's familiarity with caves. During Mao's Cultural Revolution, he told Guérin, his family had lived with his disgraced father in a village cave for seven years.

Ministry of State Security, Beijing...

Shortly after, Ma Chuntao quietly returned to China "for her next trade assignment." Her unique skills-set, both vertical and horizontal, would no doubt win her a promotion. As the Repentigny case wound up, her boss Tsaï Yong-kang of Department 2 of the Ministry of State Security, lifted a glass of Chinese 'champagne' to his country's plans...

for huge new investments in the vineyards of Champagne. As for Painteaux, Ma told any enquirers that she might indeed have met him. But only socially.

Hôpital de Jour Psychiatrique, Reims...

A week after the press conference, Hubert Repentigny died, his relatives finally accepting the doctors' urging to disconnect his life-support system. He had no hope of recovering from his coma. Family, police and a nurse accompanied Sophie-Charlotte Repentigny to the burial. They laid Hubert to rest at the prestigious Cimetière du Nord, final home of Marshal of France Jean-Baptiste Drouet d'Erlon and the most famous of the champagne widows, the Veuve Clicquot.

After another four months of treatment, doctors released Madame Repentigny to police-supervised home rest. In dropping charges against her, the prosecutor took into account two factors. First, her plainly delusional confession and mentally fragile state; and second, Painteaux's own confession of manipulating her with drug-induced prompting, false friendship and cynical exploitation of her religious devotion.

Madame Repentigny spent another six months under psychiatric home care, accompanied by a team of nursing-trained nuns. Soon after, she returned to her normal life of cultural and philanthropic work, as well as to her daily veneration of Saint-Remi. Reims society welcomed her back warmly as the admirable, respectable woman she was.

A very special event was her attendance at the Élysée Palace ceremony where President Roland Guérin posthumously awarded her late husband the highest level of the Legion of Honor, the rank of *Commandeur*. The citation: "At cost of his life, for unique and outstanding service to the nation and its vital champagne industry."

The family itself marked this extraordinary honor with a large plaque at the cemetery, and another at the visitors' entrance to the caves. As for Repentigny's grateful peers at the Union des Maisons de Champagne, they erected a two-meter-high bronze statue of their martyred defender in front of the *Maison de la Champagne*, headquarters of the Comité Interprofessionnel du Vin de Champagne. Even the growers approved.

Painteaux, a scoundrel not a baron, settled into his twenty-year sentence at Paris's *Prison de la Santé*. He fantasized that Ma Chuntao, imitating the wife of attempted-murderer Michel Vaujour in 1986, would take helicopter lessons and rescue him from the jail's roof. Chuntao, of course, had no such plan. She was far too busy scheming to replace her boss Tsaï Yong-kang as the first female head of Department 2 of *Guoanbu*, Beijing's Ministry of State Security.

Frédérique Pommier returned a second time to her life-sucking bore of a husband, recalling the wisdom that if you can't have the one you love, then love the one you have.

Sophie-Charlotte Repentigny happily remained Sophie-Charlotte. She still dreamt of Saint-Remi in ways that scandalized old Father Vladimir Farfelan. She kept up her devastating tennis backhand. But she now practiced an equally powerful serve, sometimes pretending her racquet was a champagne bottle... and Painteaux's head was the ball.

Hubert Repentigny, newly hailed a hero, lay sleeping in an imaginary champagne cave far below his old caves in Reims. As the patriot who died stopping Ma Chuntao's and Tsaï Yong-kang's plot to steal France's bubbles, he proudly fingered his *Légion d'Honneur, Commandeur* Class.

Just as Sophie-Charlotte used to finger her pendant with "R" for Repentigny. And Remi.

EPILOGUE
After Fiction, a Few Facts...

In 2013 and onwards, China continues deepening its love affair with French wines. Touted by the nation's ostentatious rich, as well as its upwardly mobile middle class, champagne is well on its way to becoming the Middle Kingdom's preferred celebratory drink. Traditional high-octane *baijiu* now blows out fewer brains.

France, tipsy with satisfaction, sees no need to fear losing its *cachet* as the home of elegance. The only question: Who will soon really *own* the home – both in France and China? China's gigantic Dynasty Winery Limited (a joint venture with France's Rémy Martin) plans a Chinese production of one hundred million bottles by 2015. Other joint ventures have engaged France's Pernod Richard and Moët Hennessy. French know-how and the vast Chinese market make a splendid marriage of reason -- and why not? – of love for the West's *dolce vita*..

French wine castles are an irresistible prize (and bargain) to newly rich Chinese: by early 2013, Chinese investors owned thirty Bordeaux castles, with twenty more under negotiation. In mid-2012, they had already snapped up one extremely prestigious Burgundy property, the Château Gevrey-Chambertin.

China's billionaires see no shame in rebuilding in China full-size replicas of French castles. Just outside of Beijing, giant winery Château Chanyu built itself a classic turreted French castle. And Dynasty, only two hours from Beijing, has built a full-scale replica of the Château de Montaigne. For good measure, it plunked in front of it a model of the *Pyramide du Louvre*. Only a real-sized model of the Folies-Bergère is missing.

Red and white wine and apéritifs are one thing. But champagne? Both Chanyu and Dynasty, though careful to say they respect trade treaties by using only the downscale *méthode champenoise*, announce sparkling wines that gracefully wink at the real thing. Says Dynasty's online pitch for its sparkling wine: "The wine has a bright and crystal-clear appearance, sharp, fruity, perfect and refreshing in taste, solid and full-bodied, in character [with] that found in good French Champagne."

China's capture of Champagne's as well as champagne's bubbles will proceed gradually, but surely. You can't blame the Chinese for being Chinese: far-sighted, enterprising and energetic.

And you can't blame the French for being French: eager to please and astonish, and rightly proud of their elegance and expertise. Like some red and white wine confrères, a few champagne growers and merchants will continue to lend their skills to China's enterprises.

Betrayal? *Mais non!* Descartes meeting Dom Pérignon, French champagne barons can gracefully rationalize their passionate patriotism to include a smidgen of practicality.

Aided by magnums of *le divin liquide* and barrels full of highly convertible *yuan*.

ACKNOWLEDGMENTS

Many thanks to my sources in the Police Judiciaire and the champagne world who were so generous with their time, advice and encouragement. If this book conveys any sense of reality, however imperfect, it is because of them – and my splendid research assistant, Ms. Mozilla Firefox.

Earlier drafts benefited from the astute readings of Marie-Jo Cerisier, Vanessa Dylyn, Ratna Ray, Paddy Sherman, Dag Spicer, Nick Spicer and Grace Spicer-Pilon. Final editing faced the demanding standards of Geneviève Spicer and Blanca Turcott. Their judgment, sharp eye to detail, and tireless commitment (in spite of illness) have made this a far better book. Their generosity in helping with practical tasks also enormously lightened production burdens.

To all, but especially to these two ladies for their loving complicity: fond gratitude and a flute full of bubbles

Very special thanks to Alan King of Helix Web Design for his delightfully horrifying cover.

K.S.

Paris

THE AUTHOR

Ilona Hurda

Born in Toronto in 1934 to English-Canadian parents, Keith Spicer attended local public elementary and secondary schools. Dazzled at 13 by a photo of his beautiful French pen-pal, he ended up making France and all things French into a hopeless love affair.

After language and literature studies in French and Spanish at the University of Toronto, he graduated from the Institut d'Études Politiques (Sciences-Po) in Paris, completing in Canada a doctorate in international relations.

He pursued careers in the media, academia, business and government. Among other universities, he taught at the University of Toronto, UCLA, Dartmouth College, N.H., University of Ottawa and the Sorbonne. He founded and ran for six years the Media and Peace Program at the UN-linked University for Peace (Costa Rica).

For seven years, he was Canada's first Commissioner of Official Languages. Later he chaired the country's national radio, TV and tele-communications regulatory body (CRTC). Between these times, he was for five years editor of the daily *Ottawa Citizen*. During a constitutional crisis in 1990-91, he led a national people's consultation called the Citizens' Forum on Canada's Future.

In 1996, he moved to France, advising Ernst and Young on Internet policy. He now savors the life of a man garrulously proud of his three children. And he is still dazzled by young girls: his three granddaughters.

Website: www.keithspicer.com
Email: kspicer22@gmail.com

CPSIA information can be obtained at www.ICGtesting.com
Printed in the USA
LVOW06s1758040913

350984LV00001B/6/P